## She hadn't known been growing insi the changes in he

Her whole focus had been on the nagging worry at the back of her mind. The worry that had ratcheted up to a whole new level a month later with the arrival of the letter and the first photograph. By the time the next one turned up in her mailbox a week before she left Stillwater, she had been half-crazy with worry. Any physical symptoms her body had been displaying had come second to the turmoil of her emotions.

Vincente frowned. Clearly, he wasn't buying that explanation. Beth didn't blame him. She wouldn't herself if she was the one listening to it. *A lot on my mind.* It was a classic fobbing-off phrase. His lips parted in preparation to ask more just as a cry from the baby monitor, for the second time that day, provided an interruption.

This cry was different. This wasn't one of Lia's usual noises. It was a high-pitched scream that brought Beth straight to her feet and had her running for the door. At the same time, out in the yard, Melon went into a frenzy of barking.

"What is it? What's wrong?" Picking up on her panic, Vincente was right behind her as she dashed up the stairs.

"Someone is in Lia's room."

* * *

**Sons of Stillwater: Danger lurks in a small Wyoming town**

* * *

**If you're on Twitter, tell us what you think of Harlequin Romantic Suspense! #harlequinromsuspense**

Dear Reader,

Thank you for journeying back to Stillwater with me!

*Secret Baby, Second Chance* is the third book in the Sons of Stillwater miniseries, and it tells the story of Vincente Delaney.

The only unpredictable thing Vincente's rancher father did was fall in love with beautiful Italian socialite Giovanna Alberti. When the marriage ended, his mother left for Italy and a series of new marriages. Vincente was left feeling out of place in Stillwater...and within his own family.

The only person with whom he ever felt truly comfortable was Beth Wade. Vincente and Beth had a unique, passionate relationship. Then, one night, she disappeared...

This story goes deeper than the mystery of why Beth went on the run and what happened ten years ago during an ill-fated expedition to the Devil's Peak.

When Vincente catches up with Beth, everything has changed. The passion is still there, but the danger they are in, together with their new responsibilities, mean they have to face a different kind of future.

I loved writing the story of how Vincente falls in love twice over. He almost lost Beth and he has to deal with that, but he is also instantly enchanted by his daughter. He never thought he would be a father, but this little person captures his heart.

I'd love to find out what you think of Vincente and Beth's story. You can contact me on my website (janegodmanauthor.com), Twitter (@janegodman) and Facebook (Jane Godman Author).

Happy reading,

*Jane*

# SECRET BABY, SECOND CHANCE

**Jane Godman**

HARLEQUIN® ROMANTIC SUSPENSE

Recycling programs
for this product may
not exist in your area.

ISBN-13: 978-1-335-45625-0

Secret Baby, Second Chance

Copyright © 2018 by Amanda Anders

Printed in U.S.A.

**Jane Godman** writes in a variety of romance genres, including paranormal, gothic and romantic suspense. Jane lives in England and loves to travel to European cities that are steeped in history and romance— Venice, Dubrovnik and Vienna are among her favorites. Jane is married to a lovely man and is mom to two grown-up children.

### Books by Jane Godman

### Harlequin Romantic Suspense

#### *Sons of Stillwater*

*Covert Kisses*
*The Soldier's Seduction*
*Secret Baby, Second Chance*

#### Harlequin E Shivers

*Legacy of Darkness*
*Echoes in the Darkness*
*Valley of Nightmares*
*Darkness Unchained*

#### Harlequin Nocturne

*Otherworld Protector*
*Otherworld Renegade*
*Otherworld Challenger*
*Immortal Billionaire*
*The Unforgettable Wolf*
*One Night with the Valkyrie*

Visit the Author Profile page at Harlequin.com for more titles.

This book is dedicated to my wider family circle
(you know who you are!).
They are always there to support me.
Thank you!

# Chapter 1

"We've found Beth Wade."

Vincente Delaney had been waiting to hear those words for the last twelve months. Waiting and dreading. Now they had finally been spoken, it was as if his mind wasn't sure how to process them and his emotions didn't know how to react. He'd imagined that, as soon as he was told, he would be torn apart by anger and pain. Instead, all he felt was a curious detachment, as though he was viewing the scene as an outsider.

"Why wasn't her body with those of the other women Grant Becker murdered?"

He was pleased to find his voice sounded normal. That he could ask the question without crumbling. He supposed it was because there had been plenty of time to prepare for this moment. Twelve months ago, the police had told him that Beth fitted the profile of those killed by the murderer known as the Red Rose Killer and she was likely to have been one of his victims. Ever since then, this situation had been at the back of his mind. He hadn't thought about it every minute of every day. Not quite that often.

Of course, it had been made worse because the man responsible for the deaths of all those women had been someone Vincente had known most of his life. Grant Becker had been his brother Cameron's best friend. Vincente and Grant had gone hunting and drinking together. To learn that Grant, the sheriff of West County, was not only a serial killer, but that he could have been responsible for killing Beth… Vincente shook his head. He still struggled to come to grips with the reality of what had happened in his hometown. Grant was dead now, but the legacy of his crimes had rocked the city of Stillwater, Wyoming, to its core.

"Oh, dear Lord, Vincente. I'm so sorry. That came out all wrong." Laurie, Cameron's wife, was a detective in the Stillwater police. She moved swiftly across the room to place her hand on his arm. "Beth isn't dead. What I came here to tell you was that we've finally found out where she's been living since she left Stillwater."

The emotion did kick in then, so hard and fast he felt light-headed with it. Relief hit him first. *She's not dead!* The long, anguished months of picturing her murder, of wondering if there was anything he could have done to save her, of thinking about all the might-have-beens… And all that time Beth had been alive.

"Where is she?" His initial relief was followed by something colder and harder. Beth was alive. Questions began to form. Dozens of them. Why had she left? And why so suddenly? What was her life like now? Was she single? Married? In a relationship? Why did those things matter? She had walked out on him without an explanation. If not in the middle of the night, near enough. It wasn't the action of someone who wanted to be with him. Nevertheless, she owed him some explanations.

Laurie shook her head regretfully. "I can't tell you that. If someone disappears the way Beth did, they do it for a reason. They don't do it because they want to be found. We have to respect her privacy." She gathered up her jacket and keys. "I wanted to come and tell you as soon as I found out because I knew what it would mean to you to know that she's alive. I'll be going to see her to question her about the Grant Becker case in the next few days. I'll let you know how she is, but that's all I can do."

Vincente didn't reply. Instead, he watched Laurie go, his body tense and his emotions raging. Beth didn't want to be found. He'd got that message loud and clear sixteen months ago when he tried searching for her. At that time, it looked like Beth had walked out of Stillwater without a backward glance. The clients in the legal practice where she worked as a lawyer had been less than happy at her departure. Her boss didn't have a clue where she'd gone. The landlord of the neat little house she'd rented out on the lake road had been bemused. She'd left most of her belongings and had paid her rent for the next quarter. When Vincente spoke to her friends they appeared genuinely bewildered…either that, or they were putting on a good performance for his benefit.

Then, four months after he had last seen her, the devastating news had emerged that Beth could have been one of Grant Becker's victims. She had the same physical characteristics as the other women Grant had murdered. Beth had dark, wavy hair, blue eyes and the sort of smile that could knock a man sideways. Her looks made her the ideal candidate to attract attention from Grant, to get his token gift of red roses…and then be brutally murdered by him.

Vincente thought back to the last time he had seen her, seeking new clues to her disappearance in light of Laurie's visit today. Beth had turned up at his apartment after more or less ignoring him for a month. The silent treatment had followed one of their fiery clashes. Theirs had always been a stormy relationship, filled with wild fights, frequent breakups and passionate makeups. Even though sex with Beth had always been explosive, that night had been one to remember. She had barely crossed the doorstep before they were tearing off each other's clothing, dropping T-shirts and jeans on the floor and kicking off boots as they kissed their way to the bedroom.

As he'd tugged her underwear down, his hands had lifted her and her knees gripped his hips. "Why are you here, Beth?" He had managed to gasp the words out as he walked her backward to the bed.

"Because I can't stay away." Her voice had been anguished as she pulled his head down to meet her lips. "No matter how hard I try. That's where the danger lies."

Those strange words were the last thing he remembered her saying to him. They had fallen asleep in each other's arms and when Vincente woke, Beth was gone. Although he had searched for her, it was only when he thought she had been killed that he realized how much the loss of her had torn him apart.

The police investigation had been one of the largest West County had ever seen. The search for women, including Beth, who had gone missing within the time-frame of the murders was wide-ranging and ongoing, but Vincente hadn't been able to leave it at that.

Guilt gnawed at him over those missing four months before the police had begun their inquiries. Sure, he had tried to discover where Beth was before Laurie had told him she could be one of Grant's victims, but had he done enough? If he hadn't simply assumed she'd walked out on him, could he have saved her?

Twelve months ago, as Stillwater was being rocked by the news that one of its sons was a serial killer, Vincente had been trying all over again to discover Beth's whereabouts. He had gone over every conversation, every confidence, every contact they'd ever had, searching for a clue. He'd even driven around the highways of West County late at night, hoping to catch a glimpse of her.

Even though his head had told him repeatedly to prepare for the worst, his heart had insisted on keeping a tiny flare of hope alight.

Now he knew she was alive and he was supposed to leave it at that? His lips tightened and his jaw clenched. *I don't think so.*

Beth Wade stared at the stack of papers in front of her with a mingled feeling of tiredness and despair. The deadline to have this paperwork completed was looming, but she'd hardly slept and her brain was refusing to cooperate. She thought briefly of her old job at E. Powell Law in Stillwater. Back then she'd have flown through a routine task like this…

Those days were gone. This was Casper, not Stillwater. She was no longer a rising star in a prestigious law firm, dealing with clients and grappling with difficult cases. She worked from home for an hourly rate and, if she didn't get started, she wouldn't get paid.

The knock on the door shook her out of her weariness. Twisting her hands together in her lap, she turned her head toward the sound. No one ever knocked on her door…

Cautiously, she rose from the kitchen table and walked silently down the hall. Maybe she could ignore it? Whoever it was would assume she was out and go away.

"Ms. Wade? My name is Laurie Delaney." The voice was pleasant and confident and… *Delaney*? "I'm an officer with the Stillwater Police."

With her mind spinning, Beth opened the door.

Her visitor smiled. "I'm also Vincente Delaney's sister-in-law." She said it as if it wasn't an earth-shattering statement. As if, even though Vincente was always at the back of Beth's mind, hearing his name spoken out loud wouldn't make her go weak at the knees.

Beth waved aside the badge Detective Laurie Delaney held out. "I'm not questioning that you are who you say you are. I'm just…"

"Bemused?" Laurie supplied helpfully.

*Bemused* was an understatement. *Stunned* would be a more accurate summary of how Beth was feeling. The woman standing on her doorstep was a police officer, and she was Vincente's sister-in-law. That was a hell of a chunk of information to assimilate on any day. Mid-morning on a Monday, after a sleepless night? It was taking a while to process the information. Realizing they were still standing by the open door, she gestured for Laurie to come into the house.

She had known when she left Stillwater that she

would miss Vincente, but she had never anticipated the depth of her longing for him. The feeling of loss was like a shard of glass lodged permanently in her heart. Even so, she couldn't succumb to her desire to ask Laurie questions about him. Just hearing his name had intensified her craving for him, ratcheting the ever-present pain up to a level where it was almost unbearable.

Beth hadn't left Stillwater to get away from Vincente. She had left because her life was in danger, and, if she'd stayed, she'd risk exposing him to the same harm. The anonymous person who was threatening her had made that clear.

*No police.* Whoever had sent the photographs and newspaper reports had included that chilling warning in the accompanying letter. But Laurie wasn't here because Beth had contacted her. And no matter how scared she might be of that letter writer, Beth could hardly slam the door in a police officer's face.

Once they were inside the narrow hall, a furry black-and-white shape trundled up to them, almost knocking Laurie off her feet. Beth hauled the wriggling, tail-wagging figure away from her visitor. "Sorry. He still hasn't got the message that he's meant to be a guard dog."

Laurie, who was clearly used to dogs, squatted and clicked her fingers. "He's beautiful. What's his name?"

Beth rolled her eyes. "Melon. He's a border collie. His previous owner named him. He thought it was funny."

"Sorry. I don't get it." Laurie looked confused.

"Melon-collie. Melancholy. They sound alike. It's meant to be a joke." Beth rolled her eyes. "I always have to explain it."

Laurie laughed. "I get it now. Melancholy? He doesn't suit his name."

Since Melon was lying on his back, with his tongue lolling as he waved his paws in the air, he seemed to be doing all he could to prove her statement correct.

"Despite appearances, he actually has a very good sense of who he should let into the house and who he should be wary of. He was trained as a search and rescue dog, but he injured his paw and needed some time out of action. When he was well again, his owner had a new K-9 partner. Luckily, it was around the time I was looking for a guard dog," Beth said. "I decided I needed one, since I'm living on my own with—" she bit her lip, annoyed at the near slipup "—no one else around."

"You can never be too careful," Laurie agreed.

Leading Laurie through to the kitchen at the rear of the house, Beth let Melon out into the yard before holding up the coffeepot. "I was just about to take a break from work."

It wasn't true, of course. Although the kitchen table was littered with papers and her laptop was still open, to say that she had been working would be stretching a point. She had been trying to get her brain in gear before she began to review the client evidence she had been sent.

If she was honest, she might have also been indulging in her regular pastime of daydreaming about Vincente. About what life might have been like if only she hadn't had to leave. About how she was ever going to get rid of the gnawing, yearning ache that came with the knowledge that she would never see or hear from him again.

Laurie didn't need to know the details of her daily struggle. And caffeine might be what Beth needed to help wake her sluggish brain cells.

"Coffee would be good." Laurie took a seat at the table.

"Did Vincente send you?" Even as she asked the question, Beth realized how foolish it was. If Vincente knew where she was, he would never send someone else in his place. He would be here himself, filling this room with his presence. With his dangerous masculinity. The thought sent a thrill of remembered longing down her spine.

"Vincente has no idea I'm here. And I won't tell him where you live." Laurie's tone was reassuring, the words confirming what Beth had just been thinking. "This is actually an official visit, but it's nothing to be concerned about."

Beth carried the coffee over to the table and took a seat opposite Laurie. "Now I'm intrigued."

"It's an intriguing story, and not a pleasant one. You may have heard about it if you've been following the news from Stillwater. Have you heard of the Red Rose Killer?"

"Goodness, yes." Beth had hardly been able to believe what she had been hearing when she had visited the grocery store and overheard a conversation about what had been happening in her hometown. Although Stillwater was a three-hour drive from Casper, the story of the murders had been gruesome and newsworthy. "I don't know all the details, but I knew Grant Becker. Was it true? I couldn't believe it when I heard someone saying he was responsible for killing all those women."

Laurie's expression was grave as she nodded. "I was a newcomer in Stillwater at the time, but I know how it rocked the whole community. I was working undercover on another job when I found out that Carla Bryan, who everyone thought had died in an accident, had actually been murdered. Carla was my cousin. Once I started investigating, it turned out that Grant had killed at least six other women who had the same physical characteristics as Carla. We're saying at least six because the investigation is still ongoing." She took a sip of her coffee. "It's the reason I'm here."

Startled, Beth raised her brows. "It is?"

"You left Stillwater very abruptly, and you have the same physical features as the women Grant Becker killed," Laurie said. "Dark hair, blue eyes, clear skin, slim figure, nice smile." She ticked the characteristics off on her fingers. "This was a huge investigation involving the FBI and the Stillwater Police Department. We couldn't rule out the possibility that you might have been one of Grant Becker's victims."

Beth took a moment to let that information sink in. "So you've been looking for me all this time?"

Laurie nodded. "Almost twelve months. When we didn't find your body with the others, we put out an alert asking you to come forward."

"I didn't see anything." Beth bit her lip. "I don't have much time for TV or newspapers." In a way, it was better that she hadn't known the police were looking for her. Knowing would have been a dilemma of epic proportions. How could she have ignored that? Yet, at the same time, how could she have responded to it? "How did you find me?"

"Even though you've been using an alias, your boss saw your picture in our newspaper advertisement and phoned in."

*And there you have it.* It was that easy. If the police could find her that way, anyone else could. Vincente could. Worst of all, *he* could find her. She always thought of the person who sent the letter and photographs as a "he", but it could just as easily be a woman.

Her thoughts must have shown on her face because she became aware of Laurie watching her with concern. Leaning across the table, the other woman clasped Beth's hand. "This is really not a big deal. Now that we know you are alive, I can cross you off our list of possible victims. I just came out here today to ask you a few questions. I hope that's okay. I certainly didn't want to worry you."

Beth forced her features into a smile. It would be very easy to confide in this woman. To go upstairs and get that envelope, lay everything on the table and tell her the whole story. That way she could hand over her cares to someone else. But she didn't have that luxury.

*It's not just my own safety that's at stake here.*

"Ask away."

The searching look in Laurie's eyes was still there as she flipped open her notepad. "I need to know whether you left Stillwater to get away from Grant Becker."

Beth shook her head. "Apart from the fact that Grant was friends with Vincente, he and I barely knew each other."

"So why did you leave Stillwater so suddenly?" Laurie asked.

At that moment—and with monumentally bad timing—a soft, demanding cry crackled over the baby monitor.

Vincente parked his car in a side street at right angles to the little house. From this vantage point, he could watch the front door without being too obvious.

Following Laurie around for the last three days had not been easy. Pursuing a seasoned detective in the small town where everyone knew them both? He had set himself an almost impossible task. But Laurie had said she would be questioning Beth about the Grant Becker case in the next few days. She had specifically said she would be "going to see" Beth. Vincente figured that, sooner or later, Laurie would lead him to Beth.

He decided the only way to check on his sister-in-law's whereabouts was to make it look like, by some fluke, they kept bumping into each other. At the end of the second day, Laurie was joking that she'd seen more of her brother-in-law lately than she had of her husband.

Chasing around town, getting in Laurie's way had played hell with Vincente's work schedule. His younger brother, Bryce, who ran Delaney Transportation with him, had sent him an increasingly frantic series of messages demanding to know why he had abandoned his office. Unable to explain that he was stalking Laurie, Vincente had feigned illness.

"You're never ill." Bryce managed to make the statement sound like an accusation.

"First time for everything." Vincente had done his best to sound feeble.

"Steffi was hoping you'd come over for dinner tonight. Cameron and Laurie will be there." Knowing how much Vincente enjoyed evenings spent around the table in his brother's rambling, comfortable home, Bryce had clearly decided to try another approach. Since his recent and blissfully happy marriage, Bryce enjoyed gathering the family together while his wife, Steffi, regaled them with stories of the animal sanctuary she was establishing. They had come a long way from the days when

Bryce had been the local stud, and Steffi was a famous Hollywood actress.

"Maybe next week when I've shaken off this flu." Vincente had turned down the invitation with real regret.

His stalking tactics had proved frustratingly unsuccessful. Until today. Today, his patience, or thinly disguised impatience, had finally paid off. Laurie had left home at her usual time this morning, but instead of going into town and making her way to the police headquarters, she had headed south.

After an hour of following her at a discreet distance, Vincente had gained an inkling about her destination. Beth's parents were dead, and she'd lost touch with most family members over the years. But he remembered that she spoke about friends of her parents who lived nearby in Casper whom she had visited now and then as a child. Although they weren't relatives, she had called them her aunt and uncle and always regretted losing touch with them. Vincente had forgotten all about them back when he had been searching for her, but he supposed it was possible that, when she left Stillwater, she'd gone to a town she knew. He became increasingly convinced he was right. The police wouldn't have known about the connection because the people he was thinking of weren't Beth's family.

Knowing Laurie would recognize his car, Vincente had rented a nondescript black sedan. Subterfuge really wasn't his style, but he was determined to find Beth and ask her the questions that refused to go away. Even in his rental car, he had stayed well behind Laurie. He had a healthy respect for his sister-in-law's powers of observation. The woman who had tracked down the Red

Rose Killer was more than capable of recognizing that she was being followed.

Once he was convinced he knew where she was going, Vincente had overtaken her on the freeway. Pulling in at a gas station on the outskirts of Casper, he had waited, hoping his hunch was correct. When Laurie's car came into view, he had released a long sigh of relief. If he'd been wrong, he wasn't sure what his next move would have been. All he knew for sure was that giving up wasn't an option.

Keeping his distance once more, he had followed Laurie to this quiet neighborhood in Casper. She had pulled up outside a house that was set back slightly from the street. Although he hadn't been able to see too much, he had watched as the door was opened and Laurie went inside. That had been almost an hour ago, and he was going half-crazy with tension, waiting for the opportunity to *do* something. He had been told more than once, by both of his brothers, that patience was not his best quality.

Finally, he saw a movement over at the house. Tilting the old cowboy hat he'd worn as an additional disguise low over his brow, but peering out from under the brim, he slunk down in his seat. Laurie came out of the house alone. No one accompanied her to the door. There could be any number of reasons why the occupant of the house had chosen not to escort her out. From Vincente's point of view, it was frustrating. Once again, he was denied the opportunity to get a glimpse of who lived there.

As Laurie made her way to her car, Vincente considered his options. Follow her back to Stillwater? Or stay here and find out if this really was Beth's hiding place?

He almost laughed aloud that he was even asking himself the question.

Once Laurie had driven away, he waited a few minutes to be sure she really had gone before leaving his car and going across to the house she had left. As he approached, he sized up the building. Nothing about it made him think of Beth. It had a slightly neglected air, as if the owner didn't have the time, energy or money to spend on it. He contrasted that with the Stillwater house she had lived in. That had been as neat as wax. Being organized seemed to come effortlessly to Beth, spilling over into how she dressed, her surroundings and how she dealt with other people. Vincente wondered, not for the first time, if the reason she had struggled with their relationship was because she couldn't neatly package up her feelings for him. When they were together there was no controlling what they felt. It had always been raw, primal…and incredible.

The thought spurred his feet up the front step. His heart was pounding so loud it almost drowned out the sound of his knock on the door. Prepared for disappointment, his nerves—already under intense pressure—were ratcheted up to crisis level when he heard a voice calling out.

"Did you forget something, Detective?" It wasn't just any voice. It was Beth's voice.

He wondered how she would react if she checked who it was through the peephole in the door. Her words indicated she thought Laurie had come back again, and he heard a key turn in the lock immediately after she spoke.

The door swung open and the smile on her lips faded. As she gazed at him in shock, Vincente took a moment to drink in her appearance. Her hair was shorter, just reaching her shoulders now instead of the waist-length mass in which he had loved to bury his hands. It was scraped back into an unflattering ponytail. She looked thinner. And tired, definitely tired. Almost to the point of exhaustion. But maybe the reason for that was sitting on her hip.

The baby wore pink sweatpants and a T-shirt with butterflies embroidered all over. Not quite a toddler, she was a perfect little girl. Her black hair clustered in a halo of curls around her head and she studied Vincente with eyes that were huge, dark and framed by thick, spiky lashes. The hint of olive to her skin and the full ruby lips were additional confirmation of his first suspicion. It was like looking in a mirror.

Vincente almost took a step back in shock as he gazed at his daughter.

# Chapter 2

The shock of seeing Vincente on her doorstep robbed Beth of the power to do anything. Thought, speech, movement—those basic functions deserted her just when she needed them most. The only thing she seemed capable of doing with any degree of competence was stare at him. Just stare…and maybe, deep down inside, feel the old longing to throw herself into his arms. But those days were gone. She wasn't that person anymore. She didn't have the luxury of acting on impulse where he was concerned. Where anything was concerned.

"What's her name?" Vincente threw her off balance with the question. *Like I was well-balanced before he asked.*

"Lia." It was surreal. She had pictured seeing him again so many times, but it had never been like this. She had imagined she would be cool and collected. Not that he would take away the ability to think of anything except how wonderful it was to see him again.

"You gave our daughter an Italian name?"

"No, my mother's name was Amelia." Even as she said the words, Beth realized her mistake. Vincente had said "our daughter," and she hadn't denied it. She lifted an impatient shoulder at the thought. Why would she deny it? Lia *was* his daughter. He only had to look at her to know that.

"Can I hold her?" Beth was amazed at the humble note in Vincente's voice. It was something she had never heard before, had never imagined he was capable of.

"She's not great with strangers." She issued the warning just as Lia decided to take matters into her own hands.

Holding her plump little arms up to Vincente, she wriggled her body away from her mother and toward him. Beth was so surprised at this phenomenon that she could only stare in astonishment as she handed Lia over. Vincente gazed into his daughter's big brown eyes with an expression of wonderment. In that instant, something inside Beth's chest lurched.

"Woof," Lia commented solemnly.

"It's her only real word," Beth explained. "She copies the dog."

"Is that good or bad?" Vincente couldn't seem to drag his eyes away from Lia's face. "I don't know anything about these things."

"Well, she's only eleven months, so she makes lots of sounds, but actual words aren't really her thing." For the second time that morning, she became conscious that she was keeping a visitor standing on the doorstep.

But this wasn't just any visitor. It was *Vincente*. "I don't think this is a good idea."

Fire blazed in the dark depths of his eyes. She could see him fighting to keep his anger under control for Lia's sake. When he spoke, his jaw muscles were rigid. "I agree. Finding out I have an eleven-month-old daughter that you didn't have the decency to tell me about is the worst idea I've ever heard of."

Vincente's moods had no gray areas, only extremes, but his anger had never scared Beth. Now, it terrified her. Not because she feared he would hurt her. This was Vincente. She knew he was incapable of doing her any physical harm. It wasn't fear of *him* that had made her flee Stillwater. But his gaze was a knife in her ribs, digging deeper with each passing second. Where once there had been warmth, there was now only contempt.

A fierce longing to tell him the truth swept over her, and she thrust it aside. Annoyance bubbled up in its place, and she hugged that emotion to her. It was typical of Vincente to do it *this* way. To confront her, invade her space, then become judge and jury and deliver his verdict all within the space of a few minutes.

"I've moved on with my life." She tried for a hard tone as she delivered the words. It wasn't true, but she needed to convince Vincente it was.

"Fine." The disdain left his eyes as they moved from Beth's face to Lia's. "Maybe we could continue this inside, since I'm not walking away now I know I have a daughter?"

Inviting him in would make a huge statement. But what would she gain by keeping him standing here? She knew Vincente's stubbornness only too well. When he said he wasn't going anywhere, he meant it. The thunderstorm was coming. Where it took place was irrelevant. She led Vincente into the family room, and he sat on one of the sofas. Lia commenced an exploration of his face, pulling at his neatly trimmed beard and trying to poke him in the eye. Her delighted squeals broke the ice, and Beth found herself smiling at Vincente's efforts to hold on to the squirming little bundle. Conscious of the untidy room, her shirt with its missing button and the stain on the front where Lia had spilled milk that morning at breakfast, Beth made a hurried movement to pick up some of the abandoned toys that littered the floor.

"Why didn't you tell me?" Even though it was the obvious question, it stopped her in her tracks. Since she had no idea where to begin with an answer, the series of increasingly anguished howls that rent the air provided a welcome reprieve.

"What the hell is that?" Vincente looked horrified.

"It's my dog, Melon. He wants to come in." Beth went through to the back of the house and opened the door.

When Melon reached the door of the family room, he paused, his ears flattening and his tail drooping. Beth could almost read the dog's mind. Visitors were a rarity, but Melon was a sociable creature, and, on the whole, he liked them. This one, however, had the audacity to place his hands on Melon's beloved baby. That couldn't be tolerated.

Crouching low, Melon bared his teeth and growled at Vincente. Since aggression toward humans wasn't in his nature, he mitigated the threat by wagging his tail.

"Sit!" Vincente's voice was stern. Beth recalled that he always did have a way with animals.

Melon, clearly realizing the error of his ways, dashed over to him, and attempted to lick his hand. "I said 'sit.'"

To Beth's amazement, Melon sat.

"He doesn't do that for me." She couldn't keep the aggrieved note out of her voice.

"You have to show him who's boss." Vincente snapped his fingers. Melon sidled forward, resting his head on Vincente's knee and gazing up at him with adoring eyes.

Beth took a deep breath. "Look, I'm not trying to avoid this conversation, but I have a huge amount of work to do and the deadline is tomorrow. And I need to get Lia's lunch ready..."

"You look tired." Vincente's eyes probed her face. Although it felt strange to have him here, a comment such as that was oddly comforting. It reminded her how well he knew her. He was the only person who really did. "More than tired. You look done in, Beth."

"You have no idea." She gave a shaky laugh. "Lia is teething, so she's not sleeping too well right now. I'm trying to fit work around her schedule, but since she doesn't really have a schedule—"

"Why don't you get some rest while I look after her?" The blunt words cut across her floundering and the hard look in his eyes had softened slightly, but the tension level between them remained high.

This was classic Vincente. Like a seasoned boxer, he knew how to cause a distraction before delivering the knockout blow. "I thought you wanted to talk?"

There was a razor edge to his smile. "Okay. Go. Tell me why I wasn't even worth a call or a message."

Beth wanted to go to him. To take his face in her hands and tell him how much he meant to her, how much their time together had meant. But although he looked like Vincente, he was a stranger. A hard, cold man who had put up a barrier between them. And she knew that, no matter what she said, it would only push him further behind that barricade.

"There is nothing I can say to make this right."

Even behind the anger, she could see Vincente's pain. In the past, she'd have known how to take the hurt away. This time, she was the cause. The knowledge caused tiny shards of ice to pierce her heart.

"You don't get off that lightly, Beth." She could see his muscles bunched tight beneath his T-shirt as he held his fists clenched. "This isn't like that time you drove my car into the wall and forgot to tell me. Or when I smashed that old china cat."

That was it. Vincente had always known how to get to her. Despite her determination to stay calm, Beth felt anger crashing through her. How dare he bring up past hurts at a time like this?

"You mean the antique figurine my grandmother left me? The one you broke and didn't tell me? The one I found in pieces in the trash?"

"Exactly." There was triumph in his eyes. "This isn't anything so trivial. This is about how we made another person and you didn't even bother to call me."

To her horror, Beth felt tears burn the back of her eyelids. When she tried to speak again, her lips trembled and her voice refused to work. Vincente started to speak again, but she held up a hand.

"No more." The word was little more than a croak and she struggled to get her voice back under control. Pointing to Lia, she shook her head. "Not in front of her." She took a deep breath. "And you're right. I'm tired."

His expression was grim, but she saw a glimmer of understanding in his eyes. "So do what I suggested.

Get some rest." The inflexible note was still there. "Because we are having this conversation, Beth. Whether you want it or not."

Flustered, she tried to hit on a reason to refuse that didn't involve going straight to ordering him out of her house. "She doesn't settle easily with people she doesn't know." Since Lia was curled comfortably into the crook of his arm, that excuse wasn't going to work. "You're not used to children."

"No, I'm not, but you'll only be upstairs. You're dead on your feet, Beth. I'm worried about you." In place of the continuing tempest, the unexpectedly gentle note in his voice shook her equilibrium even further.

She remembered that knack he had of catching her off guard. He was right. She couldn't remember the last time she'd slept for more than an hour or two at a stretch. If she didn't get some rest soon, she would fall down. And what use would she be if she was exhausted? If she didn't meet tomorrow's deadline, she would lose her job. She was already behind with the rent...

The situation was ridiculous. How many times had she pictured meeting Vincente again? Not once had the imaginary conversations she had conducted in her head included him offering to babysit. And behind the concern, she knew—because who knew him better than she did?—that his anger that was still waiting to be unleashed.

"Let me do this, Beth." A persuasive note in his voice, the one she hated because he used it to get her to do just about anything he wanted, made an appearance. "For old times' sake."

"I can't believe you just said that." She rolled her eyes.

He laughed. "Nor can I. The shock must have gone to my head."

"Okay." She had never thought of Vincente Delaney as an angel in disguise—the thought caused her to smile inwardly, since she had occasionally thought of him as a *devil* in disguise—but there had to be a first time for everything.

"All Lia's toys are in the box over there. There is pasta in the fridge for her lunch and she likes banana after it. She'll drink plain water from her own special cup. Oh, and her diapers and wipes are in this bag."

Vincente's calm deserted him slightly at those words. "I can come and get you if we have a diaper situation, right? That's something I'm going to need to do under supervision the first time." First time? The words had a confidence about them that unsettled her.

"Wake me if there's a problem."

She went to the door, turning back to look at him as he bent to talk to Lia. Although seeing Vincente here had tilted her world off course, the effect he was exerting over her pulse was not entirely due to the shock. He always did have the power to knock her sideways with his presence. Even though she had spent a lot of time over the last sixteen months dwelling on her memories of him, she had underestimated his magnetism.

What was she thinking? Every rational thought screamed at her to get him out of here. She had broken all her ties with Stillwater for a reason. A dangerous, life-threatening reason. Leaving had hurt more than she'd believed possible. Leaving Vincente? That had been its own kind of hell. She'd never known if they'd last forever. The longest they'd ever managed was a few months. Not because they didn't care. *We cared too much.* That had always been their problem. Everything between them was too much. Too passionate. Too intense. Too raw. Too hungry. It was like they burned each other up whenever they were together. But Beth had never imagined being with anyone else. Had never imagined her life without Vincente in it, even if it was only in their own, unique, on-off, tempestuous way. Until the letter and the photographs. They had changed everything.

"Get some sleep, Beth." Vincente's dark eyes seemed to read her thoughts. "Then we'll talk some more."

*Just this one time*, she told herself sternly, *and only because I'm so tired. Then we'll talk some more.*

Those words had an ominous ring to them.

Vincente's mind wanted to dwell on the shock to his system. He was struggling to know what to feel, although anger was making a strong case for being his most powerful emotion. How could Beth keep something like this from him? If Lia was eleven months old, that meant Beth had to have been four months pregnant when she left Stillwater. Vincente thought back to the roller-coaster ride that was their relationship. Yes, four months before Beth left, they'd been right in the middle of one of the most intense "on" times of their on-off periods. Soon after, they'd split up following a fight over something or other. He couldn't recall the reason, but he did remember Beth calling him arrogant and conceited before she slammed out the door.

Anger continued to bubble deep inside him, as hot and destructive as lava. It churned and boiled, desperate for release, and he knew there was a real danger of becoming too much for him to handle. He wanted to find a release. Slam his hand down on a table, kick a door, shout at the person responsible…

*Four months and she didn't tell me? She came to my apartment the night she left Stillwater and she didn't mention that she was carrying my child? She left me sleeping and walked out of my life, prepared for me to never know about this person who shares my DNA?*

He couldn't reconcile those thoughts with the Beth he knew. They'd always been honest with each other. From the moment they got together that first time they'd known what they had was different. Unique. Mind-blowing. But Beth had always known the truth about Vincente. He couldn't commit to a normal relationship. Hearts, flowers and promises of forever weren't for him. It didn't take much soul-searching to find the reasons why.

Even within his own family, Vincente had always felt like an outsider. The only unpredictable thing his rancher father ever did was fall in love with a beautiful Italian socialite. When Kane Delaney brought Giovanna Alberti home to Stillwater, she had batted her long eyelashes at him and declared that Wyoming was too boring to be her home. By the time Vincente was born, the marriage was in its death throes.

Even their son's name had been a cause for disagreement. Giovanna had wanted a full-on Italian name, while Kane had held out for something more American. In the end, they had compromised. Instead of the Italian "Vicente" or the American "Vincent," they had named him "Vincente." It was a metaphor for his life. With a foot in each world, he belonged in neither.

The ink was barely dry on the divorce papers before Vincente's mother had reverted to her maiden name and returned to Florence. Although he saw her occasionally, her aristocratic world might as well have been a million miles away from his Stillwater home.

Vincente knew Beth wasn't like his mother. He wasn't naive enough to believe that she would walk out on him and break his heart the way Giovanna had done to Kane. No, he was more afraid that *he* would be the one to hurt *her.* All he knew for sure was, however much he wanted Beth—and Vincente had never wanted anything in his life as much as he'd wanted Beth—there was something missing in his psyche. *Call it the Alberti gene. We don't do long-term.* His mother was on her fifth marriage. He was not going to put Beth through the same sort of torture.

And Beth had understood. She had always accepted him for what he was. Their relationship hadn't been one-sided. It hadn't been about her trying to get a ring on her finger and him resisting. It had always just been them. Doing it their own way.

Of course, a baby would have changed things. How? He couldn't answer that because the knowledge that Lia even existed had only just hit him. Had Beth run out on him because she thought he wouldn't be able to cope with the commitment? A wave of shame washed over him at the thought. She must have known him better than that. Surely, she must. If she thought he would leave her to cope with their child on her own, then she hadn't known him at all.

That brought another emotion to sit alongside the anger. As he looked down at Lia's perfect features, he felt an overwhelming sadness.

He hadn't wanted a child. If anyone had asked him why, he'd have said he'd be the world's worst dad. He was selfish, impatient, untidy, and he didn't like responsibility. Also, no sleep, no free time, no social life? No, thank you.

Now, he was in shock as his feelings on the subject had sharply reversed. Because how could he not want this beautiful little being? And how much of her life had he already missed? He hadn't been there when she was born. Hadn't heard that first cry or seen her first smile. She was crawling, pulling herself upright and making noises. Some of them almost sounded like words. She had a personality all her own…quite a strong one from what he'd seen so far. *She looks like me. This little person has been growing up without me.* The mingled feelings of joy and loss tugged at something deep within him.

Other than telling her Giovanna had left when he was a baby, he'd never talked to Beth about his mother, but she must have known there was a twisted branch in the Delaney family tree. It didn't take much imagination to work out that Giovanna's abandonment was at the root of Vincente's issues. The loss of a parent had impacted his whole life. Yet Beth had repeated the pattern with Lia?

He wanted to storm and rage at Beth for what she'd done, but he also needed to find out why she'd done it. This was Beth. Beth, to whom he had been closer than any other person in his whole life. There had to be a reason why she had deprived him of almost a year of his daughter's life. He had to get this right, for all they'd once been to each other, but also for the innocent child who was caught up in the middle of this.

The innocent child who was sliding from his knee with a purposeful glint in her eye. Vincente had never realized it was possible to move so fast at a crawl. Before he knew it, she had reached a vase of flowers and toppled it onto the floor. As he stooped to pick them up, she launched herself at the dog, grabbing him by the tail. Melon let out a yowl and ran for the door. That was the moment when Vincente decided it was probably a good idea to postpone the soul-searching and concentrate on the babysitting.

As he watched Lia and tried to keep up with her, some of the negative emotion coursing through him melted away. It was replaced by a new warmth as he felt an immediate connection to his daughter.

She was *his*. As well as the physical similarities, he could see other traits they had in common. When he tried to take something from her, a militant light entered her eye and she thrust out her chin, mirroring his own stubbornness. As he sat with her and tried to help her stack her blocks, she brushed his hand away, determined to try it for herself.

Although he'd been consumed by rage and shock as he'd crossed the threshold of this house, he'd resolved to do his duty. He had a child and he would take care of her. What he hadn't expected was this rush of pure joy he felt every time he looked at her.

Lia might look like him, but her smile was all Beth… or the Beth he'd once known.

He hadn't been exaggerating when he told Beth he was worried about her. Physically, she had barely changed, but there were other differences that became more apparent the longer he was with her. She was wound as tight as a coiled spring, tension apparent in every part of her slender body. The way she held herself taut as though poised for flight, the tilt of her head as if she was listening for a subtle sound and the way those glorious denim-blue eyes refused to settle on one thing.

He had thought at first it was because she was unable to make eye contact with him. Gradually, he realized her gaze was constantly moving, checking her territory, seeking reassurance that everything was normal.

She was exhausted. That had been apparent the moment he set eyes on her. And he had used it to his advantage. By offering to look after Lia while she got some rest, he supposed he had been manipulative, but wasn't he entitled to be devious in the circumstances? He had just come face-to-face with the daughter he didn't know he had. And he hadn't been entirely underhanded. Although, after the initial shock had worn off, his first emotion had been simmering rage, he could sense Beth's turmoil. Offering to look after Lia while she got some rest served a number of purposes. He got the chance to spend precious time with his daughter—*a tiny fraction of the eleven months I've lost*—Beth could recoup some of her strength for what promised to be the ordeal of the conversation they needed to have and Vincente could catch his breath.

He suspected he and Laurie were the only visitors this house had seen in a long time. Lia was immaculately dressed, but, like Beth herself, the house was clean without being exactly cared for. It was far from being a hovel, but her nervousness, together with the way she fussed around, picking up toys and plucking at the stain on her shirt, drew his attention to the details. She was clearly focused on appearances and finding them lacking. What had happened to the happy, sociable woman he'd known in Stillwater? Yes, Beth had a baby now, but would that turn her into a recluse? He didn't know enough about these things. Maybe it would.

But what worried him more than anything was the

feeling he got that all this was about more than being protective of her child. No, it wasn't a feeling. He knew her too well. It was a certainty. Beth was scared. More than scared. She was terrified.

Beth woke abruptly with a rising sense of panic. She was fully dressed, lying on top of the bedclothes. How could she be asleep during the day? What about Lia? Gradually, the events of the morning came back to her and she heaved a sigh of relief. The sensation of content-ment soon dissipated when she realized what she had done. *I left Lia with Vincente. Today might be the day I actually took leave of my senses.* She sat up abruptly. After sixteen months in hiding, she had not only opened her door to the man she had decided never to see again, she had blithely handed her daughter over to him.

*Our daughter*, she reminded herself. Lia would be safe with Vincente; there was no question about that. The problem was, now Vincente knew he had a daugh-ter, there could be no going back. He would want to be involved in her life. That was a conversation that was going to take every ounce of Beth's considerably de-pleted energy.

Pausing only to run a brush through her hair, drag it back into its ponytail and slip her ballet flats back on, she made her way back down the stairs. When she reached the family room, a scene of total devastation greeted her. Vincente was seated on the floor, half reclining against the sofa. His shirt was pulled out of his jeans and his hair and beard were smeared with something that looked suspiciously like dried banana. Lia was asleep with her head on his shoulder.

"She trashed the place," he whispered. His expression was stunned. "As soon as you left the room, she just went for it."

Every toy Lia owned was scattered across the floor. The wildflowers Beth had picked the day before were shredded into tiny pieces. The vase they had been in lay on its side and water formed a pool on the carpet around it. Cushions and throws had been dragged from the sofas and piled in a heap on the floor. It looked like a whirlwind had been through the room. And it had. Beth knew what Whirlwind Lia at full force could do. Vincente would not have stood a chance.

"I think she wore herself out." Vincente smiled ruefully as he indicated the sleeping figure in his arms.

Although she had only just woken up, Beth felt weariness crowding in on her once more. Stooping, she lifted her slumbering daughter into her arms. "I'll take her upstairs."

As she carried Lia from the room, she was aware of Vincente watching her intently. Once upstairs, she settled the warm, sleeping bundle into her crib, pulling a blanket over her. There was a draft coming through the open window, which she closed before returning to the crib. Bending to kiss Lia's soft cheek, she studied her face for a moment or two. Sleeping or waking, she could watch her forever. Right now, she supposed she should go and get the less attractive task of talking to Vincente over with.

When she reached the den, Vincente had picked up the throws and cushions and placed them back on the sofas. He paused in the act of placing Lia's toys back in their box. "No wonder you look tired."

"Laurie said she wouldn't tell you where I lived."

"She didn't." His expression was half wary, half apologetic. "I followed her without her knowledge." He ran a hand over his face and, feeling the residue of the banana, grimaced. "Is there somewhere I can clean up?"

Beth directed him to the bathroom and went into the kitchen to fix coffee, shaking her head at the normality of the situation. This was *Vincente*. The thought was on a loop inside her head. They didn't do polite conversation. They'd never needed words. The last time she'd seen him, she had kicked his apartment door shut and torn his shirt off. They hadn't exchanged more than a few sentences that night. It had almost killed her to sneak out of his apartment without saying goodbye. She had left his apartment, gotten into the car that was already loaded with her luggage and driven out of Stillwater for good. The ultimate irony had come two weeks later, when she realized that the recurring stomach bug that had been bothering her was actually a four-month pregnancy.

Vincente reappeared with his shirt tucked in and the banana removed. As Beth poured the coffee, she was conscious of those melting dark eyes watching her face. "When were you planning on eating lunch?"

"Don't do this, Vincente." She handed him his coffee and took her own to the table, grimacing as she viewed the paperwork that she still hadn't touched. If she pulled another all-nighter, she might just meet the deadline.

"Do what?" He came to sit opposite her.

"I know these tactics. This is where you soften me up before you go for the kill." She took a deep breath. "I know how angry you are. Just say what you have to say."

He didn't speak for a moment or two and she took in the tight set of his jaw, the glitter in the dark depths of his eyes and the way his clenched fist rested on his muscled thigh. "You think angry comes close to describing what I'm feeling right now? I'm so far beyond that it's not true. But I want to understand why you cheated me out of almost a year of Lia's life. I'm trying to contain my feelings so we can have some sort of rational dialogue for the sake of that little girl upstairs, and because I'm concerned about you—"

"Oh, no." Beth sprang to her feet. "I see where this is going. You think you can walk in here and pull a stunt like that?"

"What the hell are you talking about? What stunt?" Vincente looked up at her, his expression bemused.

*"Get some rest, Beth. Let me do this for you, Beth. For old times' sake?"* Her voice quivered as she mimicked his concerned tone. "What will you tell the judge when you try to take my daughter away? You turned up here and found I was incapable of looking after her? Depressed? Unstable? An unfit mother?"

Vincente got to his feet, facing her across the width of the table. "Is that what you think?" His voice was harsh. "That I've changed so much I would do that to you?"

"I'm sorry. It's just that losing her…it's my worst nightmare." He didn't know—couldn't know—what she'd been through. The debilitating anxiety and isolation of postpartum depression was something she still found hard to come to terms with, even now she was over the worst of it. At times like this, when she felt under pressure, some of the symptoms resurfaced. She no longer needed medication, but she did occasionally keep in touch with her counselor. Right now, she focused on regulating her breathing. It was one of the techniques she had learned for coping with stress.

"Beth, no matter what I'm feeling, I would never try to take Lia from you."

Beth knew Vincente well enough to sense when she could trust him. He couldn't be trusted to turn up on time to a date. She couldn't trust him to remember birthdays and anniversaries. No matter how many times she told him, trusting him to remember that she hated anchovies on her pizza never worked. But when it came to the big things? She knew he would never lie to her. This was one of those times. There was nothing but truth in those dark eyes.

"I still want an answer to my question. Why did you leave Stillwater without telling me you were pregnant?"

She took her seat again, making an effort to relax the tension in her limbs. Following her lead, Vincente sat down, as well. How could she tell this story without telling him all of it? Vincente wasn't a fool. He was the smartest person she knew. Not only was he the most quick-witted, well-read, articulate person to have made her acquaintance, but he was also the most perceptive. And where Beth was concerned, he was incredibly intuitive. He had always been able to tell when she was lying.

"It wasn't like that." She took a sip of her coffee, buying a little time. "I didn't know I was expecting a baby when I left Stillwater."

"Math is my job, Beth. I've already done the calculations. Lia is eleven months old. That means you must have been four months pregnant when you ran away—" she nodded in confirmation "—yet you didn't know?" His voice said it all. She hadn't been some kid who didn't know her own body. She had been a twenty-seven-year-old attorney with a promising career.

"I had a lot on my mind." God, those words sounded so lame. But it was true. The newspaper report had arrived two months before she left Stillwater. She hadn't known that Lia had already been growing inside her, hadn't noticed the missed periods and the changes in her body. Her whole focus had been on the nagging worry at the back of her mind. The worry that had ratcheted up to a whole new level a month later with the arrival of the letter and the first photograph. By the time the next one turned up in her mailbox a week before she left Stillwater, she had been half-crazy with worry. Any physical symptoms her body had been displaying had come second to the turmoil of her emotions.

Receiving anonymous threats had been bad enough. When those warnings became directed at anyone close to her, she had panicked. Because there was only one person close to her. Whether he liked it or not, Vincente had been the one who meant the most to her. Even though it had broken her heart to leave, even though missing him had been a constant ache ever since, it had seemed like the only way she could protect him.

Now he was here, and she couldn't tell him the truth. *I'll come after the ones you love...* Even the thought of those words made her shiver.

Vincente frowned. Clearly, he wasn't buying her explanation. Beth didn't blame him. She wouldn't herself if she was the one listening to it. *A lot on my mind.* It was a classic fobbing-off phrase. His lips parted in preparation to ask more just as a cry from the baby monitor, for the second time that day, provided an interruption.

This cry was different. This wasn't one of Lia's usual noises. It was a high-pitched scream that brought Beth straight to her feet and had her running for the door.

At the same time, out in the yard, Melon went into a frenzy of barking.

"What is it? What's wrong?" Picking up on her panic, Vincente was right behind her as she dashed up the stairs.

"Someone is in Lia's room."

## Chapter 3

Vincente got all the confirmation he needed about Beth's state of mind when she hurtled from the kitchen and charged up the stairs. "Someone is in Lia's room? What the hell do you mean?" How had she reached that conclusion from the noise she had heard Lia make through the baby monitor?

Beth didn't answer. He could hear her breath catching in her throat in a series of gasps as she reached the top of the stairs and burst through a door to her left. To Vincente's relief, Lia was lying on her side in her crib with a pink-and-white blanket pulled up to her chin. Her long lashes shadowed her cheeks and her breathing was rhythmic.

Beth made a sound that was somewhere between a sigh and a sob. She raised a hand to her lips, but it was shaking so wildly she couldn't complete the action and she lowered it back to her side. When she turned to look at Vincente, her eyes were urgent and haunted, their blue depths awash with unshed tears.

"Beth—" *just what was going on with her?* "—she's fine. No one has been in here."

The tears spilled over as she blinked, and she brushed them impatiently away with the back of her hand. "She cried out as if someone had touched her." He could see doubt creeping in now as she turned back to look at Lia. "That's how she cries when a stranger tries to hold her."

She shivered slightly as if a chill had caught her unawares. Turning slowly, she looked at the open window. "No. I closed that when I brought her up here. I know I did."

"Maybe you forgot. It's easily done."

The uncertainty and trembling were gone now. Momentarily, he was looking at the old Beth. "I know I closed the window. I felt a draft and I moved across here to close it before I came downstairs." There was a militant look in her eye. One he remembered well. "I'm not wrong about this, Vincente."

She moved to the window and leaned out. "Look." She pointed. "Someone has placed a ladder up against the side of the house, right below this window. That's how he got in."

Vincente was still skeptical. "In broad daylight? And why didn't that mad dog of yours attack whoever it was that was setting a ladder up against the side of the house and climbing in through one of the windows?"

"Because this room is at the side of the house." Beth was pacing now, wrapping her arms around her waist as though hugging herself. "Melon is in the backyard.

He was barking to warn me, but he couldn't get around to this side."

"So, this person, whoever it was, climbed in, touched Lia and made her cry, climbed out again and ran off?" Vincente said. "Why? What did he, or she, hope to gain from it?"

"He wanted to frighten me. He said if I told anyone… if I involved the police…" She struggled to regulate her breathing. "Now you and Laurie have been here. This is his way of warning me."

Vincente was about to pursue the subject further when Lia stirred and rolled onto her back. The action revealed an item that had been hidden under the blanket. Although Vincente could see it was a photograph, he couldn't make out the detail, and he didn't get a chance to look too closely. His attention was taken up by the remarkable effect the picture had on Beth.

As soon as she saw the photograph, she gave a little cry and ran from the room. Picking up the picture, Vincente straightened the blanket over Lia before following her. When he found Beth, she was on her knees beside a bed. Presumably this was her own bedroom.

As he watched in surprise, she hauled a suitcase out from under the bed and opened it. Pulling open the closet, she began to throw clothes into the suitcase.

"What are you doing?" *Apart from losing your mind?*

"Getting out of here." She brushed past him and, opening a drawer in the dresser, carried an armful of underwear over to the case. "Right now."

Beth's heart was beating so fast it felt like it was going to burst right out of her body. Her chest grew tighter as if her ribs and lungs had expanded beyond their capacity and, with nowhere to go, they were forced to stay inside her. One minute she couldn't inhale. The next, her breath was coming in great, whooping gasps as though she'd just finished running a marathon.

Then her stomach decided to join the party, giving a huge backflip that sent sick bile rising up into her throat, making her gag. And the whole time her mind was playing one thought on a loop, over and over.

*Get out.*

She raced wildly around her bedroom, scarcely aware of Vincente until he blocked her way, forcing her to stop what she was doing and look at him.

"You have to tell me what this is about."

"No." *Don't tell.* That was what the letter had said. *I'll know if you do.* "I can't."

"Beth." He caught hold of her hands, and his touch slowed some of the madness in her heart. "I am not letting you leave here like this. You may have run from me once, but it's not happening again. I will keep following you until you tell me what is scaring the hell out of you." He lowered his voice, so it became softer and more persuasive. "You have always been able to tell me anything."

She looked into those midnight eyes. He was right. No matter what crazy point they had been at in their relationship—midfight, making up, wildly in love, just friends—Vincente was the one person to whom she could always take a problem. Even when she was mad at him, she used to go to him for advice. *That was before I had a madman on my tail. And now he's after my daughter.*

The thought sent a renewed flare of panic storming through her and she tried to tug her hands away. "I can't."

Vincente pointed to the picture he'd placed on the bed. "That was placed in my daughter's crib. If you won't tell me what it's about, do I need to take it to the police?"

Beth felt the color, what little there was left of it, drain from her face. "No. Please don't."

"Then talk to me, Beth." He released one of her hands and picked up the picture. "We can go to Lia's room, if you feel more comfortable there."

She nodded. "Give me a minute to get something."

While Vincente returned to the nursery, Beth withdrew the envelope containing the letter, newspaper report, and the other photographs from the drawer in her bedside table. Was she really going to do this? She had run from Stillwater because of this. She had left her old life behind, partly because she had been in danger, but also because any people to whom she was close had been in danger. And Vincente had been the closest of all. Oh, he didn't know that. Or maybe he did…but he would never admit it. Vincente didn't do close. He was great at the physical stuff. But emotionally? *No. We never went there. Every time things strayed close to the* L *word, we'd find ourselves breaking up again.*

But this was no longer just about Beth. Someone had been in Lia's room today, and that someone had already killed two people. Beth was determined to do all she could to protect Lia, but maybe she needed help. And what better person was there to help her than Lia's father?

Even so, this wasn't going to be easy. She'd been keeping this secret for two long years and it felt like part of her. Opening up, even to Vincente, was going to be tough, particularly as there were parts of the story that were so hard to tell.

When she reached Lia's room, she leaned over the crib. The sight of that little figure always restored her equanimity and she smiled as she breathed in that unique Lia-smell. Looking up, she was aware of Vincente's eyes on her. There was only one chair in the room, and he indicated for Beth to take it while he sat on the floor nearby.

*Okay, let's do this.* She sat down, gripping the envelope tightly. "This started way back when I was eighteen. You know what happened the summer before I went away to college, right?"

They had both lived in Stillwater all their lives, but Vincente was five years older than Beth. She was closer in age to his younger brother, Bryce. As a teenager, she had been increasingly aware of the dark, broodingly handsome oldest Delaney brother, but it was only when she came back after college and started working for a law firm in town that the attraction had ignited between them.

"I remember what you told me, and I saw the news reports. I know people in Stillwater still talk about it now and then. But I was in Italy that summer visiting my mother." His lips twisted into a smile that was both bitter and affectionate. "It was one of her weddings, possibly the fourth. I've lost count. I always thought you told me a shortened version of what happened on the mountain because you couldn't bear to talk about it. Although I know some of the detail, if it's important to this story, tell me about it again."

"You're right. Even though I couldn't forget it, I tried to avoid discussing it. At that time, I loved rock climbing." *At that time*. Those words held a world of memories and meaning. "I belonged to the West County Climbing Club. It was run by a group of experienced climbers, who encouraged those of us who were new to the sport. We traveled all over the state, climbing the Tetons, Ten Sleep and Sinks Canyon. That summer, they organized an expedition to climb the Devil's Peak, the highest point on the Stillwater Trail."

"How many of you went on the climb?"

It still didn't seem real that Vincente was here in Lia's pink-and-white room. He was seated with his back against the closet—the one on which Beth had carefully stenciled teddies and bunnies—with his knees drawn up and his clasped hands resting loosely between them. He looked so big and masculine. That should be reassuring, right? His presence should make her feel safe and protected. Maybe it would…if it wasn't for the contents of the envelope she held in her hands.

"There were two instructors and eight junior climbers. Although we were amateurs, the Devil's Peak is so difficult, we had to have a high level of expertise before we could be included in the team. Although I was only eighteen, and the youngest member of the group, I had been part of the club since I was thirteen. I'd done some tricky climbs and Rick Sterling, the lead instructor, was my mentor. He had partnered me on several tricky climbs and he decided I was qualified enough to join this one." Beth tried out a smile. "I was so excited when he said I could go along. In hindsight, I wish he'd told me to stay at home."

"I don't know much about these things, but I know the Devil's Peak is a beast of a climb," Vincente said.

"I read an article not so long ago rating it one of the top ten hardest in the country."

"It's a killer." Beth winced as she said the words. "Climbing the Peak was always going to involve an overnight stay. We started out hiking through the alpine meadows at the base, then it became like a rocky moonscape before we had to tackle a vertical notch known as the Keyhole. The drop-offs from there were like nothing I'd ever seen. It was vertigo-inducing. We were about halfway up when, without warning, the weather changed. We were caught in a snowstorm. The wind was lashing around us and more snow was whipping off the surrounding peaks. We were completely exposed. Halfway up a dangerous rock face with nowhere to go."

"Surely your instructors had checked the weather conditions before you set off?" Vincente asked.

"They had. This was totally unexpected. And it was one of the recommendations that came out of the inquiry that followed. Now, climbers are warned that the weather on the Devil's Peak can change in minutes and that forecasts are not always accurate. We didn't have the benefit of that warning."

"So you had to choose whether to go up or down?"

"We chose to keep going." There had been no right or wrong choices. The only decision had been to keep moving in one direction or another. Beth recalled the tension as, blinded by the snow in their faces and buffeted by the wind, they had continued with the climb. Rick had reasoned that, once they reached the next plateau, they could set up camp as planned. "Physically, and mentally, it was the most challenging thing I've ever done. Clinging on to the rock while the wind tried to drag me off set every muscle screaming in agony. After a few hours, my arms and legs felt like Jell-O. My brain was mush, I can't remember having a single coherent thought during that time. We were almost at the top when one of the group fell. His name was Cory Taylor and, after the instructors, he was probably the most experienced climber among us. It was at a point when we'd almost reached safety. He *should* have been okay by then."

Beth paused, drawing a breath. It had been so long since she'd talked about it. The horrors of that day hadn't receded in the intervening years, but she'd thought about it less over time. She supposed that was what coming to terms with it meant. It didn't go away, but she learned to live with it. When the letter arrived, it had brought it all flooding back, of course. In the two years since then, it had resurfaced regularly.

"I know his injuries were bad." Vincente's voice was gentle.

"He broke his neck and his back." She spoke bluntly. There was no other way to tell it. "We were roped together in pairs. When Cory fell, it was only the skill of Rick's coleader, Tania Blake, that stopped him and his partner plummeting off the rock face and into oblivion."

She paused, taking a moment to collect her thoughts. Leaning forward, Vincente placed a hand on her knee, and his touch ricocheted through her like a streak of lightning. It was good and bad. Good because it grounded her, reassured her and brought her back to normality. Bad because she felt a resurgence of all the old feelings tingle through her nerve endings…and how wrong was it to feel like that in this situation?

"Between us, we got Cory to the top of the Keyhole. By that time, we were in a full-blown storm. We had no way of getting medical help for Cory. No radio or cell

phone signal. Nothing." Beth covered her face with her
hands at the memory. "It was awful. He was in so much
pain. I can still hear his screams, still hear him pleading with us to let him die. He kept saying it was what
he wanted. It was the most awful sound I've ever heard.
And we were so helpless. There was nothing we could
do. One of the team, Peter Sharp, was a paramedic. He
gave Cory painkillers, but they couldn't even touch the
pain he was in. We had pod tents that we were able to
get up in spite of the snow, and we took turns to sit with
him during the night. I was the one who was with Cory
when it happened."

"When he died?" Vincente asked.

"When he was murdered."

Lia woke up right at the point when Vincente was
going to suggest Beth needed to take a break anyway.
Telling the ten-year-old story was clearly taking its toll
on her. Although Vincente had heard a watered-down
account from Beth herself several years ago, and had en-
dured the town gossips' version of events now and then,
hearing the details was harrowing. He still wasn't sure
what the "Murder on the Devil's Peak," as it had become
known in Stillwater folklore, had to do with Beth's current problems, but he guessed she was leading up to that.

Worry continued to play in a loop as he observed Beth
and thought about what she was telling him. Either the
incident on the mountainside had some connection to
her current state of mind or her problems were out of
control. Either way, he was concerned about her.

The story she had told him was worse than he had
imagined. He knew she had been on a climb that had
ended in danger and the death of one of her companions,

but he hadn't paid attention to the details. That hadn't been because he was uncaring. It had been because he had believed Beth wanted to put the whole episode behind her. Now he knew she hadn't done so. He had been shocked by what she'd told him. Beth had lived through a nightmare. Had she ever really recovered from that?

Beth carried Lia down to the kitchen and handed her to Vincente while she fixed her formula. "Although this still feel weird, you have no idea how useful an extra pair of hands is." After the drama of the last few hours, he was pleased to see her make an attempt at a joke.

"Why didn't you get yourself a proper guard dog?" he asked as she opened the door and Melon bundled excitedly into the room.

"Melon *is* a guard dog." Beth seemed offended on behalf of her pet.

Melon brought Vincente a chewed-up tennis ball and dropped it at his feet in an invitation to a game. When Vincente ignored him, the dog pushed the toy closer with his nose. "I hate to be the one to break this to you, but that is not a guard dog."

Beth brought the bottle of milk over, and Lia reached out eager hands for it. "She'll do all the work if you sit down with her," Beth said.

They moved to sit at the table. "Are you ready to tell me the rest of it?" Vincente asked as Lia leaned contentedly back against his arm, making little gulping noises as she drank the milk.

Her weight on his arm felt right and his heart expanded with the strength of his feelings. He wanted to keep her here in his arms, safe and warm, just like this, forever.

"I don't know what happened, if that's what you

mean. I was in Cory's tent with him. The idea was to talk to him, to keep telling him everything was going to be okay. In reality, I'm not sure he even knew there was someone there, let alone that he could understand what we were saying. He was out of his mind with pain. I had my flashlight and my book with me and I was reading to him. Then I felt a blow to my head and I blacked out. Sometime later, the next person came into the tent to sit with Cory. They found I was unconscious with a head wound, and Cory was dead. He had been suffocated. We didn't know that for sure until the inquest. We thought— hoped, even—that he could have died in his sleep."

"Did you have any idea who did it?" Vincente asked. Although he was focused on what Beth was saying, part of his mind was on the warm weight of his little girl against his arm. He had started this day not knowing she existed and now having her there felt like the most natural thing in the world. If Beth was right and someone was threatening her, threatening them both…

What he felt for Lia went way beyond the natural protectiveness any normal adult felt toward a child. Within minutes of meeting her, his hard, outer shell had melted, leaving him with a new vulnerability. He had a family to care for now. The thought of anything, or anyone, harming a hair of his daughter's head had him snarling inside like a tiger. He pressed his cheek against her hair, breathing in the scents of shampoo and baby powder, feeling the hook that connected his heart to hers digging in a little deeper.

He looked up to see Beth watching him. She came within his protective sphere, as well. She always had.

"No. We thought—" she bit her lip as she answered

his question "—this sounds awful, but we thought someone had done it as a sort of kindness."

"A misguided way of ending his misery?" It was a horrible idea, but he understood what she meant.

Beth nodded, tears filling her eyes. "It can't ever be right to take a life, but anyone who heard his cries couldn't fail to be moved. The storm was over by then and Rick found a place to get a signal. He called the Stillwater Ranger Service and they sent an emergency team. Once it was known how Cory had died, there was a police investigation, but no one was ever charged with his murder. It got a lot of press attention."

"Did you bear the brunt of it because you were with him when he died?" Vincente had been out of the country at the time, so he hadn't seen the news reports.

"Some of it was brutal, suggesting that I knew what happened, that I colluded with the person who killed him, even that I did it. The attention died down eventually." Beth bit her lip. "But the memories took a lot longer to fade. I couldn't go rock climbing again after that. I think some of the club members still got together— maybe they do even now—but I couldn't face seeing any of them. Talking about what happened just seemed all wrong. Anyway, it had started to fade naturally into the background. I still thought about it, but less and less often. Then I got this."

She reached for the brown envelope that she'd brought downstairs with her. Opening it, she withdrew an old newspaper cutting. It had been written a day or two after Cory's death. The headline was Climbers' Death Storm Horror. Whoever had sent it to her had taken a red pen and carefully scratched out the words *climber* and *climb-*

*ers* throughout the text, replacing them instead with the words *murderer* and *murderers*.

"When were you sent this?" Lia had drained her bottle and was struggling to be put down. Vincente dredged up a memory of babies and feeding. "Doesn't she need to be burped or something?"

"No, she's older now. She'll be fine." Lia crawled with surprising agility over to a box of toys. Beth's eyes followed her and remained on her as Lia settled down to play. "About two years ago." She returned to his question.

"Why didn't you tell me at the time?" His earlier anger had given way to a nagging feeling of anxiety. His worries about Beth were growing by the minute, settling in his gut as a physical ache. He had a feeling it wasn't going to shift any time soon.

She withdrew the other items from the envelope and pushed them toward him. "Because of these. The letter, and the first photograph were sent a month after the newspaper article."

There were four photographs, all similar to the one that had been left in Lia's crib, and a short letter. Vincente read the letter first.

*Greetings, Murderers,*

*When you killed Cory Taylor, you took away my life. Now I'll take yours. One by one. You don't know who I'll come for first. You don't know who'll be next. Don't tell. I'll know if you do, and I'll come after the ones you love. Enjoy looking over your shoulder. One day, I'll be there.*

"Beth, this is sick, but you can't let it get to you. You should have gone straight to the police." Vincente was outraged to think that she'd been living in fear all this time because of this.

He was shaken to the core at what he was seeing and hearing. Beth had run from her life in Stillwater, from *him*, because of this hateful letter? Part of him wanted to ask why she hadn't trusted him enough to share what she'd been going through, but the haunted look in her eyes told him all he needed to know. Beth hadn't been capable of thinking of anything beyond the sheer terror caused by these threats.

Although his initial reaction was to give in to the rage he felt, Vincente knew he had to deal with this differently. Storming out of the house in search of the person who had written those words wasn't going to help Beth, or protect her and Lia.

Beth was so fragile; any wrong move on his part could tip her over the edge. He had to show her she could trust him. No matter how much he wanted to punch the wall, he had to act with compassion.

"Look at the photographs, Vincente." Beth lined them up in front of him on the table. "This is a group photograph, taken just before we set off on the climb. We all had a copy of it as a memento of the expedition. This was my copy—" She tapped an unmarked version of the picture with one fingertip before moving along to the next photograph. "And this is the one that was sent to me with that letter. It's the same photograph, but in this one there is a red *X* over Cory's face."

Vincente could see the pattern that was emerging along the line of photographs. "A month later, I was sent this picture." Beth pointed to the next photograph. "In this version, there are two red *X*s. As well as Cory's face being crossed out, there is a red *X* over the face of Andy Smith, one of the other climbers." She moved on to the next picture. "I got this picture the day before I left

Stillwater. Three *X*s. This time, the expedition leader, Rick Sterling, has his face crossed out."

Vincente had a feeling he wasn't going to like the answer to his next question. "Did you get in touch with Andy and Rick after you received these pictures?"

She lifted her eyes to his face. "I tried, but they are both dead."

Vincente took a moment to let that information sink in. "What about the police, or anyone else who was on the climb? Did you try to contact them?"

"You saw what the letter says." Her face was ashen. "Once I heard Andy and Rick were dead, I knew it wasn't an idle threat. If I'd tried to speak to anyone, I'd have been putting you in danger. The only thing I could do was leave."

## Chapter 4

Vincente envied people who sailed through life on unruffled emotional seas. In comparison, he steered through passionate storms. His feelings swooped from high to low, but rarely seemed to settle in that midrange known as calm. The only times he'd truly found inner peace had been during those times with Beth when their relationship had been stable.

Even so, he'd never known a day like this one. It had him on the emotional ropes and was pounding him into submission. Just how many sensations could a few hours throw at him? The initial anger he'd felt toward Beth for concealing Lia from him was still there. Perversely, amid everything else that was going on, he felt cheated out of the big confrontation he needed. His rage wanted an outlet and it wasn't going to get it.

In the past, there had been a script. Vincente was

good at being mad. Hard, biting comments that provoked
a reaction from Beth were his specialty. His anger craved
her response. A smile twisted his lips. Beth didn't do
submissive. She had always snapped right back at him,
giving as good as she got. The air between them would
crackle with fire and intensity. The outcome always hung
in the balance. Would one of them storm out? Or would
they end it by tumbling into bed, finding a resolution
that didn't need words?

Okay, nothing as big as a secret child had ever come
their way. Anger and hurt this bad had never featured in
their lives. Even so, Vincente's initial instinct had been
to turn his fury on Beth. When he had gotten over the
initial shock, all he wanted to do was incite one of those
huge, explosive fights.

Restraint didn't come easily to him. He choked back
a laugh. Most days, it didn't come to him at all. But it
hadn't taken him long to see he needed to find some of
it. Right around the time Lia was trying to hitch a ride
around the house attached to Melon's tail, he realized
this was a situation that required careful handling. And
things had gotten a whole lot stranger since then.

Vincente had to put aside his feelings of anger and
hurt about Lia. No matter how cheated he felt that he had
been kept out of his daughter's life, he had to rise above
it. And, once he had learned about the photographs, part
of him could understand Beth's motives.

Now, it was dusk and Vincente had offered to take
Melon for a walk while Beth prepared dinner. The dog
was bounding wildly in and out of the trees, chasing
imaginary prey and occasionally returning to check
on Vincente, his tongue lolling and his flanks heav-
ing. Guard dog? Beth had to be kidding. Melon was a

likable idiot. At least this activity had given Vincente some thinking time.

He wasn't sure there was a murderer lurking behind the anonymous messages. More likely it was a sick mind, someone who took pleasure from tormenting Beth with evil threats. But whoever it was, whatever their motive, that person had been inside Beth's house today. Inside Lia's room. That strayed beyond idle threats, and into the realms of dangerous. Even if the sender of those letters had no real intention of committing murder, it didn't matter. Beth believed he wanted to kill her, and now Lia. She was terrified by it. So terrified she had run from her home. The thought of what she had been through sent a surge of emotion through him. Beth had been in hiding for all these months, cowering in fear of her nameless tormentor, struggling to bring up their child on her own.

Alongside a renewed feeling of anger, Vincente's chest constricted. The feeling of helplessness was overwhelming. Telling himself he couldn't have done anything because he hadn't known wasn't good enough. Although it was irrational, he couldn't shake the feeling that he *should* have known.

*I should have done more to find her.*

It was all very well blaming the Red Rose Killer investigation. Had he ever really believed she was dead? A connection like theirs didn't just fizzle out when one person went away. The pain he'd felt when she left had been like nothing he'd ever known before. But he had nothing against which to measure it. Beth had been the only person with whom he'd had any sort of relationship and he'd always known their mini-breakups weren't permanent. That sounded overconfident, but that was how it was between them. They'd had a bond that was different to anything he saw in other couples around him, as unique as it was unbreakable. When Beth had left for good, the closest thing he could compare it to was the grief he'd felt when his father died. But losing Beth had felt more acute. More raw. As if he knew it was something from which he would never recover.

There had been no one he could to talk to about it. Growing up, his relationship with his half brothers had been antagonistic. They had been family in the remotest sense of the word. Vincente had been almost two when Cameron was born, and Bryce had come along two years later. Vincente didn't need any in-depth analysis to tell him that he'd been jealous of his half brothers, even though their mother, Sandy, had done her best to make him feel loved. Their childhood had set the tone for an uneasy distance between them in adult life. It was only recent events that had made the three brothers see they could be a formidable team when they put their minds to it. Taking on a vicious serial killer and then a corrupt, murdering politician had made them realize they were bound together by unbreakable ties of love and loyalty.

Even though he was closer now to Cameron and Bryce, confiding in his brothers about his emotions wasn't an option. Vincente didn't open up to others, and he certainly didn't do feelings.

Among all the other emotions fighting for dominance, there was also a powerful concern for Beth. He could understand the change in her now, but it didn't mean he was any less worried about its impact. He wasn't even sure if she had that spark in her anymore, the one that would fire up and fight back at him if he pushed her. Deep in his chest, the thought triggered a shard of pain. This scared, broken woman wasn't *his* Beth.

His shoulders sagged. The weight of his responsibility felt huge. He had no intention of shirking it, but he needed to get it right. *Had* to get it right. It was too important. He had to take charge. For Lia. For Beth. For all of them.

He stepped back inside the house, releasing the catch on Melon's lead.

"Thank you." Beth's smile hit him right in the center of his chest. "I never seem to find the time to walk him as often as I should."

"I did some thinking while I was walking." He might as well plunge right into this. "And I think you should come back to Stillwater with me."

Beth was pleased at the way she managed to get her shaking hands under control before she placed the dish of pasta in the center of the table. She gestured for Vincente to take a seat and concentrated on serving the food before she spoke.

"I can't go back to Stillwater."

"I know what you're thinking—"

"No, you don't."

No one could possibly know what she was thinking. Because no one had lived through the fear with her. She had been alone when she had experienced that feeling of her heart pounding so hard it felt like it was trying to burst out of her chest. The sensations of her muscles tensing and her breathing coming too hard and fast? They were things she had learned to deal with by herself. Lia wasn't an easy baby to settle. Beth hoped that wasn't because she picked up on her mom's anxiety… her counselor assured her it wasn't. But, each night, having spent hours settling Lia, Beth would then lie awake, her ears straining to hear every tiny sound.

Vincente joked about Melon, but the dog had been Beth's only comfort in the long, sleepless hours. She knew Melon would warn her if there was a problem.

She drew a breath. "Someone wants to kill me, Vincente. There was no mistaking what that letter said. He warned me if I told anyone, he would come after the people close to me. If I come back to Stillwater with you, it will be obvious you know about the letter and the photographs. I would be putting you and Lia in danger." Even though she had to refuse, the temptation to agree had been overwhelming. And she didn't have to look far for the reason. Ever since she had seen Vincente standing on her front step, her emotions had been on a wild rollercoaster ride…but he was *here*. Just being with him again, even for this short time, had eased some of the tightness in her chest. Leaving him had been the hardest thing she'd ever done. Even through the drama of these last few hours, his nearness had been a bittersweet indulgence. She was like an addict who had given in to her cravings. Losing him all over again would be the worst kind of hell.

Even so, she had find the same inner strength that had driven her to leave Stillwater. The thought made her shoulders droop. She wasn't sure she could still summon that kind of fight.

Vincente stopped eating. Reaching across the table, he removed Beth's fork from her hand and placed it on the table. His fingers were warm as he clasped her hand. Even though she knew his intention was comfort, nothing more, the gesture sent a shock wave thrilling from the point of contact along Beth's nerve endings. She was conscious of the way Vincente's fingers filled the spaces between hers. Of how she'd missed them there without knowing it.

"You can't keep dealing with this on your own. And you can't keep running. He found you this time and he'll do it again."

Those words said it all. With them, he summed up her terror and exhaustion. Could he tell how much she wanted to relax her body and place her head on his shoulder? How much she wished she *could* to go back to Stillwater with him? When he'd said those words, an image had come into her mind. Crisp and clear. Like a snapshot of a beloved memory. It was of her hometown on a bright, sunny day.

Stillwater was a beautiful city, cradled in the embrace of some of the most sensational mountain scenery Wyoming had to offer. The Stillwater Trail wound high above the city itself, leading on a wild adventure through pine forests, past the vast, haunting expanse known as Tenderness Lake and up toward the base of the most dramatic point of all. Devil's Peak dominated the whole area, and could be seen from most places in the city.

The residents of Stillwater congratulated themselves that the spirit of the Old West was still there, on their streets and in their hearts.

Beth had never understood the obsession some of her friends had with getting away from Stillwater as they were growing up. Small-town life had stifled them, they said. Stillwater was a place where everyone knew everyone else, where everybody knew a little *too* much about the next person's business. That was part of what Beth loved about it. She liked that there were no strangers. She liked walking down Main Street and greeting people by name, going into the stores and getting the latest news—okay, the latest *gossip*. She still felt a thrill of pleasure each time she entered the memorial hall, the place where Stillwater held its barn dances, rock concerts, bake sales and children's Christmas parties. When she'd gone away to college, she'd enjoyed the contrast of living in a big city, but it had only confirmed what she already knew. She was a small-town girl and Stillwater was her home.

"Come back with me, Beth. Stay with me. I'll keep you safe." Those midnight eyes were magnetic. Vincente's eyes were so beautiful it actually hurt her to look into their depths. They had been the first thing that attracted her to him. Unusually for such dark eyes, Vincente's were expressive, conveying the extent of his emotions. Now, they were telling her she could trust him. And Beth did trust him. She knew he wouldn't let her down. But it wasn't that simple.

"Rick Sterling and Andy Smith are already dead." She pulled her hand away. Saw the flash of fire in his eyes and felt a corresponding pang of regret. "They probably thought they could keep themselves, and those around them, safe."

"We don't even know if they had received letters and photographs from this guy before they died. Maybe that's something we should check out."

"You make it sound so easy." Suddenly everything was easier. From taking a nap in the afternoon to walking Melon, to thinking about a way out of the nightmare that had haunted her for almost two years. Because Vincente was here, her heart felt that little bit lighter.

"It may not be easy, but it has to be done." His expression was resolute. "How did they die?"

Beth gazed down at her untouched plate of food. She didn't want to do this. Didn't want to have a conversation about people in that photograph with crosses through their faces. *Because what if I'm next when he gets his red pen out?* The panic began to rise again, its hateful fingers gripping her throat. There were a dozen excuses she could make to get up from the table and end the discussion. She still had that work to finish. There was a pile of Lia's laundry that needed to be folded. Melon had shredded a newspaper and hidden the pieces under Beth's bed...

But she knew Vincente. Knew that determined look. He wouldn't let this go. It would be unfair to cheat him out of the whole story. And, when she thought it through, what options did she really have, other than to place her trust in him? If she ran again, she had nowhere to go, no money, a car that was held together only by rust, and a baby and a dog to care for. Maybe handing Lia's safety over to her father was the smartest move she could make right now. By involving Vincente, Beth would be instantly doubling up on the people looking out for Lia. That could only be a good thing.

She was worried for his safety if he became involved, but he was already involved. The person who had been in Lia's room earlier in the day had entered the house while Vincente was there. Maybe *because* Vincente was there. The timing of that day's warning could have been a coincidence. Or it could have happened because Laurie and Vincente had found her. Either way, Beth had to accept that she needed help. Most of all, she needed Vincente.

"Rick Sterling died on a climb and Andy Smith was killed when he took an overdose of painkillers." She looked up, a challenge in her eyes. "I know what you're going to say."

"But I'll say it anyway." His voice was surprisingly gentle and un-Vincente-like. "Those deaths could have been accidents. Even suicides."

Beth shook her head so hard her ponytail swung from side to side. "Not when you link them to the photographs."

"Think of it another way. When did they die?"

She blinked. "I don't understand."

"Did Rick die before or after you got the photograph with the red *X* over his face?" Although his voice remained calm, there was message in Vincente's gaze. He was urging her to see something she could have missed.

Beth raised a hand to her lips. "I didn't check. I don't know when they died."

"If someone with a grudge knew that Rick and Andy were already dead, he could have hatched this plan with the intention of scaring you. If the photographs were sent *after* Rick and Andy passed, then it's possible these were just accidents and the sender of the letters has been exploiting that."

What Vincente was saying made sense. Beth had been so spooked to discover that Rick and Andy were dead, she hadn't considered the timeline of events. She had simply assumed that the photograph showing Rick's face crossed out had been sent before he was killed, and that the same had happened with Andy. Her terrified brain had made the connection that both men had been murdered by the person sending the pictures. But if they died *before* the pictures were sent, then Vincente was right. Their deaths could have been accidents and the sender of the letters and photographs was a nasty opportunist. Someone who had used their deaths as a chance to spread fear and anxiety. It could still be someone close to Cory, of course. A person seeking revenge for his death. But they might not be prepared to go as far as murder.

She hadn't tried to investigate Andy's and Rick's deaths. Fear of what she might find, together with her pregnancy and subsequent post-partum depression, had left her incapable of taking control of the situation. Now Vincente was offering a different approach.

Vincente pointed to the envelope that was still on the table. The photograph that had been placed in Lia's crib was on top of it. Facedown, because Beth couldn't bear to look at it. "Whose face has been crossed out on that one?"

"Danielle Penn." Beth shivered slightly. "She was the closest thing I had to a friend in the group. Although she was about five years older than me, we were the only girls in the team. There was Tania Blake as well, but she was an instructor, so she felt like an authority figure."

"I'll ask Laurie to do some investigating into the deaths of Rick and Andy. At the same time, she can check out Danielle. We may find out she's alive and well and has no idea what this is all about."

"The letter said no police." Vincente was offering her a glimmer of hope, but Beth had been too scared for too long. She didn't know if she could take it.

"Laurie is my sister-in-law. She'll do this in a way that won't draw attention to you."

Vincente was watching her face, waiting for her response. Beth managed a slight smile. Hope. It had been missing for so long, she hardly dared let herself feel it now it had come along.

"Your apartment isn't suitable for a baby and a dog," Beth said. The modern apartment block overlooking both the Ryerson River and Savage Canyon had been the scene of many of their most passionate encounters. It would feel strange to go back there in different circumstances.

"I wasn't thinking of staying there. Remember the Dawson ranch out on the road to Park County? Cameron and Laurie bought the place when they got married. Cameron plans to sell his other house, the place by the lake where he used to live, but he hasn't gotten around to it yet." Vincente cast a glance in Melon's direction. "I take it he can swim?"

Beth pictured the beautiful, designer house perched high among the pine trees above Stillwater Lake. Designed by Carla Bryan, Cameron's late architect girlfriend who had been murdered by the Red Rose Killer, the lake house was the perfect hideaway. With its private beach, encircling cliffs and high-tech security system, it was about the safest place Beth could think of.

Even so, there were still things that worried her. "Once I go back to Stillwater, *he* will know where I am. Even if we're not talking about a murderer, things could get nasty."

"You can be as visible or invisible as you choose. You can show yourself to the people you trust, but you don't have to let anyone know where you are staying. And don't forget—" he took her hand again "—I'll be with you."

She swallowed hard. "I don't have any money. I can't let you keep me until this person is caught, Vincente."

He speared a piece of cold pasta and placed it in his mouth. "You know how hopeless I am at cooking. You can help me out by ensuring that, while we are together, I don't have to survive on takeout pizza and microwavable meals."

*While we are together.* Beth didn't have to wonder if he picked up on the irony of those words. She caught the flare in the depths of his eyes as he said them.

Together was in the past. She wasn't sure what the future held, but so many things had changed when she'd walked out of Stillwater sixteen months ago. Walking back again wasn't going to magically turn back the clock.

The logistics of getting Beth, Lia, Melon and all their belongings to Stillwater had proved to be more of a headache than Vincente had originally envisaged. Cameron was away at a political conference, but when Vincente called him, he had come through for him on the lake house. It was a relief, even though Vincente hadn't expected anything less from him.

"Of course you can stay there." There had been a note of mild surprise in his brother's voice when Vincente made the call. "Is there a problem with your apartment?"

"Not exactly. But I'll have a few houseguests." He watched as Beth neatly placed Lia's clothes in a suitcase. Each time she turned away, Lia pulled them out again. "Look, I have to go. I'll explain it all when I see you. Can you ask Laurie to call around and see me tonight?"

He scooped Lia up under one arm and she squealed delightedly. "Will your car make it to Stillwater?"

If Beth owned the vehicle he'd seen out in front of the property, it didn't matter what the answer was. That old rust bucket was a death trap and there was no way she and Lia were traveling to the end of the street in it, let alone driving for three hours to get to Stillwater.

The corners of Beth's mouth turned down. "I'm not sure…"

"Here's the deal. We'll transfer Lia's baby seat to my rental car, take the basics with us now and I'll get someone to come out here later to pick up the rest."

Beth pushed her hair back from her face in a familiar gesture that tugged at a specific point just south of his abdomen. *Be honest.* It was *well* south of his abdomen. A delicious, if inappropriate, reminder of the sort of control she once had over his body.

"I'd forgotten how decisive you can be."

He grinned. "Decisive? That's not what you used to call it."

She returned the smile. "Okay. I'd forgotten how *bossy* you can be."

It was a bright moment after the drama and tension of the previous day. A day that had ended with Vincente cramming his long limbs onto one of those small sofas for what had to be the worst night's sleep of his life. Now, he was tired, aching and in need of a shower and a change of clothes. He wanted to get back to Stillwater and get on with this. Beth wouldn't feel safe until she had some answers, and he was determined to provide them.

"These are the essentials?" Vincente regarded the mountain of baggage with a disbelieving eye.

"Welcome to the world of living with a baby." Beth ticked the items off on her fingers. "She needs her crib, her high chair, her bottles and formula, diapers, wipes, changing mat, favorite toys and you have no idea how many outfits she can go through in a day…"

Vincente handed Lia back to her. "I surrender. I'll load this into the car while you get ready."

When Beth emerged from the house with Lia in her arm and Melon's leash in her hand, Vincente held the passenger door open for her. Beth shook her head. "I'll travel in the back with Lia. Melon can sit up front with you."

Melon bounded onto the front seat. "Why is that?" Vincente asked.

"Because Melon likes cars and Lia doesn't," Beth explained.

Her statement became clear as they set off. Lia maintained a high-pitched wail that nothing Beth did could diminish. Beth tried singing, storytelling, pointing out features of interest on the roadside…none of it worked.

"Is she in pain?" Vincente asked. It was the only thing he could think that would explain such anguish.

"No. She doesn't like being strapped in." Beth sounded remarkably serene in the face of so much distress.

Melon, meanwhile, gazed out the front window and sniffed the air coming through the slight gap in the window with evident delight. After about half an hour, the screaming subsided and became snuffling sobs before turning into silence.

"She's asleep." Beth heaved a relieved sigh.

"Does she do that every time you get in the car?" Vincente wasn't sure how Beth coped with that when she was in the driver's seat.

"We don't go out much." He sensed a world of information in that sentence. Vincente glanced in the rearview mirror, but Beth's dark head was bent close to Lia and he couldn't see her face.

They continued the drive in near silence. When they reached Stillwater, Vincente drove along Main Street, secure in the knowledge that the tinted windows would protect Beth from prying eyes. His hometown was doing what it always did. Sarah Milligan was brushing the sidewalk outside her general store. The chalkboard menu outside The Daily Grind invited customers to try a slice of homemade lemon cake with their coffee. In front of Dino's, the restaurant owner, also named Dino, leaned against the door frame, chatting to a passerby…as he did every day. It was all safe and familiar.

As he turned onto Lakeside Drive, with its backdrop of pine trees and mountains on one side and the sparkling expanse of lake on the other, he risked another glance in the mirror. Beth's cheeks were wet with tears.

## Chapter 5

The lake house fitted perfectly into its environment. All glass and natural wood, it perched above the rock face, jutting out over the lake so every room seemed to be suspended above the water. The large family room had floor-to-ceiling windows that opened onto the wrap-around deck. Furnished in colors reflecting the pine forest outside, it managed to be elegant and comfortable at the same time.

Hauling their belongings from the underground garage hadn't been an easy task, but it was done. Beth was glad she'd brought the baby gate. The house was all on one level, but the deck led to steep steps down to the lake. Having the gate in place meant the door could remain open and they could enjoy the fresh air while keeping Lia safe. Melon had hurtled straight down to the lakeside and could be seen darting back and forth at the water's edge.

Beth had taken in the features of the property when they'd arrived. Its beauty was obvious, but safety was her main concern. The house ticked all the boxes. Turning off Lakeside Drive, Vincente had approached the house along a narrow lane. When he reached the gates, he used an electronic fob to open them and drove directly into the garage. He explained that Cameron had upgraded security following an incident a few months ago when a group of men had broken in and attacked Bryce and Steffi. A camera system on the gate regulated visitor entry. No one could gain admittance unless someone in the house granted them access. Visitors didn't drive into the garage. There was a small courtyard at the front of the house where they left their cars.

"The alarm system also includes cameras on the exterior wall, so you can see who is approaching." Vincente had pointed them out to her. "The only other way to reach the house is from the lake itself."

It was so different to the little house they'd just left. There, she'd felt exposed all the time, as though she had needed three-hundred-and-sixty-degree vision. It felt like staying safe had just gotten a whole lot easier. But maybe that had something to do with the man who was standing next to her as she looked out at the view. Vincente was over six feet of lean, hard muscle and he was dedicating himself to taking care of her and Lia. She'd take that over a sophisticated electronic method any day.

Lia was awake and displaying no ill effects from the trauma of the car journey. Having tested the baby gate and found it wasn't budging, she was crawling around, exploring her new surroundings.

"It doesn't affect her for long," Beth explained. "Like I said, she hates to be strapped in. She wants to roam loose around the car and can't understand why she has to be confined in one place. She's an explorer."

"She must take after you."

Beth smiled. "I seem to have lost my intrepid spirit lately."

Her rock climbing days had ended abruptly with Cory Taylor's death, but she had continued to enjoy other outdoor pursuits. Hiking, kayaking, caving, snowboarding… In the past, anything that allowed her to explore the natural beauty of her home state had appealed to her. It was only since her abrupt flight from Stillwater that her love of adventurous activities had been curtailed. She felt a tiny flicker stir inside her. Maybe it was nostalgia. It could even have been excitement at the thought of new possibilities.

The scent of the lake mingling with pine forest and mountain air—the aromas of home—must be getting to her.

"I put Lia's crib in the master bedroom. You sleep in there. I'll take the guest room."

Was it her imagination, or did something slide quietly away with Vincente's words? But it would be silly to think of it as a missed opportunity. An opportunity for what? To pick up where they left off? To relive the past? Too much had happened for that. She wasn't the same person. She didn't want the same things from life that she had sixteen months ago. *And he wouldn't want me now anyway.*

Her spirits had been tested to the limit in the time they had been apart until she no longer felt like the same person. The impact had been physical as well as emotional. She'd lost weight. Always slender, she knew she looked in the mirror now and saw a woman who was thin and drawn. Why would Vincente, himself so vigorous and full of life, want anything to do with the shadow she had become? The thought made her raise a hand to self-consciously fix her ponytail.

"Why do you do that?" Vincente gestured to her hair. "Why scrape it back that way?"

"Oh." Her hand fluttered in midair, caught in surprise at his words. "It's easier. I don't have time to style it anymore. What with Lia and everything…"

Why was she floundering as she explained her hairstyle choice to him? She sighed. Because it was Vincente. No matter what she tried to tell herself, how he looked at her, how he thought of her, mattered. *He* mattered. They might have both moved on, but he would always have this power over her. The thought caused her breath to catch uncomfortably in her throat. She knew, without a shadow of doubt, that no other man would ever affect her the way Vincente Delaney could. Maybe he picked up on her self-conscious thoughts, because Vincente looked away, releasing her from his probing gaze.

"I need to get a shower and borrow some of the clothes Cameron keeps here." Vincente tugged at the front of his T-shirt with a grimace.

"I'll make coffee." Cameron's kitchen had some basic provisions, and Beth had thrown enough into a bag to feed them for a day or two. After that? She was relying on Vincente's ingenuity.

While Vincente showered, Beth checked the family room for hazards. The decor was minimalist and there wasn't much that could harm Lia. Beth moved a few large chunks of quartz from the coffee table to a higher shelf and secured the screen more firmly in front of the log fire. Lia followed her, babbling contentedly.

Beth swung her daughter up into her arms, carrying her to the window so they could look down at Cameron's private beach. "What do you think?"

Stillwater Lake was a huge body of water. In the far distance, Beth could just make out the sailboats close to the leisure marina. It was a popular place with water-skiers and speedboat enthusiasts. Across the other side was the spot known as Catfish Point. It had been named by the fishing enthusiasts after the most popular activity over on the quietest part of the lake. But where she stood now—on the deserted side—this was the most beautiful view.

Steep cliffs rose on either side of the small bay and behind the house itself, making it impossible for anyone to accidentally access this cove. Melon dashed along the pebbly shore, occasionally darting into the water. His tongue lolled from one corner of his mouth as he patrolled the shoreline, already protecting his new territory.

"Woof," Lia commented, raising her hand to wave in the dog's direction.

There was a warm feeling in the pit of Beth's stomach. Contentment. Security. Confidence. All those words were too soon, too strong. She was going to settle for calling it an improvement on what she'd left behind. Back in Casper, she'd been alone, looking over her shoulder all the time. Now she had Vincente's protection... and she was no longer alone. It almost felt like they were a family, safe and enclosed in their own little world.

When Bryce called for the fourth time that day, Vincente had decided he couldn't postpone the explanations any longer. "I'm out at the lake house. It'll be easier to explain face-to-face. Before you come out here, stop by my apartment and pack a suitcase full of my clothes. And bring lunch…for three-and-a-half."

When he went into the kitchen, Lia crawled over to him and tugged at his pants, demanding to be picked up. Something in his chest gave way each time she did that. He didn't need to do anything to bond with her. He only had to look into those big brown eyes and he fell deeper in love with each passing minute. He lifted her into his arms, and Lia pulled sharply on his beard, giggling delightedly at his exclamation of surprise.

Beth carried their coffee through to the family room, where she had placed Lia's toy box in one corner. Vincente set his daughter down to play, while he explained to Beth that his message was likely to make Bryce drop everything and tear down to the lake house to find out what was going on.

"I'll have to tell him why I can't be in the office. We divide the running of the company between us. Bryce is in charge of operations and I take care of finance and administration. He's going to need to find someone to replace me."

Beth bit her lip. "Is this going to leave your business in a mess?"

He shook his head. "No. It would leave it in more of a mess if I handed the financial side of things over to Bryce. Luckily, he knows his own limitations when it comes to bookkeeping as well as I do. Will you be okay with seeing him?"

"Oh, goodness, yes. There is no way I would distrust either of your brothers." She smiled reminiscently. "It will be good to see Bryce again. Half my friends were in love with him when we were growing up."

"The days when he was known as the Stud of Stillwater are behind him. He's a happily married man."

He couldn't possibly envy the little smile that crossed Beth's lips when she spoke of Bryce, could he? He should be glad to see her smiling, not experiencing this sudden caveman-like desire to growl and beat his chest. Reminding himself that those days were over, he turned his attention to Lia. She was systematically taking each toy out of the box and discarding it. Vincente wondered what Cameron would think if he could see his beautiful family room looking like a…family room.

"Will she be okay with the move?"

"I think so. Where she is doesn't matter. All she really needs is me. And probably Melon, who she loves. Although—" Beth smiled shyly "—she has taken an instant liking to you, which is good. We don't see many people. She's always been wary of strangers." A frown flitted across her brow. "I worry about what the seclusion does to her."

"She's probably too young for it to affect her. But it's another reason to resolve this and do it fast."

Beth was about to respond. Instead, she looked up sharply as a voice rang out. Vincente frowned. He should have warned Bryce not to use his key to get into the house. He got to his feet as Bryce came into view. His wife, Steffi, was with him.

There were shocked looks all around. Beth gazed in amazement at Steffi, the woman who, until she went on the run following an accusation of murder, had been Anya Moretti, one of Hollywood's most famous actresses. Bryce stared at Beth, whom he, along with the rest of Stillwater, believed had been murdered by the Red Rose Killer. Steffi stared at the beautiful baby girl who, having emptied her toy box, was carefully pushing her toys under the sofa.

The silence was broken by Melon, who appeared at the baby gate and launched into a volley of angry barks at the strangers who had invaded his new home.

"When I said it would be easier to explain it face-to-face..." Vincente raised his voice above the onslaught. "I hadn't taken into account the guard dog."

Bryce managed to tear his gaze away from Beth's face. "That's not a guard dog."

The comment provoked a number of reactions. Vincente started to laugh at the way his brother had repeated his own words.

Beth fired up in defense of her pet. "Melon is the *best* guard dog."

Steffi dropped to her knees beside the baby gate and ruffled Melon's ears. "He's a sweetheart." Melon rolled his eyes in delight.

"I think some introductions are needed." Vincente raised his brows at Beth, seeking her permission. She understood what he was asking and nodded in reply. Nothing in his life had ever matched the feeling of pride that swelled his chest as he stooped and picked up Lia. "I'd like you to meet my daughter."

Beth couldn't quite believe that Steffi Delaney was Anya Moretti, and that the woman helping her serve lunch was also the woman who had starred in some of her favorite movies. She seemed so...normal. Pretty, lively and clearly devoted to Bryce, but down-to-earth and fun. She made Beth laugh by comparing Melon to some of the dogs at the animal sanctuary she ran.

"Believe me, I would rather live with my pigs, goats

and horses than the more dangerous animals I knew in Hollywood."

"It sounds like you have an amazing place." For the first time in a long time, Beth was having a conversation with a stranger about something other than groceries or rent. Talking to Steffi was easy. Beth was amazed to find she was relaxing, even starting to enjoy herself.

"You should bring Lia out to visit," Steffi said. "She'd love it."

Beth gave a noncommittal reply. No matter how much she might want to get to know Steffi better, no matter how much she might want to take Lia to see the animals, leaving the lake house might be a dangerous option.

There was a curious atmosphere in the room, as though everyone had a dozen questions to ask, but no one quite knew where to start. When they sat around the kitchen table to eat lunch, it was Vincente who turned the conversation in a serious direction.

"I'm going to take some time away from the business."

Beth sensed an unspoken communication pass between the two brothers. It was almost as though, in that fleeting instant, Bryce was checking that everything was okay with his older half brother. Once he got the reassurance he needed in Vincente's answering look, the tense lines of his body relaxed slightly. Something had clearly changed in the time she had been away. Before she left, Vincente's relationship with both his brothers had been strained. Although the three of them worked together and ran the company well, they didn't get along personally. Beth had known Vincente's feelings were clouded by hurt in his past, and her heart had ached for him. His antagonism toward Bryce had been particularly strong, stormy clashes a regular feature of their encounters.

"How long will you be away?"

"I'm not sure. Which is why I think Trey Reid should step up and take my place while I'm gone." Vincente's eyes seemed to challenge Bryce.

"Isn't he a little new to the company to take on that kind of responsibility?"

"In the time he's been with us, he's demonstrated that he's got flair and he's willing to learn. We don't have anyone else with his brains, initiative and leadership skills," Vincente said. "If I'm going to be out of action for some time, you'll need that sort of support. And I'll keep in touch with him by phone and email."

"Are you able to tell us what's going on?" Steffi's voice was gentle. "I don't want to pry, but we may be able to help."

"Beth has a stalker, someone who has been sending pictures and letters, threatening to kill her. That's why she left Stillwater and went into hiding. I knew the police had found her, so I followed Laurie to Beth's home in Casper. The person who has been trying to intimidate her has also said he will harm those closest to her if she tells anyone or goes to the police." Somehow, the way Vincente told the facts, coldly and calmly, made it sound even worse. "While I was at her house yesterday, he gained access to the property and left another picture in Lia's crib."

Steffi reached out and covered Beth's hand with her own. "How horrible."

Bryce frowned. "But if your intention is to hide from him, you could be here for a very long time."

"The plan is to keep Beth and Lia safe by staying here

at the lake house, but the most important thing is to find out the identity of the stalker and put a stop to what he's doing," Vincente said. "That's why I've asked Laurie to come and see me tonight. Although this person has insisted on no police, Laurie is family. She'll be able to keep her inquiries quiet."

"Before Bryce and I got married, I had a problem— not a stalker, but a dangerous killer who was on my tail—and Laurie helped me out." Steffi's words triggered a vague memory. Even from her hiding place, Beth had caught snippets of headlines and grocery-store gossip about Anya Moretti disappearing and going on the run.

"Ahem." Bryce cleared his throat, raising his brows at his wife. "I seem to recall I helped a little too."

Steffi laughed. "Did you? I don't remember."

He growled. "When I think of how I chased across the country with you…"

Steffi patted his cheek. "You are my hero, and you know it."

Their obvious, glowing happiness brought a sudden, unexpected lump to Beth's throat. She looked up and caught Vincente's eyes on her face. There it was again, that feeling of losing something they never had. *Domestic bliss was never on our horizon, so why am I craving it?* Maybe it was the situation she was in. She felt like a prisoner who had been reprieved. Given a snippet of normality, she wanted more.

The long months of fear, of not feeling safe, of starting at every phone call or knock on the door. That sense of being hunted. She had dreaded having to leave the house. Every time she got in the car, it became a nightmare journey during which she spent more time checking to see if she was being followed than she did concentrating on the road. What if *he* tried to snatch Lia as she lifted her from the vehicle? What if *he* tampered with her car when she parked it outside the bank?

Routine had been her enemy. Never going anywhere at a set time. Appointments she made for herself and Lia were fraught with fear. She remembered in the darkest days of her postpartum depression, begging her doctor not to write anything down, not to keep any records about her. Unable to explain why, she had watched with a feeling of helplessness as he gently overrode her wishes and made his notes anyway. *I am not being irrational.* She had wanted to pluck the pen from his hand and make him listen to her. *Someone wants to kill me.* Instead, she had subsided into tears. The only way she had been able to deal with her fears had been to use the strategies her counselor had given her. Although she didn't share her story, the techniques had helped with both her postpartum depression and her anxiety that the person who had threatened her might find her.

Even inside her little rented house, there had been no escape from fear. Sleep, going online, going into the yard…the uncertainty about who might be watching, waiting to pounce when she least expected it. Those things might not have occupied her mind constantly, but they were always at the back of it.

Her pregnancy had been a lonely one. Nothing had prepared Beth for the feeling she got when she held Lia in her arms for the first time. It had been like reaching into her soul and finding an unbreakable connection between her and this tiny, squawking person. *I made you.* That had been her first thought. Her second had been a brief moment of sadness that Vincente couldn't be there to share it. It was a bond of adoration and protectiveness so perfect it took her breath away. And it never faltered. But bringing up a baby was hard work. Doing it with no adult company was even harder. She hadn't left Stillwater only to put a new set of people in danger.

She decided it was no wonder she was envious of Bryce and Steffi. It wasn't surprising that her thoughts should turn to Vincente and think of what might have been. He was Lia's father. He had turned up on her doorstep like a knight in shining armor. He had been uncharacteristically understanding about what had happened… the anticipated fireworks hadn't happened.

*But "might have been" for us was never forever. And now we don't even have that.*

If she was going to stay in the same house as him, she might need to give herself regular reminders about that. With difficulty, she tore her gaze away from the melting depths of his dark eyes and forced herself to focus on what Bryce was saying.

## Chapter 6

"We can take a picnic." Vincente gestured to the mirror-still lake and the perfect, clear blue skies. "Catfish Point will be quiet. There's no chance that anyone down there will recognize you. They won't look up from their fishing rods and nets long enough to pay us any attention. And even though there's no chance we'll need it, I'll take a gun."

After Vincente and his brothers had been forced to take action against Grant Becker twelve months ago, Cameron kept a locked gun in a cupboard in the house. Knowing he had one of his own licensed weapons close by gave Vincente an added feeling of security.

He could tell Beth was wavering. After a week spent cooped up in the lake house, or on the beach below, she needed to broaden her horizons...and stop living in fear. His words about the dedicated fishermen made her laugh. Despite not going beyond the confines of the house, she had been doing more laughing as the week went on. Could he take credit for that? Hell, he was going to.

"Are you seriously proposing to introduce a baby and a dog into the midst of a quiet sport like fishing? And you think no one will notice us or object?"

"We'll find a place a little way down the bank from the most popular fishing locations." He moved a fraction closer. Close enough that he could feel the warmth of her arm. Not touching, but better than touching. The anticipation of touching was a thrill, a tiny spark of magic in the air between them. He watched Beth's eyes, seeing the moment they darkened as she felt it, too. There had been more of these moments between them over the past day or two. Unspoken exchanges. Maybe it was wrong to read anything into it…but it sure felt right.

They'd never had this. This sweet, slow burn. Their relationship had been a microwave: touch a button and they were horny and all over each other. This was different. This was a slow cooker. The heat was building, simmering, growing hotter all the time.

Was it going anywhere? He had convinced himself it wasn't a good idea to pursue it. But he sure as hell was enjoying the burn. Sixteen months without sex was probably to blame for his overheated imagination. After Beth left, he hadn't wanted anyone else, had not even been able to contemplate the idea of being with another woman. A week of being in close proximity to her and his sex drive was back with a vengeance…along with some very erotic memories. Memories that were keeping him awake at night with the knowledge that there was only a wall between them.

*Still not doing anything about it.*

He had convinced his mind, but his body seemed to have other plans.

Catfish Point was a spectacularly beautiful location. The jagged peaks in the distance allowed only a glimpse of clear blue sky above, but the day was bright and warm. Summer was fading into fall and the colors of the trees on the shore were a tapestry of green, brown and gold. From this angle, only part of the lake could be seen. It was easy to imagine that Stillwater Lake was smaller and quieter. The boats, water-skiers and swimmers who dominated the other side of the water might not have existed.

Vincente chose a spot farther down the bank from where the serious fishermen would be.

"Although this is not the season for fishing these waters," he explained as Beth placed a blanket on the grass. Lia was asleep and Vincente placed her carefully down. Melon dashed off into the trees to explore. "Anyone coming out here today is unlikely to have much success."

"I forgot you used to come here with…" Beth's voice trailed off.

Vincente knew what she had been about to say. "Yes, I used to fish with Grant Becker."

She grimaced. "I didn't know how comfortable you were with talking about that."

"It still doesn't seem real. I'd known him for most of my life and never suspected anything. Even though we weren't close friends, I still wonder if I should have known he was a killer, if I could have done something."

Beth sat down, and Vincente joined her. "I don't know much about these things, but it seems to me that the reason serial killers are successful is that they are able to hide their crimes for a long time. There is something in their makeup that means they can do that. When they are finally caught, it's always a shock to the people who knew them."

He relaxed, half reclining so he could study her face as he spoke. "It was a horrible time for the town. Grant was born in Stillwater and he was a well-known figure in the county. This city is too small for something like a serial killer in our midst not to rock the community to its core. And it hit our family hard. It made us take a closer look at ourselves."

"It seems to have worked out well." He could see Beth treading cautiously and realized it was because conversations about his family had always been off-limits. He hadn't felt able to open up to her before, even though she'd been closer to him than anyone. "You and Bryce seem to be getting along better than before."

"The three of us had to work together to rescue Laurie from Grant and then again when Bryce and Steffi were in danger. I guess we forgot to be angry and remembered that we loved each other."

"And you thought I was dead." She wasn't looking at him, her eyes were fixed on a point somewhere beyond the lake, but he could sense the tension in her.

"That was the hardest thing of all." Could he explain his emotions during that time to her? Could he explain that feeling of a giant hand ripping apart the fabric of his life and leaving his heart in tatters? "It was bad enough when I thought you'd left. I couldn't understand why you'd gone, and I was hurt and angry. But when Laurie told me you could have been one of Grant's victims—" he drew a breath and tilted his head back at the sky, battling with his emotions "—I didn't want a world without you in it, Beth."

She was silent for a long time. When she turned to look at him again, her eyes shimmered with unshed tears.

"I'm so sorry I hurt you…"

Vincente acted on instinct. To hell with restraint and resolve. He reached out a hand and slid it behind her neck, drawing her face down to his. The instant their lips touched it was as if all those months of being apart had never happened. There was only this. This rightness. The touch, taste and feel of Beth was all that mattered. It was all that would ever matter.

As her lips parted, urgency took over and Vincente moved his hands to her waist, drawing her closer. At the same time, Lia gave a cry and sat up, rubbing her eyes.

Vincente groaned, pressing his forehead to Beth's. They were both breathing a little bit harder, and he liked the familiar blaze of desire he saw in her eyes. "I don't know whether her timing is good or bad, but I do know we have some unfinished business here."

Vincente had been right. A few hours away from the house had done Beth good. The sunshine, fresh air and glorious views had refreshed her. Throwing sticks for Melon, stopping Lia from crawling into the water, laughing with Vincente over memories of other times they had visited the lake…all of those things had done her good. Maybe kissing Vincente had also contributed to the overall feeling of well-being she had as she packed their belongings away. No matter how much she tried to tell herself it had been a mistake, her lips—and other parts of her body—tingled insistently at the memory.

He had said they had unfinished business. She watched him now as he chased Lia toward the water one last time, turning it into a game that made the little girl giggle as she tried to crawl faster than he could run.

*We'll always be unfinished business.*

The thought sent a shiver down her spine. Beth was scared by the intensity of that brief kiss. It confirmed what she had already suspected. She wanted Vincente as much as ever. The hold he had over her body was stronger than her own will. He only had to touch her and she melted. Nothing had changed, yet everything was different.

She didn't know if she could resist him, but she had to try. Because she was frightened of the consequences if she didn't. The fight back from postpartum depression had been long and hard; she had never discussed the letters and the photographs with her counselor. Beth always wondered whether there might have been contributing factors. She would never know for sure, but she had been in a bad place before Lia's birth. Leaving her hometown, leaving her friends—leaving *Vincente*—and fearing for her life: none of those things had helped make her pregnancy an easy one.

When her counselor had spoken to her of risk factors for depression, two things had resonated with Beth: stressful life events and lack of support. Both of those had been features of her pregnancy. She had been vulnerable after Lia's birth and had succumbed to a very dark time.

*I won't go back there.*

Vincente had always been honest about his inability to commit to a permanent relationship. In the past, she had been able to accept that. Things were different now. *I'm different now.* She didn't want the free-wheeling lifestyle they'd once had. She needed stability, for herself and Lia. The temptation to give in to what she felt for Vincente was overwhelming, but she knew where it would lead them. And she couldn't risk a mood-lowering breakup. Her name-calling, door-slamming days were over. That had once been part of who they were; it had driven them to greater passion. In a way, it saddened her to let it go.

*It's called growing up. And, my God, I've had to do a lot of that in the last sixteen months.*

The problem was, she couldn't see anything in Vincente that told her he'd changed in any way. He'd forged a new bond with his brothers, and that was a positive thing, but she couldn't imagine his approach to romantic ties would ever change. The damage went too deep.

As he charged up the riverbank with Lia slung over his shoulder, the laughter in his eyes was infectious. And dangerous.

As he drew closer, he studied her face. "Are you okay?" He'd always had this knack for being able to pick up on her moods.

Beth tried out a bright smile as she took Lia from him. "Fine."

Those dark eyes missed nothing. "You never could lie to me, Beth. I don't know why you try."

She sighed. "Just sad, I guess, at having to leave the open air and go back to a sort of captivity."

His phone buzzed and he reached into the pocket of his jeans to get it, scanning the message quickly. "Good or bad, Laurie has perfect timing. She's coming over this evening."

Beth's heart gave an uncomfortable thud. "Does that mean she's found some information?"

For the past week, Laurie had been making inquiries into the deaths of Rick Sterling and Andy Smith. She had also promised to find out what she could about Danielle Penn. To keep it low-key and not draw attention to the case, she was doing this outside of her working hours. She had explained that the task would take longer than usual. To Beth it felt like forever.

"She didn't say, but it seems likely." He took her hand and every sensible thought about keeping her distance grew wings and flew over the mountaintops. "Look on the bright side, it could be good news."

She felt her lip wobble. "I haven't had many bright sides lately."

Vincente placed a hand over his heart in mock hurt. "I'm not a bright side?"

That made her laugh. "You always were hopeless at flirting."

"That's not true and you know it." He stooped to pick up the rug and picnic basket. "I'm actually very good at it."

"Ah, I must have not been around at the time."

They strolled back toward the car, squabbling light-heartedly about his ability to charm the birds out of the trees. Picking up on the mood, Lia babbled excitedly. An exhausted Melon trotted alongside them. Beth could almost believe it was idyllic. If she discounted the death threats and danger. She knew what Vincente was doing, and was grateful for his thoughtfulness in trying to distract her from the looming meeting with Laurie.

A lone hiker was walking toward them as they neared the car. It was an unusual sight. Stillwater Lake wasn't an easy place for walkers. The shoreline wasn't accessible all the way around. There were sharp cliffs and places where dense pine forest came all the way down to the water's edge. Most hikers preferred to take the Stillwater Trail, which led them to Tenderness Lake, a smaller, prettier body of water, higher in the mountains, the shores of which could be walked around in a day.

As the man drew level with them, he halted, turning his head to look at them.

"Beth?" His voice was familiar, his tone shocked. "Bethany Wade?"

Hours after the encounter, Vincente had run out of curse words to describe the crazy twist of fate that had led them into a chance meeting with Beth's old boss. What the hell had possessed Edgar Powell, who knew the area well, to come out walking at Catfish Point? And why did he have to do it today, of all days? Interpreting one of Lia's lengthy babbled monologues would be a better use of his time than attempting to answer those questions. Ask anyone in Stillwater and they would tell you the same thing. Edgar Powell was a well-respected lawyer, a stand-up citizen, the nicest guy you could ever wish to meet…but he was eccentric.

Fortunately, Beth seemed to take the encounter in stride. Meeting Edgar again, after she'd left her job without giving him any notice or a reason for going, must be difficult, but Vincente wasn't able to detect any resentment on either side. Edgar seemed genuinely delighted to see Beth, and Vincente recalled the affection with which she had always held her boss. Going to work had never been a chore for Beth. She had always loved her job at

E. Powell Law. If Vincente remembered rightly, before she left, there had been talk about her becoming a partner.

They didn't linger. Edgar accepted the excuse that Lia was tired. As he turned away, Beth cast a quick glance at Vincente before hesitantly stepping up to the older man. Placing a hand on his arm, she pressed a quick kiss onto his cheek. "One day, I'll tell you the whole story. In the meantime, would you mind keeping this meeting to yourself? I'd prefer it if no one knew where I was."

Edgar patted her hand. "I always knew you wouldn't have gone the way you did without a very good reason. I only wished you'd come to me so I could help." He fished in his pocket and produced a business card. That was Edgar Powell. The man who took his business cards on a hike. "Call me if you need anything. Or if you want to do some freelance work. The office hasn't been the same without you."

As Beth prepared dinner, the card remained on the counter and Vincente was aware of her casting the occasional glance at it. When they sat down to eat, Lia, fiercely independent, insisted on feeding herself and was soon covered in spaghetti and sauce. She preferred a collaborative style of dining, one that involved a handful of food for herself and then a few morsels dropped on the floor for Melon.

"I'm glad Cameron can't see his pristine kitchen right now," Beth said.

"We may have to do something about her table manners before we take her to Dino's Restaurant."

Beth started to laugh. "I can just picture Dino's expression if she decided to use one of his elegant dishes as face cream."

It occurred to Vincente in that moment that all his

happiest moments had been with this woman. But this one was different. Sitting at the kitchen table, enjoying a family meal, a shared appreciation of the antics of their daughter…there was a new note to his happiness. The laughter froze on his lips as he tried to analyze the feeling. Could it be contentment? How would he know when he'd never experienced it before? He was aware of Beth regarding him with a puzzled look.

That was when Lia decided things would probably be even more amusing if she tipped her bowl upside down and placed it on her head. At the same moment, the buzzer signaled the arrival of Laurie.

When Vincente answered it, he rolled his eyes at Beth. "She's not alone. Cameron *is* going to get a look at his kitchen."

Beth placed her head in her hands. "Do I need to start looking for a new place to stay?"

The visitors paused on the doorstep. A twinkle lit Cameron's eyes as he surveyed the scene. "Bryce told me there was a new addition to the family. Does anyone mind if I don't kiss her right now?"

"You take Lia for her bath." Vincente rescued Beth from her embarrassment. "I'll clean up in here and make coffee."

It turned into a group effort, with Cameron making the coffee while Laurie helped Vincente with the cleanup operation. By the time they'd finished, Beth had brought Lia through from the bathroom. The baby was pink and glowing from her bath and clearly sleepy. Although she regarded the new arrivals with curiosity, she was more interested in her bottle and fell asleep halfway through drinking her milk.

"I'll take her." Vincente held out his arms and Beth

placed the sleeping figure in them. He was aware of Cameron's gaze on his face as he cradled Lia close to his chest. His brother's expression was hard to read. "I'll be back in a minute or two."

After settling Lia in her crib and turning on the baby monitor, Vincente returned to the family room. Cameron was still regarding him with that same fixed expression. It was unnerving, as though his brother was seeing him for the first time.

"Do you have some information for us?" There was a nervous hitch in Beth's voice, and Vincente moved closer to her, hoping to offer her some comfort with his nearness.

"I do." Laurie withdrew a notepad from her shoulder bag. "As you'll already know, Beth, the members of the West County Climbing Club came from right across the county. My investigations would have been easier if the people I was trying to find information about had lived in Stillwater, meaning I would have access to the police records here, but none of them did. I started my inquiries with Andy Smith, who resided in Elmville at the time of his death. I spoke to one of the detectives I know in the Elmville Police Department. I wasn't able to find out a lot more than you already told me. Andy had recently separated from his wife of ten years, had started drinking heavily, was in danger of losing his job. He'd called his wife the day before his death. She said he was drunk. It was a long, rambling call, during which he told her there were reasons for his decline—" Laurie consulted her notes "—forces at work behind the scenes, things he couldn't divulge. Those were his exact words. She thought he sounded paranoid and urged him to get help. The next day, she tried calling him and contacted the police when she got no response. He had taken a lethal cocktail of prescription drugs washed down with alcohol. Although the police believed it was suicide, the coroner returned a verdict of accidental death. There wasn't enough evidence to prove he knew what he was doing."

Beth shook her head in disbelief. "I know a lot can change in ten years, but the man you've just described is so totally different from the person I knew. Andy was the most easygoing guy you could ever meet. He was the joker on our team. We could always rely on him to lift our spirits and make us laugh. And when Cory died, Andy had recently gotten married. He was devoted to his wife."

"The only thing that may be relevant to your problem, Beth, is that, at the time of his death, Andy had been burning old letters and photographs."

"What?" Vincente sat up a little straighter.

Laurie held up her hands in a helpless gesture. "There was very little left of the items. No way of knowing exactly what had been burned."

Vincente was aware that Beth's face had paled. "If Andy Smith had been sent the same letter, newspaper article and photographs as Beth, why would he burn them? Especially if he planned to take his life?"

"He wouldn't." Beth spoke mechanically "But he didn't kill himself. The person who sent the photographs killed Andy and made it look like suicide. Then the murderer got rid of the evidence by burning it."

## Chapter 7

Beth decided Laurie must be very good at those parts of her job that required her to reassure members of the public. She had a calm, authoritative manner, but she managed to be approachable at the same time. "There is no way of knowing for sure what happened inside his house on the day Andy Smith died."

"Andy's words were that there were forces at work, things he couldn't divulge. He meant he was being sent the same letter and photographs as me. He couldn't tell her because if he did, she would be in danger."

"That's one possible explanation." Laurie's voice was cautious.

Beth didn't respond. Getting into a discussion about it wasn't going to achieve anything. She *knew*. That was enough. She was aware of Vincente's gaze on her profile. Did he think she was going to fall apart? She had never felt more in control in her life.

"What happened to Rick Sterling?" Beth leaned forward, her eyes on Laurie's notebook.

"He died in a climbing accident." Laurie was searching for the right page.

Beth felt her lip curl in an expression of disbelief. "Rick was the most experienced climber I knew."

"That was pretty much what everyone told the police in Jackson who investigated the incident. Rick had been working as a guide in the Grand Teton National Park for the last five years when he died. On the day it happened, he was taking a small group out on a climb. It was straightforward. There was nothing about it that should have presented a problem, even to the most inexperienced climber. They were almost finished when Rick called to his deputy to take over. He said that one of the group had slipped and was stuck on a ledge. Rick was going to climb down to the rescue. No one saw Rick again."

"His body must have been found, surely?" Vincente said.

Laurie shook her head. "The ledge he climbed down to was above a steep ravine. If he fell from that—and the Grand Teton rangers have no other explanation for what happened to him—Rick would have fallen into a very deep, fast-flowing river. His body was never recovered."

"What about the person who was stuck on the ledge?" Cameron asked. "Did they fall, as well?"

"That was the strange thing. None of the group *had* been stuck. They were all accounted for at the end of the climb, and no one knew what the deputy was talking about when he asked if anyone had needed rescuing from the ledge. There was some speculation that Rick had lost his nerve after the Cory Taylor incident and that maybe—out of guilt because he hadn't been able to save Cory—he'd imagined someone was in trouble this time. Then, as he went to the aid of this nonexistent person, he'd gotten into trouble himself and fallen."

"Oh, don't you see?" Beth couldn't sit still any longer. Getting to her feet, she started to pace the room. "There *was* someone on the ledge. It wasn't one of the group, it was the murderer. When Rick went down to help, he was pushed off the ledge."

Even if it wasn't obvious to the police, it was crystal clear to Beth. She had known Rick Sterling. He had been her friend and mentor. She could picture him now, the most upright, honest, honorable man she had ever known. It wasn't just his muscles that had been powerful. Everything about Rick had been strong, including his character. There was no way the person on that ledge had been conjured up by a disordered mind.

"Did Andy Smith die before or after Beth received the photograph with his picture crossed out?" Vincente asked.

Laurie went back to her notes. He got the feeling she already knew the answer to his question and was buying a little time to give Beth some breathing space. "He died two days after Beth was sent the picture."

"And Rick Sterling?"

Laurie checked her notes again. "Beth was sent the photograph and Rick died four days later."

"So we're not dealing with an opportunist who knew these men were dead and decided to use that as a chance to scare Beth with these photographs." Vincente's expression was grim. "This person sent the photographs to Beth and then killed Andy and Rick."

Laurie nodded. "I'm afraid so, but we can't jump to conclusions."

"You're not going to try and say this was a coincidence?" Vincente's voice was incredulous. "That this guy just got lucky and both times he crossed out a face in those photographs, the people he chose just happened to die a few days later?"

"I'm not saying anything right now." Laurie remained calm in the face of her brother-in-law's skepticism. "I'm going to keep an open mind and I hope you'll do the same."

Beth waited for the terror to hit, the overwhelming darkness that had sapped her strength for so long. This last week had brought some respite from the worst of it. Not because she truly believed that it was all okay, but simply because she was no longer alone. And maybe that was the reason why it didn't come back full force right now. Or why it came back differently. When Vincente came to stand beside her, although the fear was there, her spine straightened and her chin came up and...*oh, my goodness, I feel like* me *again.* From somewhere deep inside, her old fighting spirit surged, just a little, and she welcomed it, seizing it eagerly.

"What happens now?"

Laurie gave her an approving look. "Now you're staying here, you are within the jurisdiction of the Stillwater Police Department and I have informed my colleagues of the situation. There is an alert on this address and on calls from your cell phone number or Vincente's. You've done all the right things so far. You are staying on a very secure property. You're being careful about who you see and where you go. Don't relax that vigilance. If there is any further contact from this person, let me know immediately."

"You're saying you can't do anything unless he harms me, right?" Beth tried to smile, but it became something more like a grimace.

"I'm saying we'll do everything we can to protect you." Laurie's gaze was steady. "I'm getting back to my colleagues in Elmville and Jackson about reopening these cases in the light of the threats against you—"

"But the letter said no police," Beth interrupted. "If you reopen the cases, he'll know I've talked to you."

"Trust me, Beth. Your name won't come into this."

Trust. After everything that had happened, it didn't come easy. Until the sender of the photographs was found, it was all she had. She looked up at Vincente and he smiled, an expression that warmed her in spite of everything. Maybe trust wasn't the only thing she had.

"What about the photograph that was left in Lia's crib last week?" Vincente asked. "This killer found out where Beth was living and got into her house."

"Do you have any idea how he did that, Beth?" Laurie asked.

"No. I thought I was being careful." Beth managed a rueful smile. "But you found me, as well."

"And now the woman in that picture is in danger," Vincente said. "What was her name?"

"Danielle Penn." Beth remembered Danielle from the climbs they had done together. Recalled the pretty, fun-loving woman with a mischievous smile, who loved the outdoor lifestyle and the wide-open spaces as much as Beth did. Did she want to hear that Danielle had killed herself, or died in a so-called accident?

"I was hoping you might be able to give me some

more information about her, Beth. When Cory Taylor died, Danielle lived in Cedar Hills, right at the opposite end of the county from Stillwater. She left soon after, and I haven't been able to trace her," Laurie said.

"Although she'd lived in Wyoming for several years, Danielle was Canadian. Is it possible she went home?" Beth asked. "I think she was from Toronto."

Laurie scribbled a few notes. "That helps. I'll get right on it tomorrow. And, of course, I'll be speaking to Cory Taylor's family to see if I can find out who might be responsible for sending the letter and photographs."

"What about the other surviving members of the West County Climbing Club?" Vincente asked. "If Beth is right and the items that had been burned in Andy's house were the same photographs and letters she's been getting—and the letter is not addressed to Beth, it's general, as if it *has* been sent to more than one person—then it seems likely other people have been sent them, as well."

"I've been thinking about that." Laurie flipped her notebook open to a clean page, as she got ready to take more notes. "The problem is that, if they've been sent the same letter as Beth, containing the same threat, they are going to experience the same reluctance to speak to us. If I turn up at their houses or at the next meeting of the West County Climbing Club and start asking questions, they are going to take to the hills."

Cameron placed a hand on her knee. "That was a really bad pun, my love."

Laurie frowned. "Take to the hills?" Her expression lightened when she realized what she'd said. "Sorry. But you see my dilemma. Ten people went on that climb. Nine of them returned. We know that two more have since died, and I have to tell you that, despite my offi-

cial line about not jumping to conclusions, I don't like
Danielle Penn's chances. If I'm right, and Danielle is
dead, that leaves six survivors, including Beth. Those
other five people are not going to talk to the police. It's
highly likely they won't even admit they've been sent
copies of the photographs."

"They might not open up to the police." There was
an urgency in Vincente's voice that made Beth turn her
head sharply to look at him again. "But I wonder if they
would talk about it to each other."

It was late when Cameron and Laurie left. After Beth
gave Laurie details of the other surviving climbers, Vincente had opened a bottle of wine and switched the conversation to other matters in an attempt to lighten the
mood. Although he wasn't sure he would ever succeed
in taking her mind completely away from the murders,
Beth had smiled and laughed in the right places.

Laurie's news had hit Vincente like a thunderbolt. He
supposed a small part of him had been prepared for Beth
to be right and for the person who sent the photographs
to be a murderer. But if he was honest, he had convinced
himself that they were dealing with a poisonous schemer.
Someone who had loved Cory Taylor and who was hurt
and suffering. A person who wanted to frighten Beth
because she had been with Cory when he died.

When Laurie confirmed they were likely dealing with
a killer, Vincente's initial reaction had been shock. Then
concern for Beth had kicked in. He had been afraid she
might be too fragile to deal with this. Although she had
always believed that Rick Sterling and Andy Smith were
murdered, a clinical delivery of the facts from a police
officer might have been too much for her to cope with.

Instead, she had surprised him. He'd seen a flash of fire in the depths of her eyes. Her voice had been calm and her hands steady. He could tell she was scared, but she wasn't going to let fear pull her under. A fierce sense of pride washed over him. Although she had run from Stillwater when she got the first photographs, she had done it with the best of motives. And she had kept herself and Lia safe in difficult circumstances. She hadn't spoken about that time, but he could tell, more from what she left unsaid, how tough it had been. Now, when the tension had been ratcheted up to a new level, she seemed to have found new reserves of strength. No. They weren't new. He could see elements of the old Beth emerging. She was starting to heal, and he wanted to nurture that. At the same time, he wanted to bring this nightmare to a speedy end.

"You asked if the members of the climbing club would talk to each other." Beth was curled into a corner of the huge, squishy sofa. "What exactly did you mean?"

Vincente had dropped that idea into the conversation and deliberately not elaborated on it. He had just let it sit there, but he had known she would pick up on it. And he knew she had already guessed what he meant.

It was late at night. They were alone together. Lia was asleep. They'd both had a glass or two of wine. The only sound was Melon snoring quietly on the rug and the wind outside stirring the pine trees. Physical contact was probably a bad idea.

To hell with it. Vincente moved closer and took her hand.

"Could you go back to the climbing club?"

Her eyelashes fluttered down, shadowing her cheeks as she looked at their entwined fingers. "I thought that might be what you meant." When she looked back up at him, her eyes appeared bluer that ever. "Honestly? I don't know. I haven't done any climbing since Cory died."

"Maybe we could go on a climb together and see if that helps your confidence?" He rubbed his thumb in a circle around her palm. The way he used to. "I'm not in your league, but I've done a few of the lower peaks on the Stillwater Trail."

"Aren't you forgetting something?" Her mouth curved in amusement. He should focus on what she was saying, not on how much he wanted to press his lips to the point where the corner of her mouth creased when she smiled.

"Hmm?"

"Short, dark, likes Jell-O, hates diaper changes…" Beth jerked a thumb in the direction of the baby monitor.

"We could ask Steffi to babysit."

A look of panic swept over her face. "I've never left her with anyone. I don't know if I could."

"Why don't we start by taking Steffi up on her offer of a visit to the animal sanctuary? We could take Lia out there tomorrow. We'll only ask Steffi to care for her while we do a climb if you feel okay with it."

Beth did that thing he'd noticed a few times. It seemed to be some sort of breathing exercise. "Shouldn't we stay here? At least when we're inside the house we know it's safe."

"Beth, this could take a long time. You heard what Laurie said. At this moment in time, no one else is even treating these deaths as murders, let alone linking them. You can't let him turn you into a prisoner." Even though he didn't want her to stay locked up inside the lake house, he wasn't going to take any chances with her safety. "At Delaney Transportation, we have a number of vehicles in the depot. I'll get Bryce to bring me a car with tinted windows tomorrow morning and swap it for mine. We'll change transport regularly and only go places where you feel safe. I'm not suggesting you walk down Main Street waving and smiling."

Although there was still a hint of reluctance in her manner, she nodded. "You're right. I can't hide away forever. It's just been good to feel safe again." Her grip on his hand tightened. "With you."

Vincente wasn't sure who closed the distance between them first. Perhaps they moved at the same time. All he knew was she was in his arms. His hand cupped her chin, tilting her face up to his. When their lips met, it was as soft and warm as the first sip of hot chocolate. The familiar feeling of Beth's body melting into his was like coming home. He kissed her the way he'd dreamed of doing in the long months when she'd been gone. All his feelings were there as his lips caressed hers and his tongue stroked hers. That kiss was the words he hadn't been able to say. The missing her, believing he'd lost her, aching to hold her one last time: it was all there in the sweet wonder of his mouth on hers. He felt his own emotions reflected in the tremor that ran through Beth's body.

When they broke apart, they were both breathing hard. Wanting hard. Beth got to her feet.

"Good night, Vincente." There was an unspoken question in the words.

He remained seated, a battle going on inside him. His emotions were raging out of control. If he listened to his body, he would go to her now and drag her into his arms. He knew from the look in her eyes how she would respond. Knew her well enough to predict the night of wild sex that would follow. But things had changed between them. No matter how hard and ready his body might be, it was time to start listening to reason. And his rational self was telling him what they'd had in the past—wonderful though it had been—wasn't going to work anymore. That, until he figured out what *was* going to work, he needed to keep his distance.

"Good night, Beth." It cost him every ounce of self-control he possessed to say it.

The animal sanctuary proved to be the perfect antidote to the drama of the previous night. Beth had worn a baseball cap and shades on the drive, and was relieved that the car Bryce had delivered to the lake house had tinted windows. Despite her nervousness, it was good to be out of the house and in a different environment.

"The primary aim of the center is to find new homes for abandoned or abused domestic and farm animals. If we can't find a home for them, they stay here." Steffi swept an arm around her, indicating the acres of land, including stables, kennels and other buildings. In the distance was the large, rambling house where she and Bryce lived. "Oh, and we also take in wild animals if they are injured or suffering."

"It must be quite a change from making movies." Beth was still finding it hard to accept that the woman showing them around had once been famous for the designer outfits in which she'd graced Hollywood's red carpets. Now Steffi wore faded jeans, a sweater in an indeterminate color and galoshes that were splattered with unmentionable sludge.

Steffi brushed her hair back from her face, leaving

a streak of grime on her temple. "I guess so, but I always used the earnings from my movies to fund an animal charity. I just did it anonymously. When I retired from that life, I decided this was what I wanted to do full-time. Now I get to do the fun parts, as well." She laughed. "Bryce complains that he only married me for my money and he doesn't see any of it because it all gets spent on animal feed."

Vincente was showing Lia around the different pens of farm animals, and she was clapping her hands together delightedly as she observed pigs, hens and goats. Steffi cast a sidelong glance in Beth's direction.

"I've never seen that look on Vincente's face."

Beth followed the direction of her gaze. "What look is that?"

Steffi didn't answer immediately. Instead, she leaned over the barrier of one of the pens, watching a group of rabbits enjoying the grass. "When I first came to Stillwater, Vincente was the person who gave me a job. I was scared out of my wits and barely able to think straight, so I hardly noticed him. What I did notice was that he wasn't happy. And as I got to know him better, that impression stayed with me. He was Bryce's brother, and he helped us when we were in a dangerous situation. But I always knew he was sad." She looked back across at Vincente. "He's not sad anymore."

"You think he's happy?" Vincente was smiling as he watched Lia's face. "I suppose it's hard to be miserable when there is a baby around."

"I don't think he's decided what he's feeling."

"That's very cryptic." Beth turned back to look at Steffi.

"You know him better than I do. I'd say Vincente's

feelings are very deep and very powerful. I don't think he'd let them out until he was absolutely sure about them. Bryce once told me that when they were growing up Vincente was the outsider, because he never tried to be anything else. He said Vincente enjoyed being the stereotypical half brother. Although Vincente was the one who displayed all the signs of jealousy, he was the one with all the gifts. Strikingly good-looking, Vincente is the artistic, intellectual one in the family, yet he can still outrun, outshoot and outswim his brothers if he chooses."

"That's the secret to Vincente." Beth smiled. "*If* he chooses. Life on Vincente's terms is never straightforward."

Steffi nodded wisely. "That's another thing Bryce said. He described living with Vincente as like wrestling an eel."

The image struck Beth as so funny that she laughed out loud. When Vincente and Lia joined them, she and Steffi were still chuckling. It felt good. It was a long time since she'd enjoyed the company of a friend and Steffi was easy to get along with.

"I never knew rabbits could be so entertaining." Vincente looked over the barrier.

"You had to be there." Steffi held out her arms to Lia, who studied her solemnly for a moment or two before returning the gesture.

Beth exchanged a glance with Vincente as he handed Lia over to Steffi. "She doesn't often do that."

"Possibly she just guessed that she's going to have a new baby cousin soon and wanted to be the first to congratulate me." Steffi seemed entranced by Lia as the baby tugged on her ear.

"Hey!" Vincente kissed his sister-in-law on the cheek. "That's wonderful news."

Steffi blushed. "I checked with Bryce and he said it was okay to tell you both today, even though he isn't here to share the celebrations."

Beth managed to reach out and give Steffi a congratulatory embrace without trapping Lia between them. She cast a glance in Vincente's direction. She had made up her mind. She would be happy to leave Lia with Steffi while they went climbing. Interpreting her look, he nodded. "If you'd like to get some practice before your own little one arrives, we have a favor to ask you…"

# Chapter 8

The next day, they took Lia to Bryce and Steffi's house, then headed straight out to the Stillwater Trail. Leaving the car close to Tenderness Lake high up in the mountains, they followed the winding trail that led to Tarryn Point. Even though he had lived in this area all his life, its wild, dramatic beauty never failed to fill Vincente with awe. Gigantic trees rose on either side of them, crisp, clean air filled their lungs and a sparkling stream tumbled alongside the path.

Beth had chosen Tarryn Point for their introductory climb. They had both scaled it before, and she had decided it would be a good starting point for rebuilding her confidence. It was a popular place with first-timers, and likely to get busy later in the day.

Although Beth hadn't kept any of her equipment, Vincente had borrowed most of what they needed and purchased a few items at the store on Main Street that specialized in outdoor activities. Luckily, Laurie had been able to loan Beth a pair of climbing shoes in the correct size. Between them they carried ropes, harnesses, a bag of chalk, carabiners and quickdraws. Beth wore a woolen hat with her hair tucked up inside, and she had a pair of wraparound shades pushed up on top of her head, ready to be pulled down when they came in sight of other people.

The day was cloudy, with some sunny spells forecast. There was no rain predicted, which was good. As Beth pointed out, they didn't want to end up abandoning this first attempt because the rock was too slippery.

"I haven't worked out in months." There was an added sparkle in Beth's eyes, a spring in her step and a restlessness in her manner that Vincente hadn't seen before. "This could be a disaster if I find out my muscles aren't strong enough."

His smile was teasing. "I've seen ten-year-olds do this. I think you'll be okay."

Beth pulled a face at him and bumped her shoulder against his. The mood was lighthearted, and Vincente was glad. There had been no soul-searching from Beth about coming here today. If anything, she appeared to look forward to it. The only thing he had noticed as they approached Tarryn Point was that way her eyes were drawn beyond it. The peaks of the Stillwater Trail were an impressive sight, gaping out of the earth like jagged teeth from the jaws of a dinosaur, but one towered above the others. The Devil's Peak was a hauntingly beautiful rock spire. Actually part of a series of the three most inaccessible, it soared higher, steeper and sharper than its lesser-known sisters.

Vincente didn't feel any compulsion to climb the high peaks. Although he enjoyed competitive sports, he didn't look at the Devil's Peak and feel a surge of desire to conquer it. But no one could live in Stillwater without knowing its reputation.

Among the rock climbing community, the Devil's Peak was a coveted prize. It was technically difficult and presented even the most experienced climber with a set of unique challenges.

When they reached Tarryn Point, it was still early and there were only a few other climbers at the base of the rock. Beth chose a place several yards away from them. Placing the equipment on the ground, she began checking the length of rope with her fingers.

"The guy I borrowed it from is an experienced climber. He said it's almost new," Vincente said.

Beth pointed to the sheer rock face. "When you're halfway up there, what would you rather trust…his word, or my fingers?"

He held up his hands in a gesture of surrender. "You're the boss."

She wagged a finger at him. "Don't you forget it."

Because they were alone, they faced a choice of who should lead climb the route and who should remain at the base of the rock and belay. Vincente didn't want to push Beth, but to him, the choice was obvious. Beth was the more experienced climber. She should be the one to go up the rock and prepare the way for him. Having studied the rock face in silence for a few minutes, she began to do warm-up stretches. It seemed to Vincente that she had slipped automatically into a well-rehearsed routine.

When she reached for her shoes and harness and chalked her hands, he breathed a sigh of relief. Beth was going to do this. She was going to climb the rock face and put her trust in him to belay the rope for her. The look of steely determination told her what they both already knew…she was getting her life back on track.

With Vincente belaying, Beth started climbing. It was obvious straightaway that she had a grace and fluidity way beyond anything he had ever seen before. Her technique was relaxed, her grip easy, as she moved with her body close to the wall. Totally in control, using tight muscle movements, she climbed all the way to the top. Vincente had watched other people do this, but he'd never seen anyone as fast as Beth. Once there, she attached a quickdraw to a bolt already cemented into the rock, anchoring the rope in place before rappelling down.

"Your turn." She unhooked her carabiner.

"Wait a second." Vincente paused before he changed places with her. "That's it? No applause? No celebration? You just did your first climb in ten years. Doesn't that at least deserve a high five?"

Beth laughed. "High five? I think it deserves a hell-yeah hug."

Vincente gave a whoop of delight. Sweeping her into his arms, he swung her around in a circle.

"It felt amazing," Beth gasped when he set her back on her feet. "Like I'd never been away."

Even though her eyes were smiling, he noticed the way they slid past him again toward the dark, threatening crags. He wondered if it might have been better to go somewhere else. Somewhere where they couldn't see that towering spire that pierced the clouds. But the Devil's Peak dominated the Stillwater landscape. If Beth was hoping to come back to her old life, she would have to get used to seeing it again.

"I swore I'd climb the Devil's Peak again one day." Her voice was slightly dreamy, almost as though she was talking to the mountain, rather than to him. "To prove it hadn't beaten me."

"And will you?"

She lifted her shoulders, and the gesture seemed to break the spell. "No. I have Lia to think of now. Extreme sports and motherhood don't mix." Her smile became mischievous. "Are you going to stand around here distracting me, or are you going to get some actual exercise?"

They did several climbs, moving to a more difficult part of the rock each time. Beth called a halt when they both could feel the strain on their muscles. "We'll be sore anyway tomorrow without pushing ourselves too hard."

Instead of hiking back down the trail immediately, they found a secluded place close to the lake. Leaning against a rock, they downed their energy drinks and ate the cookies Beth had brought.

"This is my favorite part of rock climbing." Vincente leaned back against the stone, closing his eyes as the sun broke through the clouds and warmed his face.

"I can do it, Vincente." Beth's words made him open his eyes again. "I can go back to the West County Climbing Club. On one condition—"

"What's that?"

"I'd need you to come with me."

While she and Vincente were climbing, Beth hadn't had time to worry about Lia. Once they reached the car and set off to collect their daughter, her anxiety levels started to increase.

Steffi had no experience looking after a baby. What

if there had been an accident? What if the murderer had discovered Lia's whereabouts? The what-ifs became a dozen different nightmare scenarios chasing each other around inside her head.

*I should never have left her.*

By the time they reached the animal sanctuary, Beth's anxiety levels were almost off the scale. Her whole body was rigid with tension; only her hands seemed capable of movement, twisting together in her lap like tormented animals seeking escape. She knew Vincente was occasionally taking his eyes from the road to study her with concern, but she was so wound up, she couldn't speak.

And, of course, when they got there, Lia was fine. Neither she nor Steffi had suffered any ill effects from the time they had spent together. The worst that could be said was that Lia was a little tired and cranky from the excitement of being somewhere new. With a real effort, Beth forced herself not to seize her daughter and hug her so hard it hurt.

By the time they reached the lake house, Beth was calm again. Going through Lia's usual routine—bathing, changing, feeding, reading a story, tucking her into her crib, kissing her cheek—finally restored her equilibrium. Once Lia was asleep, she sat for long, still minutes watching her. Then she made a decision.

After switching on the baby monitor, she went through to the family room.

"I need to talk to you."

Vincente set aside the book he had been reading. "I hoped you would say that."

Beth took a seat at a right angle to him. "After Lia was born, I suffered from severe postpartum depression. I was never a danger to her, or to myself, and I was never hospitalized. I was on medication for several months and I had counseling. Although I don't attend face-to-face therapy anymore, I still occasionally call my counselor." The words had tumbled out faster than she wanted them to, and she paused to catch her breath. "I'm mostly okay now. But I have...flashbacks. I had one today."

Then she did what she had been hoping to avoid. She burst into tears.

Vincente had always been surprisingly good with tears. He wasn't embarrassed or uncomfortable with them. He wrapped his arms around her and held her, letting her lean on his broad shoulder until the worst sobs had subsided. Then he went and found some Kleenex. Using one to dry her tears, he handed her another so she could blow her nose.

"Do you need to call your counselor now?"

"No. I just wanted you to understand that I'm not going crazy. Leaving your child with someone different for the first time is going to be hard for any parent. But it was always going to be worse for me." She scanned his face to see if he could understand what she was saying. "I know what Jenny, my counselor, would say. She would tell me to celebrate today. Even though I got horribly anxious, I did it. I left Lia with Steffi... and look at me. I'm not a hopeless mess." She blew her nose again. "Not totally."

"No, you're not a hopeless mess, Beth."

The look in his eyes sent a spark of something sinful shooting down her spine. The feeling settled farther south. Surely she shouldn't be getting aroused during *this* conversation? *Ah, Vincente. What you do to me.*

"I'm glad you told me. It was very brave."

She gave a watery laugh. "Brave. That's me. I run

away. Hide behind locked doors. Don't climb a mountain for ten years after a bad experience." Could she say the next words? The intensity of those dark eyes made it difficult, but she forced herself onward. "Lie awake each night thinking about you in the next room, wishing we were together, but too scared to do anything…"

He surged toward her, hauling her to her feet. "I swore I wouldn't do this."

"So did I." She breathed the words into his lips. "But you know what, Vincente? This whole mess has taught me that life's too short. Maybe we should stop thinking about this and just have sex."

"Are you sure?" His hands gripped her hips hard. Wonderfully, painfully hard. "That's what you want? Just sex?"

"So much." She nipped his lower lip with her teeth, and he growled.

"I can give you that, Beth." As their lips met, everything crackled. A firestorm started up inside her and burned along her nerve endings. It scorched the air around them, making it hard to breathe. Hard to think. But as Vincente scooped her up into his arms, Beth decided thoughts were overrated.

When he kicked the door of his room shut and placed her on her feet, they were already tearing at each other's clothes. By the time they reached the bed, every garment had been flung to the four corners of the room. How had she lived without this—without him—for so long? The fierce wanting that had been so much a part of who she was powered through her as she wrapped her arms around him.

Vincente's groan was despairing. "No condoms."

"I went on the birth control pill after Lia was born."

His answer was to move his lips to the point where her neck met her shoulder. He knew exactly what he was doing. It was Beth's most sensitive place, and he sucked her skin, driving her instantly wild. Electricity shimmered from her neck, down her shoulders to her arms, and all the way to the tips of her fingers. Vincente kissed his way across to the hollow of her throat, the scratch of his beard a glorious contrast to his soft lips.

He dipped his head to her breasts, his breath scorching her skin.

"Ah, Beth." His voice was hoarse with need. "You'll never know how much I've dreamed of this."

*He'd* dreamed of it? All those long, lonely nights when the memories of this were all she'd had to drive away the fear… Then his mouth closed around her nipple and she forgot how to do anything except respond to the commands of his mouth. Her back arched, pushing her breasts closer to him. He devoured her, licking and sucking, his teeth grazing the tender bud until her breath was coming in short, ragged bursts. Beth's core was aching, throbbing in time with each movement of his mouth on her nipple. This was what she'd dreamed of. But more. It was so much better than any fantasy.

As he moved down her body, Vincente gazed at her. Beth remembered that look. He had always stared at her that way. As if she was a goddess and he worshipped her. It made her feel incredible.

Vincente took her hand in his, moving it down her body. With Vincente guiding her, Beth could feel her own arousal beneath her fingers. Vincente groaned as he lifted her hand to his lips, sucking her fingers into his mouth one by one. Beth's eyes fluttered closed as sensation after sensation buffeted her body.

"Keep them open," Vincente rasped. "We've both waited too long to miss a second of this."

His dark head moved between her legs. The heat of his mouth was like a brand against the inside of her knee, inching slowly higher. Beth jerked her hips upward just as Vincente's hot, hot breath whispered against her clitoris. The anticipation was too much and Beth writhed, throwing her head back. Then his mouth was on her and her whole world was reduced to the touch of his tongue and his lips. Nothing in her imagination had come close to this. He sucked and licked and flicked. Beth cried out, arching again, trying to press closer to that magical mouth. Shivers rolled over her skin, and her whole body tensed. It had been too long, and she was so close. Pressure was building inside her body, pulling everything taut like a giant elastic band getting ready to snap and launch her into the orgasm she craved.

"Vincente." Her hands clawed wildly at his hair. "I'm going to…"

And then it hit her. So hard and fast that she cried out. She was soaring out of control, falling over the edge of a cliff and swooping down into nothingness. Letting go of everything but that perfect sensual release as a current of pure bliss burst over her.

Vincente's beard grazed her breasts as he moved back up her body. Beth murmured against his lips as his touch sent new tingles over her swollen mouth. Then Vincente was on top of her, spreading her thighs apart with his knees. She pressed impatient kisses along his jaw, his neck, his ear.

When he thrust into her, it was fast and hard. Beth clenched her muscles tight around him as he pulled out, then pumped into her again. Over and over. The feeling of him filling her was so achingly familiar, so perfect, that tears stung the back of her eyelids. Everything in her pulsed in perfect time with him. This was theirs. Their time. Their rhythm. Their lovemaking.

She could feel Vincente's need matching her own. Could hear it in his ragged breathing. Feel it in the bunched muscles of his shoulders as she tightened her arms around him. See it in the blaze of passion in his eyes.

The longing was building inside her again. Her body was tightening, ecstasy building once more. The heat became a flame as Vincente placed his hands beneath her buttocks, lifting her closer to him, driving harder and faster, letting her feel him fully embedded. The furnace sparked, then roared, then exploded.

Her release rushed through her, a crescendo of sensation that just kept coming. Wave after wave crashed over her as she called out Vincente's name. He plunged deep one last time, then gasped out his own completion.

After a minute or two of catching their breath, Vincente pressed his forehead to Beth's. "I am so glad my imagination didn't lie about how great it's always been between us."

She gave a shaky laugh. "It's the one thing we never got wrong."

He moved to lie next to her, drawing her into his arms. They lay like that, in silence for a long time. "I think I'm going to need a repeat performance." She tilted her head in time to catch the wicked smile on his lips. "Maybe more than one. How do you feel about a change of room?"

She nestled closer. This felt good. *Just sex, remember?*

"We can hear Lia from here, and she was used to her

own room in the house in Casper, remember? I don't have a problem with a new roommate." She returned the smile, resting her chin on his chest. "Particularly when the benefits are so enjoyable."

Vincente gave a groan of submission as she kissed her way down his body.

## Chapter 9

Vincente woke slowly the next morning, vaguely aware that it was still early and that his arms were full of Beth's soft, warm curves. He lay still, not thinking, just feeling, enjoying the little things he'd missed. The difference in size between her slender arms and his muscular ones. Her pale skin compared to his tan flesh. The smattering of golden freckles across her shoulders. The way she burrowed her head deep into his chest, her hair tickling his chin. The way his heart felt lighter when she was with him.

His emotions were a riot of confusion. The overwhelming need to protect Beth and Lia, to shelter them from harm, was radiated back at him by her nearness. Holding Beth in his arms didn't make every care and stress disappear, but they faded into the background. This moment was so good he never wanted it to end. All he wanted to do was bury his face in her hair and drift away on the scent of heaven.

As he came further awake, he analyzed his choices. He *should* get up, shower and dress, and be ready to call Trey Reid and find out if he needed any help. His temporary replacement at Delaney Transportation was doing a good job, but Vincente still checked in every day to make sure. He *could* obey the promptings of his body and wake Beth with a kiss. Since he was perfectly content, he decided to lie still, feeling her warmth, absorbing her comfort and indulging in the moment.

When his cell phone rang sometime later, Beth murmured a protest. Slipping from the bed, Vincente pulled on his jeans and left the room to take the call. It was Laurie.

"I've got some information about Danielle Penn. Can I come over?"

Vincente scrubbed a hand over his face. "I guess that means it's not good news."

"You guessed right."

He ended the call as Beth emerged from the bedroom wearing the shirt he'd discarded the night before. She looked half-awake and unbearably sexy. The urge to drag her back to bed was almost irresistible. Almost.

As she rose on the tips of her toes to press a kiss on his lips, he caught hold of her waist. Draw her too close and he would be lost. Instead, he returned the kiss lightly.

"You are way too tempting for this time of the morning." His voice was filled with regret. "But Laurie is on her way over."

Her expression changed instantly, becoming wary. Before she could speak, there was a shout from the master bedroom and Lia started rattling the bars of her crib, her usual demand for breakfast.

"You see to her, I'll fix coffee." As she turned to go, Vincente caught hold of her wrist, halting her. "Last night was amazing."

Her smile was pure mischief, chasing away the look of fear. "Which time?"

He groaned. "Go now…or I won't be responsible for the consequences."

By the time Laurie arrived, they had, between them, achieved the remarkable feats of both showering and dressing, eating breakfast and getting Lia ready.

"Even the guard dog has been fed," Vincente said with a note of pride as he buzzed Laurie in. "No one would ever guess we've hardly slept."

"You have your T-shirt on inside out," Beth pointed out as she gulped down her third cup of coffee.

Laurie looked far too alert as she strode into the kitchen with a bright smile. Accepting the offer of a drink, she followed Vincente and Beth through to the family room. Lia, who had developed a newfound confidence, insisted on spending a few minutes on Laurie's knee, examining her badge before crawling away to play with her toys.

Laurie got straight to the point, pulling the familiar notebook out of her shoulder bag. "It's not good news. Danielle Penn died a week ago."

Beth reached for Vincente's hand, the color draining from her face. "How did she die?"

"Initially, it looked like she committed suicide." Laurie delivered the facts in her usual no-nonsense way. "She hanged herself. But even before I explained about Rick Sterling and Andy Smith, and the photographs and letter you'd received, the Toronto Police Service had some doubts. They already suspected it could be murder."

"Why?" Beth leaned forward, her gaze intent.

"Because she died on her wedding day…and she was wearing her bridal gown."

Beth's face paled even more, her fingers tangling tighter with Vincente's. Even though he hadn't known Danielle, he winced at the image of a bride with her head in a noose. "It's a pretty extreme way out, but maybe she just couldn't go through with it?"

"That was how it was meant to look," Laurie said. "But there were some things that didn't add up."

"Such as?" Since Beth seemed incapable of speaking, Vincente continued with the questioning.

"Danielle had fresh scratch marks on her wrists at the time she died. The coroner speculated that she could have been self-harming, but there was no evidence to suggest she'd done that in the past. Nothing was found under her nails to either suggest that the marks were self-inflicted, or that she'd scratched another person. There were no older injuries—no one had ever seen any signs that she had harmed herself previously. The other possibility was that she had been involved in a struggle. Also, the heel had broken off one of her shoes." Laurie shrugged. "We can speculate about how, in a distressed and suicidal state, she damaged the shoes she was going to wear for her wedding. Equally, we can picture a scene where she was wearing them as she fought for her life."

Beth exhaled audibly. "She'd have fought. That's the sort of person she was. But Danielle was tiny…and on her wedding day? When she was already in her gown? Even if she'd been sent the letter and the photographs and been taking care of her safety, she wouldn't have been prepared for *that*."

"Exactly." Laurie nodded. "I told the detectives investigating Danielle's death about the letter and the photographs. They questioned her family and her fiancé, but no one knew anything about them. If she was sent copies, she never told anyone."

"Were there any other reasons to suspect she was murdered?" Vincente asked.

"The other reasons are more feelings than facts. Danielle was just so darned happy to be getting married. It's hard to get inside someone else's head, but everyone who knew them described her and her fiancé as the most loving couple ever. One of the detectives sent me a video clip of the wedding rehearsal dinner that the family released. It gives a flavor of Danielle's mood." Laurie withdrew her cell phone from her jacket pocket. "It's just a couple of minutes, if it's not too painful for you to watch it, Beth?"

"Okay." Beth gave a determined nod.

Vincente took the phone and held it so they could both see the recording. It showed a couple dancing with a group of people around them laughing and clapping. The person filming it had focused on Danielle. Petite, blonde and pretty, she couldn't have smiled more if she'd tried. And she couldn't take her eyes from her husband-to-be. Laurie was right. Danielle's happiness was so infectious it came right out of the screen and grabbed him.

"Stop." It was a sharp demand from Beth.

He pressed Pause and handed the cell phone back to Laurie. He guessed seeing her friend so full of life and knowing how she had died had been too much for Beth. "I'm sorry…"

He turned to her, expecting to see tears. Instead, he saw dawning shock. She held her hand out to Laurie in an impatient demand for the return of the cell phone. Rewinding the recording a few seconds, Beth paused it again.

"Can you enlarge a still of this frame?" She held the phone up so Laurie could see the blurred image.

"I guess so." Laurie's face was bemused. There was nothing much to see. Just a group of people smiling as the camera panned and Danielle twirled in the arms of her fiancé. "Why?"

Beth tapped the screen with one finger, singling out one of the guests. "Because this guy here is Rick Sterling."

The West County Climbing Club was situated in the town of Whitebridge, on the southwestern edge of the county. It was an hour's drive from Stillwater, and Beth spent most of that time explaining to Vincente why she refused to accept that Rick Sterling had killed Danielle. In the end it came down to one simple, unshakable belief.

"Rick is a good guy."

"Things can happen to good guys and turn them into killers." Vincente was driving another of the cars from the Delaney Transportation fleet. Lia was with her aunt Steffi again. Both of them were so delighted at the arrangement that Beth had been able to quell the flurry of nerves she felt when they left. "What happened to Cory Taylor had an impact on all of you. And Rick was in charge. Who knows what effect it had on him?"

Beth turned away to look at the landscape flashing past. The countryside had taken on brighter tones in the past few weeks, changing from the brown-and-green hues of summer to the red-and-orange tones of fall. The cottonwoods had assumed a yellow hue so flashy it looked like the trees had been sprayed with reflective paint. Beside their neon brightness the other trees put on a more dignified show as they prepared to shed their leaves. In the past, this display had never failed to soothe her. Fall was her favorite time of year, bringing thoughts of walks in the cooler weather, hot, sweet drinks, pumpkin pie and cowl-neck sweaters. This year it only made her wonder if her nightmare would still be going on when the first snows of winter came.

Vincente placed a hand on her knee, his grip light but steady. "If Rick is such a good guy, why did he fake his own death? And why was he at Danielle's wedding rehearsal?"

His voice was gentle, but she couldn't ignore those questions. She slumped farther down in her seat, tilting her baseball cap down over her face. There was a killer on her tail, and right now Rick looked guilty as hell. Laurie had passed the information on to the detectives working the case in Toronto. They were enhancing the image from the video clip and interviewing the other guests about Rick. Laurie said Rick would be long gone and Beth suspected she was right.

Even though the climbing club was still located in the same sports center in which the group had rented space ten years ago, it had moved on in other ways. Beth had been able to find details of meeting dates through the website, and the membership appeared to have grown. There was a thriving kids' club and there was now an indoor climbing wall and gym.

"In my day, we ran around the track, then climbed the nearest rock face," Beth said with a touch of envy.

Vincente laughed as he parked the car. "In my day? How old are you again, Grandma?"

She was glad things hadn't gotten awkward between them. The thought almost made her laugh. Awkward? Things had gotten very, very good. This "just sex" thing was working out fine. Better than fine. As distractions went, Vincente was the ultimate way to divert her mind from unpleasant thoughts. The only problem was, she might just be a little bit obsessed with the diversion...

"Vincente is kind of a unique name in West County." Beth emphasized the Italian pronunciation. "It singles you out. If the murderer is here, he could trace us back to Stillwater through your name."

"What do you suggest I call myself?" He leaned against the car, folding his arms across his chest and smiling down at her. Even though she was about to walk back through that door for the first time in ten years, her heart did a double somersault and her mouth watered. All because Vincente Delaney, the man she had woken up with this morning, was giving her *that* look.

"I don't know." She pretended to concentrate on the question instead of on how much she wanted to run her tongue along his lower lip. "You don't look like a Vinnie."

"Vinnie?" The word came out as a growl.

"Maybe just plain Vincent?"

"Honey." He hooked his fingers in the waistband of her jeans, tugging her closer. "I've never been 'plain' anything."

Beth wriggled free. Making out in the parking lot was tempting, but possibly not the wisest thing to do when she was supposed to be lying low. "I'll introduce you as Del. Short for Delaney."

That brief exchange meant she walked toward the climbing club with a slight smile on her face. And she guessed that had been Vincente's intention.

As they neared the club doors, they passed an old Ford Mustang parked in one of the bays. There was a sticker in the rear window announcing in giant letters that *Rock climbers do it up against the wall!*

Vincente rolled his eyes. "If that's a sample of climbing humor, remind me to give the Christmas party a miss."

The first thing Beth noticed when she stepped inside was the smell. It instantly transported her back in time ten years. It was a sporty aroma. Varnished floors, someone's forgotten, unwashed gym clothes and the scent of sweaty bodies. The room the climbing club used also added another layer. Cheap coffee. Beth guessed they were still using the same nose-wrinkling brand.

There was a table set up just inside the door, and a man and a woman were seated at it, taking names. The woman's mouth dropped open in surprise and her pen clattered to the floor as she stared at Beth.

"Bethany Wade! Oh, my Lord. How wonderful to see you after all this time."

She had risen and was coming around the table with the clear intention of embracing Beth. It was only when she got up close that Beth finally recognized her. That was how much Tania Blake had changed since she last saw her.

Ten years ago, Tania had been the coleader with Rick Sterling on the ill-fated Devil's Peak climb. Beth remembered a woman in her thirties. While not exactly beautiful, Tania had been strikingly attractive, with a stunning figure. A strong feature of her personality had been her confidence. Vocal, opinionated and loud, the one thing Tania had never done was conform.

This woman was a shadow of the one Beth had known. It was hard to tell if Tania still had her stunning curves, since her figure was hidden beneath baggy, unflattering clothes. Her brown hair was gray at the temples and cut in an unflattering, uneven style. Her face was drawn, her skin pale and blotchy. The dark circles beneath her eyes added to the impression of ill health. As Tania drew her into a quick, awkward hug, Beth noticed the way the other woman's hands shook.

"This is my friend Del. I hope you don't mind if we sit in on the meeting. I haven't been climbing for a long time, and I'd like to get back into it." Beth didn't have to fake the emotion in her voice. "But it's been hard…"

Tears filled Tania's eyes as she pressed Beth's hand. "I know exactly what you mean. It took me a long time to come back here. There are a few other people from the Devil's Peak climb who are still members. You may see them here tonight."

"Who are they?" Beth scanned the room. There were a number of people occupying the seats that had been set out in rows facing the low-level podium that was used by visiting speakers. Most of them had their backs to her, so it was difficult to judge whether she knew them.

"Peter Sharp is already here." Tania nodded toward a man seated near the front of the room. "And Isaac Harper sometimes stops by. The meeting will be starting soon. Why don't you take a seat, and we can catch up over coffee?"

They moved away and Vincente caught hold of Beth's arm before she could take a seat. "That woman is living on her nerves. Was she like that when you went climbing with her? No way would I trust her as my partner."

"No. She was the coleader with Rick, and she was one of the most capable people you've ever met. Unlike Rick, climbing wasn't her full-time profession. She also had a high-powered job as a computer systems analyst."

"She is definitely not coping now. I wonder if there's a chance her anxiety could be related to the murderer." Vincente cast a glance over his shoulder at Tania, who was fussily tidying the table. Her companion gave a definite eye roll as she knocked a pile of papers to the floor. "She looks like a woman who could be living in fear."

"I'll see what I can find out when I talk to her later." Beth led the way to where Peter Sharp was sitting.

Peter had been the oldest member of the team on the Devil's Peak expedition. He would be a useful person to talk to, having been Cory's climbing partner for many years. He was also the paramedic who had tried to relieve Cory's pain during that nightmare on the Devil's Peak. He was a quiet, modest man; Beth hadn't known much about him except that he and Cory had seemed unlikely friends. Peter was an introvert, while Cory had been such a big personality.

"Peter?" He looked up as she approached. "I don't know if you remember me—"

As soon as he saw her face, Peter flung up a hand as though warding off a possible attack. "Please go away."

"I just wanted to say hi." Beth was shocked at the pain on his features. "It's been a long time."

"I don't want to talk about what happened back then. Not to you. Not to anyone. Not ever."

Vincente placed a hand on her arm. "I think it would be best if we sat somewhere else."

Beth nodded, allowing him to draw her to a seat toward the back of the room. She felt stunned by what had just happened. She had to force her mind off the encounter and onto what was being said as the man who had been at the door with Tania moved to the front of the room and introduced himself.

"For those of you who don't know me, I'm Neil Stone…and yes, I've heard every joke there is about my name and rock climbing." There was a ripple of polite laughter. "I'm the president of the West County Climbing Club, and I'd like to extend a warm welcome to our new members and to our guests."

Stone proceeded to spend the next half hour outlining recent successes and proposing future plans. He had a mind-numbingly dull voice, and Beth was aware of Vincente shifting restlessly in his seat. She turned her head to look at him and encountered one of his scorching looks.

"Are you bored?" She kept her voice low so that only he could hear.

"Not when I can look at you."

"Flirt." She mouthed the word at him.

He shook his head. "Honest."

Aware of someone watching them, Beth glanced around and caught Tania's gaze on them. Feeling like a kid caught passing notes by the teacher, she felt the color flood her cheeks as she hurriedly focused her attention back on Stone.

## Chapter 10

When the meeting ended, most people stayed for coffee. Beth noticed Peter didn't hang around. He was sprinting out the door almost as soon as Stone said his last word.

"Why does he come here if it makes him so uncomfortable?" she asked Vincente the words that had been bothering her ever since she had spoken to Peter.

"Was it being here that affected him, or was it seeing you again? He seemed quite composed until you approached him," Vincente said. "It's possible seeing you brought back painful memories."

Beth was unconvinced. "If that's the case, wouldn't he feel the same when he sees Tania? And she said Isaac Harper sometimes comes to meetings."

"Who knows? But you were the one who was with Cory when he died. Maybe that was why he reacted so strangely to you. Since Peter has gone, there isn't much we can do about him right now. Let's concentrate on Tania. You talk to her while I socialize."

Beth went to the table where the coffee was being served. She knew from past experience that the only way to make it palatable was to add plenty of cream and sugar. Having completed this task, she searched the room, seeking out Tania. The other woman had returned to the desk and was sorting through a stack of papers.

"Can I get you a coffee?" Beth's words as she approached made Tania jump. "I'm sorry. I didn't mean to startle you."

"It's okay." Tania let out a long, shaky breath and attempted a smile. "I guess I just startle easily. Coffee would be good."

"Cream and sugar?"

Tania nodded. "Plenty of it."

When Beth returned with the drinks, they went to sit in a corner of the room. Beth noticed Vincente in the middle of a group of people who were having a very animated conversation. She contrasted their laughter to her own companion. Tania's hand shook so badly as she held her cup that some of her coffee slopped onto her jeans. She looked at the stain as if she wanted to cry.

"Here." Beth took a Kleenex from her purse and placed it over the spilled coffee on Tania's knee.

"Oh." Tania stared at the tissue for a moment, then rested her coffee cup on it. "Thank you."

"Is everything okay with you, Tania? You seem… tense." *Tense?* The woman was wound tight as a spring.

Tania's gray eyes lifted to her face. "I haven't seen you for a long time, but it was no secret among the people who knew me. I had a tough time dealing with what happened." Her lip trembled. "With Cory's death."

"We all did." Beth kept her voice gentle. She tried to remember what happened immediately after Cory's death. How had Tania reacted? She couldn't recall. If anything, she'd have said the two coleaders went into a kind of automatic response mode, shutting down feelings and simply moving from one action to the next. But once the immediate aftermath was over, Beth had distanced herself from everyone and everything to do with the climb. She hadn't seen anything more of Tania.

"No. You don't understand." Tania made a gulping noise as she swallowed. "I had a breakdown. Oh, it was a gradual decline, but Cory's death was the trigger. I just couldn't cope with the feelings of guilt."

"Did you get any help?" Beth placed a hand on Tania's other knee, the one that was free of coffee stains.

"They told me later—after I was diagnosed with severe depression—that I left it too late. If I'd asked for help sooner, things wouldn't have gotten so bad." From her own experience, Beth knew it was never too late to get help. It seemed an odd thing for a medical professional to say, but she didn't want to upset Tania further by questioning her. Tears spilled over, but Tania appeared not to notice them. "You know what I was like back then. I thought it was a weakness to admit I couldn't deal with it by myself."

Having suffered from depression herself, Beth knew exactly what she meant. That first cry for help was one of the most difficult parts. For someone like Tania, someone once so assured and confident, it must have been that much harder.

"I've been in the same situation." One thing she had

learned from her own experiences was that taking the stigma away was important. Mental health issues were often seen as something shameful, something that should be hidden away. Tania had been brave enough to open up to her. The least Beth could do was reciprocate. "I suffered from postpartum depression. Our experiences were probably not the same, but I can relate to what you are saying."

For the first time, there was a flash of emotion other than grief in the washed-out depths of Tania's eyes. There was a spark of interest, and something more. Was it gratitude? Beth wasn't able to interpret it.

"I was hospitalized." The words were tumbling out now, as though Beth's own admission had released them. "For a long time. And my life changed. *I* changed. I lost my job, my friends—even my family changed their attitudes toward me..."

"But you came through it. You survived." Although Beth used the encouraging phrase, she wasn't sure it was true. Was she talking to a survivor? She wasn't convinced. Cory was the one who had died on the mountain, but they were all victims to varying degrees. Tania was alive, so in that sense she had come through the experience. But the damage it had caused meant her life had been destroyed.

Although she sympathized with Tania, Beth was here for a reason. If Tania's anxiety had been made worse by threats from the murderer, she had to find a way to approach the subject. She sipped her coffee, grimacing at the oversweet taste and tried to find a way to start. Tania's next words startled her.

"Nine people came down from that mountain alive, and three of them have died in the last year and a half."

Tania's stress levels seemed to have been ratcheted up to crisis point. She was shaking so hard her teeth were chattering. Beth took her coffee cup from her and placed it on the floor.

"Breathe in deep through your nose and out slowly through your mouth." She waited while Tania followed her instructions. After a few minutes of deep breathing Tania appeared calmer. "It's horrible to think of people we knew dying, but we have no reason to believe that Rick's, Andy's and Danielle's deaths were linked." Beth hated to push her when Tania was clearly already so distressed, but both their lives could depend on this. "Do we?"

Tania looked nervously around the room. "Not here." Her voice dropped to a whisper. "I don't want to talk about it here."

Beth's heart gave a thud so loud she wondered if Vincente might be able to hear it all the way across the room. "Why don't we meet for lunch tomorrow?"

Tania nodded. "Give me your number and I'll call you."

Beth drew a piece of paper and a pen from her purse. She might be excited at the prospect of getting information, but she wasn't about to get sloppy. Tania was as frail as a young tree in a thunderstorm, but if the murderer somehow got to her and found Beth's details…

"Why don't I call you?"

"I've decided to speak to Edgar about doing some freelance work."

Vincente had noticed a change in Beth since they had returned from Whitebridge. On the drive back to Stillwater, she had told him about her conversation with

Tania, and her conviction that the other woman, although fearful, wanted to talk about the deaths of their fellow climbers. They had discussed ways she could meet with Tania the next day without exposing herself to danger. Eventually, they had come up with a plan with which Vincente was happy.

Then Beth had lapsed into silence. Vincente, casting occasional glances her way, had been unable to interpret the expression on her face. Something about the visit to the climbing club had triggered this mood of deep intro-spection. She had shaken it off when they collected Lia, laughing as Steffi filled them in on the details of their daughter's stay with her. Now, as they took some post-dinner exercise by strolling along the pebbly shoreline of the private beach beneath the lake house, Beth's ex-pression was determined.

Vincente, who was carrying Lia on his shoulders, paused in his stride. He had wanted Beth to break free of the restraints imposed on her by the murderer. But Dani-elle's death changed things. The video clip of Rick Ster-ling heightened the danger. At the same time, it meant they had a clearer idea of whom they could trust. Not that there had ever been any doubt about Edgar Powell. His concerns were more about logistics.

Beth appeared to be reading his mind. "I'll work from home."

*Home*. He glanced back at the lake house. The lights were on, casting a golden glow through the protective pine trees and onto the deck. Home was what it had become over the last few weeks. His, Beth's and Lia's. Melon dropped a stick at his feet as if to give him a not-so-subtle reminder. Okay, it was the damn guard dog's home, too.

It occurred to him, in that brief moment of clarity, that nowhere had ever felt like home to him until now. Not properly. His stepmom had done everything she could to make the house he grew up in feel comfortable for him. Sandy Delaney, Cameron and Bryce's mother, had been a big-hearted woman who had included Vincente in every aspect of family life. It wasn't her fault his own mother had already done too much damage. Later, when he left home, he had resided in a series of bland apartments, finally settling in the luxurious downtown riverside complex where he now lived. And that was the point. It was where he *lived*. It wasn't home. Just like his mother's increasingly lavish Italian villas weren't home when he went to visit her.

Because home wasn't about the place. It was about who was there. He could take Beth, Lia—and Melon—to a shack in the mountains and they would make it home. The thought took his breath away.

"Vincente? Are you listening to me?"

*No. I am scaring myself senseless.*

"Yes." He recovered quickly. "But how will you communicate with Edgar? I mean, I'm assuming the stuff you guys will be dealing with won't exactly be straightforward. Will a phone conversation work?"

Her brow wrinkled. "I thought about that and I don't think it would. I wouldn't be able to go into Edgar's office. Sitting in a busy law office in the middle of Main Street wouldn't exactly be following Laurie's instructions to keep a low profile. Which is why I wondered how you would feel about letting Edgar know where I'm staying. That way, he could bring the work to me and we could have a regular meeting about it here at the lake house."

Vincente considered it, weighing up the different sides of the argument. Laurie had told them to stay vigilant. They needed to remember that now more than ever. Yet he wanted to see that new spark in Beth's eye. The one that said she was ready to move forward. And they were talking about Edgar Powell, one of Stillwater's most well-respected citizens. If they couldn't trust him, they couldn't trust anyone.

*But we can't trust anyone…*

"Let's ask Laurie. We'll be seeing her tomorrow."

Beth nodded. "Good idea."

They turned back toward the house. "What made you decide this today?"

"I'd been thinking about it ever since Edgar gave me his card, but there seemed to be too many reasons not to do it."

He kept his eyes on Beth's profile, watching the sweep of her lashes and the curve of her lips. She had stopped dragging her hair back into a ponytail and was wearing it loose in the old style he preferred. He didn't flatter himself that it had anything to do with him. It was another statement about how she was getting back to the way she wanted to be.

It was a pleasant evening and Lia's feet were warm and bare in his hands. She tangled her fingers in his hair and made the soft cooing noises that told him she was getting sleepy. He didn't need to analyze the feeling anymore. Vincente was thirty-three years old and he was finally able to recognize contentment.

"Then today, after talking to Tania, I realized how close I'd come to being like her."

Vincente frowned. "You are nothing like her."

"I could have been." She turned her head to look at

him. "We both fought a mental illness. The only difference is in the degree to which it got a hold on us. And, when I looked at her, it just made me more determined than ever not to let *him* control my life. Getting back to work may only be a small thing, but it would be a start."

They reached the wooden stairs that led up to the deck. Beth placed her foot on the first step, turning back to look over her shoulder. "And, Vincente?"

He was swinging Lia down from his shoulders to his arms, ready to carry her into the house, but something in her voice made him pause. "Yes?"

"I'm glad you decided to follow Laurie to Casper that day. Until you came along, I couldn't see a way out of the hopelessness I was feeling. Without your help, I'd have just sunk deeper." She laughed. "Now come on, let's get that sleepy baby inside."

She ran lightly up the steps, and Vincente followed at a slower pace. That had been a perfect moment. Beneath a star-studded sky, gazing into Beth's eyes, he'd been tempted to tell her what the last week or so had meant to him. But how did he put what it had meant into words when he didn't understand it himself? That word, the one that scared him half to death, danced enticingly just out of his reach.

Did he love Beth? Did he even know how to love? He had always believed the part of him that should perform that function was broken. Now, as he watched her trim rear end sway just above him, a tight feeling gripped his chest. He had let that important moment slip away, and the sense of loss was overpowering.

He had no idea what he was feeling, but he was being flung in every direction by the storm of emotions coursing through him. He had always felt more for Beth than for any other person in his life, but there were other layers to their relationship now. Some of them were to do with Lia, but most were simply about *them*. And Vincente didn't know what the hell to do with this newness. His customary decisiveness had deserted him. There were so many unknowns, he didn't know where to begin. Beth had said this was just sex. Was that true? Or had it been her way of getting past his fear of intimacy? Had he used up any chance he had of more? Did he even want more? More importantly, did she?

He was so terrified of screwing this up, he didn't know how to act around her anymore. And that was making him crazy. In the past, Beth had been his best friend as well as his lover. Now she felt like a stranger. Someone whose next move he was constantly trying to analyze.

He wanted to sit her down and talk for hours about his feelings…and hers. But if he didn't know what outcome he wanted, what use would that be? Over the last year, he had seen both his brothers fall in love. Cameron and Bryce were blissfully happy with their wives. But Vincente had long ago convinced himself that long-term wasn't for him. He believed the Delaney capacity for domesticity had bypassed him. When it came to family life, he was an Alberti. He had inherited his mother's destructive genes. For the first time ever, he allowed himself to wonder if he might have been wrong in his assessment of his own genetic code.

And if he was, where the hell did that leave him and Beth now?

Kissing Vincente had always been heavenly. It was everything the fairy tales promised, and more. More, because his kisses hinted at a wickedness and spice those genteel princesses in the storybooks knew nothing about.

The first touch of his lips on hers fanned the flames of passion that had been rising between them all evening. His mood had been hard to interpret. Brooding, but not dark. Introspective, but not low. Every time she looked his way, he was watching her. Almost as if he'd never seen her before. When she finally quirked a questioning brow in his direction, he moved toward her and initiated this scorching kiss.

Beth lost herself in his heat. Vincente's beard was rough against her skin, the familiar sensation delightfully abrasive. His mouth searched hers, his tongue flicking and caressing. Beth moaned at the sensation. Moaned at how much she wanted him. It had always been this way. Ever since that first kiss.

"Do you remember the first time?" She was breathing hard when they broke the kiss. But so was he.

"Of course I do. I was shocked. You came on to me so hard I didn't know what hit me."

"*I* came on to *you*? Your memory is failing you, Delaney. What actually happened is you could barely wait until we were outside Dino's before you slammed me up against the wall and…oh!"

The breath left her body with a combination of surprise and the sudden force of being pinned to the wall with Vincente's big hands holding her shoulders in place. "You mean like this?"

"That's exactly what I mean." Beth ran her fingers over his forearms, moving up to explore the hard muscles of his biceps and shoulders.

"I think my memory might be returning." His dark eyes glittered with desire, exactly the way they had that night. The same shivery feeling tracked its way down her spine. "Remind me what came next."

She looped her hands around the back of his neck brought his head down to hers. "Then I guess things may have gotten a little out of hand."

Beth explored his mouth, sucking and nipping at his lower lip as she arched her body into his. There had been other kisses before Vincente. She'd dated, had boyfriends. But nothing had prepared her for what she would feel when she kissed Vincente. Her whole body reacted, became part of the kiss, was controlled by him. Wanted his domination. She trembled with desire, instantly needed more and knew he felt the same.

Vincente growled against her mouth. "Damn it, Beth." He may have uttered something similar back then.

His erection pressed hard into her belly, and she pushed up onto her toes to press herself more intimately to it. Vincente placed his hands under her buttocks and lifted her even closer. Wrapping her legs around him, she held on tight, not breaking the kiss as he strode down the hall toward the bedroom.

His mouth moved lower, nuzzling a trail of fire as he kissed and licked along her jaw and up to her ear. He kicked the bedroom door closed and set her on her feet, immediately yanking her blouse open. Beth helped him by tugging it the rest of the way off. Her other clothes quickly followed and Vincente's gaze was soon devouring her naked body.

"You're beautiful." He'd said those words that first time in the same hoarse, worshipful tone.

He stripped off his T-shirt and jeans, and molten heat flooded Beth's core at the sight of his erection straining against his black boxer briefs. Vincente moved toward her with a determined look in his eyes, catching hold of her around her waist and almost throwing her down onto the bed. He joined her, straddling her and pinning her arms above her head with one hand holding her wrists. The raw need in his eyes matched her own, and Beth arched her back toward him, offering herself to him. His hold on her hands was light, but she was excited by it, turned on at the thought of him dominating her.

Vincente changed position, moving between Beth's thighs and using his knees to spread her legs wide. As his gaze slid down her exposed body, Beth squirmed, enjoying the sensation of him looking at her. Enjoying her. Vincente raised his eyes to her face, and she moaned, signaling her need to be touched, or licked or sucked. Now.

Vincente's mouth was hot on her breast, his tongue a hungry rasp on her nipple. Her core tightened with pleasure in response. Vincente slid one finger along her center, and she jerked as though he'd applied electrodes to her nerve endings. He swirled his fingertip around her clitoris for one amazing moment, before he plunged two fingers into her, hooking them into a tender spot deep within. Beth bucked and writhed against his hand as his fingers continued their magic while his thumb teased her sensitive nub.

It felt like too much sensation. She was breathing hard and fast, her heart thundering out a drumbeat against her ribs, her entire body pulled taut. Her orgasm was building in every part of her, in her skin, her bones, even in her teeth. Building, pulsing, burning. Demanding to be let out.

Her muscles clenched around Vincente's fingers as he drove her relentlessly on. She cried out as her release finally came, flooding through her in warm, honeyed waves.

"That was…"

"Just the beginning."

Vincente released her hands so he could remove his boxer briefs. Even though she had just come, the sight of him made her mouth water, and she reached out a hand to caress him. Vincente groaned with pleasure at her touch.

Gripping her thighs, he hauled her against him, holding her in place so she could feel him hot and hard at her entrance. Beth licked her lips. "Hold my hands again."

Fire flared in the depths of his eyes as he gripped her wrists. "You like that?" he rasped. "You like it when I'm in charge?"

She squirmed against him, the words firing her hunger up even higher. "Yes, Vincente."

"Then I'm in charge all the way. You don't come until I give you permission. Understand?"

Beth moaned. She felt like he'd just triggered a series of heavenly electric shocks along her nerve endings. This was so far beyond any boundaries they'd pushed before. It was so deliciously wrong…and she loved it.

Vincente pushed against her, then paused. "Understand?"

"Yes, Vincente."

His name turned into a cry on her lips as Vincente thrust himself into her, ramming his erection so deep Beth saw stars. Her tight muscles stretched to accommodate him, and that wonderful aching feeling filled her. Vincente dragged out of her and drove back in, the angle hitting her deep inside at just the right place. Beth rocked her hips up to meet his next thrust. Pressure was already building inside her. She was a geyser threatening to blow, her internal muscles clenching around him.

"Not yet, Beth." Vincente gripped her wrists harder, his dark eyes glittering a warning as he raised his head. "I haven't given you permission."

He pumped harder and faster, and she bit back a sound close to a sob at the delightful torment. She was teetering at the edge of release. So close it was painful. Clamping her muscles tight around his pounding shaft, she managed to delay her orgasm. It was the most perfect torture. She had never felt so alive. Her whole body buzzed with a new awareness. The fluttering inside her vagina was building, spreading throughout every cell in her body.

Vincente fit into her so perfectly, keeping the sensations growing, bonding their bodies together. Beth started to shake uncontrollably. Her spine arched and her toes curled. She needed to grip something, but her hands were restrained.

"Vincente, please." She could barely speak. "I need…"

He released her hands and she grasped his shoulders, her nails piercing his flesh. Burying his fingers in her hair, he gazed into her eyes.

"Now, Beth. With me."

He thrust into her once more, and Beth came. The intensity of her orgasm devastated her. It was as if a ball of fire had traveled from the point where her body connected with Vincente's, up her spine and out through the top of her head. The experience left her boneless and weightless, floating on a cloud of bliss. Her entire body shuddered with wave after wave of aftershocks. Through it all, Vincente's gaze remained locked on hers while his own body tightened with his release.

After what felt like hours locked together in ecstasy, Vincente slowly withdrew from her and moved to lie at her side. Still stunned by the emotional roller coaster, Beth curled into his arms.

Beth wanted to explain what she'd felt. To tell him about the strength of her feelings. What had just happened between them had transcended anything physical. And she knew, when he'd looked into her eyes as they climaxed together, that Vincente had experienced it, too.

She tilted her head back to look at his face. And that was when, through the thin drapes covering the bedroom window, she saw the silhouette of someone standing on the deck.

# Chapter 11

The note of horror in Beth's voice as she cried out jerked Vincente out of his post-sex drowsiness. He opened his eyes to find her already scrambling from the bed and diving into her clothes.

"A man. On the deck." She pointed as she ran toward the other bedroom. To Lia.

Vincente bounded up, grabbing his jeans and tugging them on. If there was someone on the deck, why the hell hadn't Melon raised the alarm?

When he thought about the layout of the house, the answer became obvious. There was only one way for an intruder to get onto the deck outside the bedroom window. He, or she, would have to come down the cliff face, onto the roof of the house, and climb down from there. There were no alarm sensors there, because no one ever imagined a trespasser would seriously make the attempt to get in that way. Melon was in his bed in the kitchen, overlooking the lake. That meant he was on the opposite side of the house to the bedroom. As long as the guy had climbed down from the roof stealthily, Melon wouldn't have heard anything.

"Lia is okay." Beth emerged from the bedroom, her face pale, but relieved.

"Stay here. I'll check outside."

"Be careful. And take Melon. He is search-and-rescue trained."

There was a flashlight in one of the kitchen drawers and Vincente took his gun, as well. He took Melon with him on his search as Beth had instructed. His assessment of Melon's capabilities wasn't as high as Beth's, but Melon was a collie. He enjoyed herding things. Livestock, other dogs, people, cars, bikes, crawling babies... if it moved, Melon's instinct was to round it up. He didn't bite, but he was obsessive. If his object didn't cooperate, he would push and poke it into submission. If there was someone hiding on the grounds of the lake house, that person wouldn't escape Melon's sheepdog instincts.

At this time of night, the lake had a different feel to it. The darkness somehow emphasized its size, giving the impression of endlessness and timelessness. The twin disks of the moon, one in the sky and the other shimmering on the lake's surface, were huge and mystical. There was something menacing about its cold, primal beauty.

The house and its surrounding area were an easy place to search. The boundaries were clear. There were cliffs on three sides of the house and the lake on the fourth. The house fitted neatly between them. It was part of the genius of its design. The architect who had planned it was Carla Bryan, Laurie's cousin, one of the victims of the Red Rose Killer. Carla's vision had been for a home that appeared to be part of the cliff face itself. She had succeeded. It also meant the house was protected by its surroundings.

Melon, delighted by this middle-of-the-night game, dashed along the water's edge while Vincente trained his flashlight on the building. Although they walked along the shoreline twice, neither of them found anything to cause them concern.

Which left Vincente with a dilemma. Either Beth had imagined what she saw, or the trespasser had found a way of escaping before Vincente left the house. The most logical conclusion was that Beth's mind had been playing tricks on her. But Vincente was reluctant to accept that, to dismiss what Beth was saying. Because if he did that, he was gambling with Beth's and Lia's lives. And his gut told him Beth had too much control to jump at shadows. He wasn't prepared to take a risk. Which meant he had to go with the unlikely explanation that a trespasser with superhero qualities had paid them a visit in the night.

"Nothing." He returned to the house, locking the door behind him.

Beth wrapped her arms around her. "I know what I saw."

He unloaded the gun and placed it back in the secure cupboard before pulling her into his arms. "I believe you."

She melted against him, resting her head against his chest. "He must have rappelled down the cliff." Her words confirmed what he had already guessed.

"Could he climb back up again on his own?"

She raised her head with a frown. "I'm not sure. Let's go and take a look at it."

They went through to the bedroom, and Vincente unlocked the sliding full-length glass doors that led onto the deck. Melon followed them, clearly having decided this was still part of the fun.

Vincente shone the flashlight onto the cliff face. It rose steep and dramatic as if extending up from the roof of the house itself. Beth studied it for a few minutes.

"It's not easy. But it could be done. And see up there—" she pointed to a deep fissure in the rock face "—I figure an experienced climber could have got to that point really fast. When I shouted out, he could have reached up to that crevice. As long as he knew what he was doing, it would be easy enough for him to climb most of the way inside that cleft. He would have been hidden away inside there while you were searching the beach. Once you came back inside the house, he was safe to come out onto the rock face and finish his ascent to the top."

Vincente gazed up at the cliff; although he was worried for Beth's and Lia's safety, he couldn't help being amazed at the skill and daring it had taken to undertake a stunt like that. His thoughts were interrupted when Melon dropped an item at his feet.

"What the hell…?" Vincente stooped to pick it up, turning the metal object over in his hand. It was a carabiner, a clip that attached onto clothing or equipment to enable climbers to move up and down a rock face.

The next morning, Laurie arrived earlier than they had originally planned, after Vincente called her and explained what had happened during the night.

"How can you be so sure it was a man?" she asked Beth. "All you saw was an outline through the drapes."

"Because of his height and body shape. I've never seen a woman so tall and muscular."

Vincente watched her face for any signs of strain, but she looked remarkably calm under the intensity of Laurie's gaze. It was even more remarkable, considering that she hadn't slept after Melon's discovery of the carabiner. Vincente had left Melon outside overnight, secure in the knowledge that the dog would kick up a rumpus at the slightest sound. Sending Beth back to bed, Vincente had commenced his own all-night vigil. He had spent most of the time in the family room, from which vantage point he could see the front door and the passageway that led to both bedrooms. Every half hour or so, he had walked all around, checking that everything was okay. Each time he had done so, Beth had been awake.

"You really think someone would attempt that climb alone and in the dark?" Laurie looked skeptical. "Even in daylight, that cliff is a killer. In the dark, it would be a hell of a dangerous thing to do."

Beth hunched a dismissive shoulder. "Not if you know what you're doing. I could do it."

Vincente pictured the way she had shimmied up Tarryn Point. "She could," he assured Laurie. "She climbs rock the way a marine climbs rope. I'll call the alarm company and get them out here today to look at an upgrade to the security system. We need sensors on the roof and on the decking." He turned to Laurie. "Do you have any more information on Rick Sterling's whereabouts?"

She shook her head. "Nothing. He seems to have disappeared after he left Toronto. Why?"

"The figure Beth saw was tall and muscular. That describes Rick Sterling. He's certainly capable of rappelling down the cliff and getting onto the roof last night. And I'm guessing he wouldn't think twice about Beth's suggestion that he climbed partway back up the cliff, concealing himself in the crevice so I couldn't see him when I shone my flashlight around."

Laurie turned to Beth. "Wouldn't any member of the West County Climbing Club who was on the Devil's Peak team be capable of this?"

"Yes," Beth said. "We were all experienced. And we'd all be able to do a tricky solo climb at night."

"That means we can't focus on Rick as our only suspect," Laurie warned. "While he may look guilty as hell after being there when Danielle died, we can't rule anyone out."

Her words reminded Vincente of Beth's desire to get back to work. "How would you feel about Beth letting Edgar Powell know where she's living so she can start doing some freelance legal jobs for him?"

Laurie pursed her lips. "We're talking about a serial killer who has threatened you and the people around you, Beth. While I know Edgar Powell and I don't believe he is that killer, we can't risk him slipping up and giving away details of your location."

"What about if we arranged for Beth and Edgar to have a regular meeting in a neutral place?" Vincente asked.

"That could work." Laurie nodded. "Did you have somewhere in mind?"

He thought about it. "My apartment. It's secure, and no one can get in without being admitted through the intercom system. I could take Beth there once a week and wait with her while she meets with Edgar."

Beth laughed. "Just you, me, Edgar and Lia?"

He grinned. "If that's what it takes."

Her eyes were warm on his face. "Thank you." She picked up her purse and jacket. "I'll call Edgar when I get back from Whitebridge."

Laurie got to her feet. "Ready?"

Beth nodded. "I guess it's time to find out what Tania Blake is so scared of."

Tania was already waiting in Sweet Cakes Bakery in Whitebridge when Beth arrived. Laurie entered a few minutes later and took a table at the back of the restaurant, where she could watch them but not be seen by Tania.

Although Beth had called Tania that morning and finalized the details of the meeting, she had half-expected her not to show up. As she slid into the booth, she was struck again by Tania's decline. She had never seen anyone whose nerves were pulled so tight. There was nowhere else for Tania's tension to go; she could only snap. By the way she was trembling, her breaking point wasn't far off.

They ordered sandwiches and coffee, and Beth made light talk while they waited for their orders to come. It was hard to call it conversation, since Tania was barely engaged in it. She responded to Beth's comments about a couple of local news stories with one-word answers.

"I can't do this…" Tania got to her feet, spilling the contents of her large shoulder bag on the floor as she did.

As she got onto the floor to pick up her belongings, Beth knelt beside her. Their hands met on an envelope that was partway open. As Tania snatched at it and Beth released it, she could see part of the contents. The photograph was unmistakable. It was the copy of the group picture…and this one also had Andy Smith's face crossed out in red.

"We need to talk about that." Beth tried to disguise the hammering of her heart by concentrating on keeping her voice level and quiet.

Tania swallowed hard, her eyes shifting warily around the room as she slid the envelope back into her bag. "I don't know if I can." A tear fell onto the back of her hand, and she stared at it as though she didn't know where it had come from.

"I've been sent the same pictures." Beth got to her feet, holding out a hand to help Tania up.

Although the other woman hesitated for only a few seconds, it felt like hours. As she waited with her hand outstretched, Beth was aware of Laurie's gaze on them. She wished there was some way she could communicate what she had just seen to the watching detective. Instead, she concentrated on her breathing. Not any mindful technique. She found she didn't need her usual exercises to stay calm. Just the regular rise and fall of her chest. In and out. Normality.

Slowly, Tania reached up her hand and placed it in Beth's. Together, they returned to their seats. At the same time, their food arrived.

Once the waitress had made sure they had everything they needed and left them alone, Tania spoke in a low voice. "You were sent copies of the photographs?"

"Yes. Did you also get a copy of the newspaper article and a letter?" Tania nodded. "And the last picture you got, was that a couple of weeks ago…the one with Danielle Penn's face crossed out?"

Tania's hand was shaking so hard she had to put her coffee cup down again. A strangled sob issued from her lips. "Yes. I thought it was just me. That he was coming for me. I've been so scared."

Beth took her hand. "Me, too. But now we know two of us were targets, it increases the possibility that all of the Devil's Peak team were. Because the letter threatened the people who were close to us, it's possible we've all been living in our own little hell, too frightened to say anything. What about Peter Sharp and Isaac Harper? You've seen both of them regularly—do they seem scared at all?"

Tania shook her head. "I don't know. I never thought about it. Peter comes along more regularly than Isaac, but that might be because he lives locally. Right here in Whitebridge, in the same house he was brought up in. The one next to the church. Although he might stop coming so often now." Her face took on a new expression. The nervousness dissolving to be replaced by a disapproving frown. "I heard he met someone through one of those internet dating sites."

She was starting to ramble and Beth tried to get her back on track. "You didn't notice a change in either of them around the time you got the first photograph?"

"No, but I was so scared, I probably wasn't concentrating."

Given Tania's reluctance to talk to her, the answer to the next question seemed obvious, but Beth felt obliged to ask it anyway. "Have you spoken to anyone else about this?"

Tanya shook her head. "I couldn't. You saw what the letter said…"

"What about Peter and Isaac? Do you think they discussed it?"

"I don't know" She twisted her hands together on the handle of her bag. "They barely speak to each other, and Peter never wants to talk to anyone. Whenever he come along to meetings, he seems uncomfortable. But who could it be? Who would do such a terrible thing?"

Beth and Laurie had discussed how to handle this on the drive. Beth wasn't going to reveal any information she had about the murders, or about Rick Sterling. "It could be anyone. Did you ever think of going to the police?"

Tania sprang back as though Beth had slapped her. "We can't. The letter said…"

"Don't panic. I'm not suggesting we do it. I just wondered." Beth thought for a moment Tania might be about to bolt out the door. "Who do you think it is?"

Tania shook her head. "It can't be anyone who was on the climb. None of the group would do something like this."

"You sound very sure." Beth wasn't hungry. The drama of the previous night, followed by this meeting, had drained any appetite she might have had. Forcing herself to appear normal and take an occasional bite of her sandwich was hard work.

"I got to know everyone on that climb." Tania seemed calmer now. "And I've given it plenty of thought."

"Do you think the photographs were sent by someone close to Cory who had a grudge against us? Possibly that person thought we didn't do enough to save him?"

There was a flash of anger in Tania's eyes. "We didn't.

Someone killed him." Her newfound fire didn't last. She slumped in her seat. "I did everything I could to help him…" Tears spilled over and flowed unheeded down her cheeks.

"You were the one who saved him. If it wasn't for you, he'd have plunged off the side of the mountain."

Tania's lips seemed to make an attempt at a smile. It wasn't successful. "Looking back, I wonder if it would have been better if I'd let him fall."

Stillwater was a small city, and the Delaney brothers were influential businessmen. While Beth had been in Whitebridge, Vincente had spoken to the owner of the alarm company about upgrading the system.

"He said it will take a few hours and they can do it the day after tomorrow."

The corners of her mouth turned down. "This is not a big house. Where do you want me and Lia to hide while they do the work on the alarm?"

"You can come with me and hide out at Cameron and Laurie's place. We're invited for lunch."

She smiled. "You think of everything."

"I do, and right now I'm thinking of opening a bottle of my favorite Chianti. Join me?"

Beth nodded, rolling her neck and shoulders to relieve tense muscles. "That sounds like heaven. Did you and Lia enjoy yourselves while I was away?"

Although Beth had told Laurie the details of her encounter with Tania on the drive back from Whitebridge, Laurie had come back to the lake house so they could discuss the situation in more detail with Vincente. Once Laurie had gone, Beth had called Edgar to talk about a part-time working arrangement. By the time she had ended the call, they were into the evening routine of dinner, followed by getting Lia ready for bed. This was the first chance they'd had to talk alone.

"We did. We have a new game. I build a tower with her blocks. She knocks it down. One of us shrieks so loudly with laughter it makes Melon run away and hide. We can play it endlessly and never get bored."

Beth laughed as they took their drinks into the family room. "Two years ago, if someone had asked me what you'd be like as a father, I wouldn't have been able to answer. I'd have said it was a stupid question, not worth answering because it was never going to happen."

Vincente remained silent as he drank his wine. She was right. He hadn't wanted children. It had been part of not seeing a long-term relationship in his future. If he didn't do commitment, he sure as hell couldn't do family. If he'd had any regrets about that, he'd buried them long ago. Too selfish. Too busy. Too damaged by his own experiences. They were the reasons—excuses, he could call them any damn thing he wanted—he had used.

Now Lia was here, and he had never known a feeling like it. Every time he looked at her, his heart soared. The little things about being her dad were the most amazing moments of his life. Her hand in his, the way her face lit up when she saw him…even the way she pulled on his beard in excitement. Her laughter could make him forget every bad thing that was going on around them. Lia was his greatest achievement, and she made him believe in himself. No way would he repeat the mistakes his mother had made. There would be no Alberti gene when it came to his daughter. Only Alberti lessons.

Beth placed her hand over his. "I'm sorry, Vincente.

I didn't mean that the way it sounded. You are a wonderful father."

He laughed, lightening the mood. "Tell that to Lia when I don't build her tower fast enough."

They sat in companionable silence for some time. "I don't think the guy on the deck last night was the murderer." Beth's sudden pronouncement startled him.

"What makes you say that?"

"Because we haven't been sent another photograph." She was curled up into the corner of the sofa, and he wondered how she managed to get her limbs into such a small space and still be comfortable. "When he is ready to come after me, he'll send everyone a picture with my face crossed out. I haven't had that and neither has Tania."

Vincente frowned. "Are you saying it was a random intruder who just happened to be proficient at rock climbing?"

"No. There has to be a connection, but I don't think he came here to kill me," Beth said.

"Maybe he came to leave the next photograph, but when you cried out it startled him?"

"There are easier ways to get the photograph to me. If he figured out where I'm living, he could just leave it in the mailbox. Or, if he had it with him last night, he could have left it on the deck before he ran. And as I said, Tania hasn't received the next picture, either." Beth shook her head. "Until we get that, he's not ready for his next murder."

"You're probably right, but we're dealing with a serial killer. I don't know if I want to get inside his head and try to predict his next move."

"No, let's not get complacent. I don't like the idea that

we have a connection to the killer, even if it's only that we know how he works. I suppose it's possible he could change tactics." She shivered. "Something Tania said got me thinking that we could be looking at this all wrong."

"What do you mean?" Her face had always been like an artist's canvas, displaying the range of her emotions. It fascinated him to watch as they changed and deepened. Now, she was intent on her thoughts, lost in the memory of her conversation with Tania.

"She said it maybe would have been better if Cory had died when he fell. At first, I was shocked at the brutality of those words." Beth raised troubled blue eyes to his face. "For Tania, the woman who saved him from plummeting to his death, to say such a thing sounded so cold. But, when you think about it, what she said made a horrible sort of sense. If Cory had died in that way, he wouldn't have suffered such awful pain, and none of these consequences would have followed. The person who killed him would not have felt compelled to take such a dreadful step. Whoever is sending these pictures and committing these murders would not feel they had to avenge his death. When Tania saved Cory, she did it with the best of intentions, but her action set in motion a chain of outcomes no one could have foreseen."

"How does that mean we are looking at it all wrong?" Vincente asked.

"I think we should be trying to find out who killed Cory."

Vincente took a long, slow sip of wine. "Ten years on, that's a very big job. If the police couldn't find out at the time who killed him, what chance do we have now?"

"Probably none, but we have a lot better motivation." He tilted his wineglass her way in acknowledgment.

She had a point. Given recent events, the murder of Cory Taylor should be a higher priority. They would have to talk to Laurie about reopening the case. The police could openly question the remaining members of the Devil's Peak team about the decade-old murder and put some pressure on them to reveal new evidence. In the meantime, maybe Beth, who had known him, could offer some insights that had been missed at the time.

"Tell me about Cory Taylor."

# *Chapter 12*

Beth placed the photograph, the original of the group picture, on the coffee table. She pointed to Cory Taylor with one fingertip. He was standing in the center of the group with one arm around Danielle Penn and the other around Peter Sharp. Beth recalled posing for that photograph. It had been taken the night before they set off on the climb. They had gathered at the sports center to check the equipment and Rick had asked the janitor to take the picture. The mood had been relaxed, but excited. Just before the janitor had taken the shot, Andy Smith had made one of his corny jokes and they'd all laughed. Cory's hundred-watt smile had been captured by the camera, but the flash had dimmed the perfection of his dazzling green eyes.

The photograph had come to mean something else since it had been taken. It had always been a reminder of the ill-fated expedition during which Cory had died. Lately, of course, it had taken on a more sinister meaning. Beth tried to look at it now as it had been on that night. And tried to remember the man at its center. It wasn't difficult. Cory had been very memorable.

"This picture doesn't do him justice. Cory was the most handsome man I had ever seen." She gave Vincente a smile. "Present company excepted, of course. He was also very charming. But he never took those things for granted." She sighed. "I don't know if I can explain what I mean by that. I think some people—men and women—who have both looks and charisma, rely on those things to get them what they want in life. Cory never did. He was just a genuinely nice guy who had time for people. He'd remember the little details of your life. If I told him something, he'd always ask me about it the next time I saw him. But it wasn't just me—Cory did that with everyone."

"It sounds like you were a little bit in love with him."

"Maybe I was." She looked back at the picture and felt the smile touch her lips again. "Maybe we all were. I don't think what I felt for him could be described as romantic. You just couldn't help loving Cory."

"What did he do for a living?" Vincente asked.

"Cory was an artist. A very talented one. When he died, he'd already had a few successful exhibitions. That was another sad aspect to the whole thing, if there weren't enough of them already—his career was really set to take off."

Vincente frowned as though he was chasing a memory. "I think I've seen his work. Did he paint Wyoming mountain scenes?"

"Yes. He said he had traveled around the country getting different perspectives, but the light here was unique and compelling. And there was enough material to last him a lifetime." She gulped down a mouthful of wine. "Turns out he was right, because his life was cut short."

"And you have no idea who killed him?"

Beth closed her eyes, remembering what it had been like inside that tent. It had been difficult to move in her bulky clothing. Having completed the climb, she had piled on the rest of the garments in her backpack, relying on layers for warmth. The interior of the tent had been surprisingly bright, the snow outside providing a natural glow. Although the wind had died down, it still roared wildly, howling around the tents as though testing their strength. Beth had been lying on her side, tucked into her sleeping bag, facing Cory with her back to the entrance flap.

"Let me die…" His voice had been a pathetic croak.

"We'll be able to get help soon." She remembered how hard she had worked to keep the tears out of her voice. "The storm is almost over now."

"…wanted to die so bad…"

She hadn't heard the tent flap open. A slight movement behind her caught her attention. Before she could turn to look, there had been a flash of searing pain in the back of her head. The next thing she'd known, there was blood all over the sleeping bag and Peter Sharp was examining her, while a group of people was gathered around Cory.

"No." She opened her eyes. "Obviously, I thought about it, but I have no idea."

"Who discovered what had happened to you and Cory?"

"It was Mike Bradbury. He was the next person to

come and sit with Cory. He had a flashlight with him and when he saw the blood on my sleeping bag, he raised the alarm." She swallowed hard. "As well as attending to my injuries, Peter Sharp, who was a paramedic, checked on Cory. That was when he found out Cory was dead."

"You said Tania saved Cory and his partner. Who was his partner on the climb?"

"We were paired according to ability. An experienced climber with a less skilled one. I was the least experienced climber, so I was paired with Rick, who was the most proficient member of the team. Cory was quite an expert. He was with Peter, who was by no means a novice, but he'd spent less time on difficult peaks than Cory had. They had been climbing partners, and good friends, for several years."

"So, when we saw Peter Sharp, and he said he didn't want to talk about what happened back then, he probably had more traumatic memories than anyone…except you?" Vincente asked.

Beth had never considered it that way. "You're right. When Cory fell, Peter must have thought he was going to die too. Except—" she frowned, trying to remember "—I don't know how it happened, but Peter *didn't* fall." Her expression was puzzled as she thought back to that day. Her memories were clear, even if she saw them through a blizzard. "He didn't do anything much. It was Tania who started to haul Cory up, then Rick moved across to help her."

"How common is it for a climbing rope to snap or break?"

"It can happen," Beth said. She pointed to the photograph. "But that's what we were doing that night. We were checking the equipment. Every inch of rope had been carefully tested. And there was no mention of a damaged rope, either when we reached the top of the Keyhole and made camp, or later during the police investigation."

"We thought Peter didn't want to talk about what happened on the Devil's Peak because the memories were too painful...

"...but maybe he has another reason why he doesn't want anyone to inquire too closely into what happened."

Edgar Powell had always seemed to be a fixture of the city of Stillwater, as much a part of the scenery as the Devil's Peak or the Ryerson River. Vincente remembered going to the office of E. Powell Law as a child a few times. The attorney didn't seem to have changed since Vincente's father, Kane Delaney, used to do business with him. The office in the center of Main Street looked exactly the same as it always had. Yet there was something at the back of Vincente's mind. He was sure his father had once said Edgar wasn't from Stillwater.

"I don't know." Beth wrinkled her nose when he asked her. "I always thought he was from around here. I've never heard him talk about his family. I'm not sure he has any."

Vincente shrugged. "Maybe I got it wrong."

There had been a time when the downtown area of Stillwater was in danger of dying out. The railway line used to run all the way out to the Hope Valley coal mine, but the established industries of the region had experienced a slump. The railway tracks were rusted over and weeds grew between them. No coal had been mined in Hope Valley for decades and it was now better known as the place where Grant Becker had hidden the bodies of his victims.

Other Wyoming traditions had been hit hard in recent years. Ranches like the one Cameron and Laurie had bought were standing empty, and young people had been leaving the area to find work elsewhere. Cameron and the council had been faced with the huge task of bringing people back to the city. Although there was still work to be done, they had succeeded in promoting the town and the surrounding area as a tourist destination. Hotels, bars, restaurants, coffee shops, craft shops, farmers' markets...these days, anything quaint and Western was thriving. The ranches were reopening as travelers flocked to sample the scenic delights.

As a result, the city had begun to expand beyond its original boundaries in order to make room for the sudden increase in its population. A few years ago, Vincente had moved into a new apartment complex overlooking the river. Ryerson Heights was the sort of development Cameron and his fellow local politicians were keen to encourage, even though some traditionalists sneered at the modernization of their hometown.

When creating this apartment block, the designer had seen the advantages of a unique plot of land. The source of the Ryerson River was high up in the mountains. As it wound its way down toward the town, it had carved out some dramatic geological features. The developers had advertised this building as having not one, but two of the best, but most contrasting, views in Stillwater. At the rear was the stunning but inhospitable gorge known as Savage Canyon. In front, the Ryerson River took a wide meander before it tumbled into the cascade known as Eternal Springs.

As he pulled into the parking lot, Vincente thought how strange it was that this apartment no longer felt like it belonged to him. In such a short space of time, the place he had called his home for several years had become just another building. He had never felt any emotional connection to anywhere he had lived before, but if he was told he would have to walk away from Ryerson Heights right this minute and never see it again, he would be able to do it and not feel a pang.

His apartment was on the second floor, and Beth smiled reminiscently as they entered. "Your bachelor pad."

He grimaced. "Why does it always feel like that's a derogatory term?"

"It wasn't intended that way. I have some fond memories of this place." She laughed. "In fact, I'm more likely to call it your 'den of iniquity.'"

He took Lia from her, placing the baby on the floor. Lia scooted away in search of new adventures and they both followed her, checking for anything that could be a hazard.

When they were sure the place was safe, Vincente gripped Beth by the waist, drawing her to him. "I don't remember you complaining about my den of iniquity."

She caught hold of the front of his shirt. "No. I think we can safely say I never did that." Passion flared between them. Hot and hard as ever. "Not then. Not now." She rose on the tips of her toes, fitting her body to his. "Not ever."

He groaned. "There are two reasons why we have to stop this right now." Beth raised a brow. "One is that

Edgar will be arriving any minute. The other is that Lia is about to eat the TV remote control."

Laughing, she went to rescue the gadget from Lia's plump fingers. Sure enough, the buzzer sounded seconds later. When Vincente answered it, Edgar's slightly pompous voice filled the room.

"Come on up." Vincente pressed the button that would release the door at the front of the building. "Make sure no one else follows you inside, please."

"Naturally."

Even through the intercom, Vincente got a sense of Edgar's outrage that he would suspect him capable of such a transgression. He knew Laurie had visited Edgar and, without telling him the reasons why Beth had been forced into hiding, had impressed upon him the need to protect her privacy and safety. Knowing Edgar, he would follow Laurie's instructions to the very last letter.

The best word to describe Edgar was *round*. He wasn't very tall, and Vincente wondered if his waist and height measurements might be the same. But it would be unfair to suspect that Edgar was unfit. He hiked, cycled and swam. Vincente had no idea how old he was, but the attorney managed to do all of those things with the same vigor and enthusiasm he had put into them twenty years ago.

Edgar's eyes sparkled with pleasure as he folded Beth into a hug, and Vincente noticed again the genuine affection between the two of them.

"I'm so glad you offered to do this. Things have been a little crazy in the office lately. You'll be doing me a real favor."

After a few minutes, they had their heads buried in a pile of paperwork. Vincente left them to it, taking Lia on a tour of the apartment. The views were spectacular, particularly now that fall was here. His home state was always beautiful, but the fall colors added an extra layer of vibrancy. From the front windows, the wide sweep of the river with the snowy mountain peaks in the distance offered a lush, panoramic aspect.

The contrast with the vista at the rear of the building was striking. His apartment had views that were Wyoming in miniature, with the waterway at the front and the wild fissure at the rear.

Savage Canyon didn't get its name by chance. As he gazed out at the dark, brooding view, Vincente noticed with surprise that someone was entering the canyon. He'd never seen anyone go inside the ravine. Locals didn't go there. Stillwater was popular with hikers, climbers and kayakers, but even those who were the most dedicated to outdoor activities steered clear of Savage Canyon's hostile environment. There were plenty of other places to get their adrenaline buzz…ones where there was a better chance of coming out alive.

There was no reason for him to feel uneasy about what he was seeing. The council hadn't issued any specific warnings about Savage Canyon. There was no reason why a lone hiker shouldn't go in there. It just felt… wrong. But with everything that was going on in his life right now, wasn't it possible anything out of the ordinary would feel wrong?

He shrugged the feeling aside, a task that was made easier when Beth called out from the other room to tell him she and Edgar had finished their meeting.

Beth knew the Dawson ranch well, although the property had been empty for several years. Renovating it was an ambitious project, but as Vincente parked the car at the side of the house, she could see exactly why Cameron and Laurie had fallen in love with this place. The view offered everything Wyoming had to offer, with grass and wildflowers in the foreground rising up to meet a pine-topped ridge and snowcapped mountains in the distance.

Laurie stepped down from the porch to meet them. In jeans and a lightweight sweater, and with her hair loose, she appeared more relaxed than in her formal work attire. She linked arms with Beth and led her inside, showing her around the rooms that were already completed, while Vincente took Lia through to the kitchen. Melon was greeted with cautious interest by Cameron's two dogs before the three of them raced off into the distance in a cloud of dust.

"It's stunning." Beth sighed with a touch of envy as she looked out at the mountain views. The furnishings had all been chosen to reflect the colors of the landscape. "I love the lake house, but I can see why you chose to move out here."

"I had other reasons for not wanting to live at the lake house," Laurie said. "It was Cameron and Carla's home. Even if she hadn't been his girlfriend before we met, it would have felt very strange for me to have moved into the home my dead cousin designed."

"Even though we've only been there a short time, I forget it was Cameron's," Beth admitted. "Maybe it's because of the enforced seclusion of the last few weeks, but it's almost like I've never lived anywhere else."

Laurie's gaze was steady, almost as if she was attempting to read her thoughts. Beth decided she really would not want to be on the receiving end of an interrogation from Detective Delaney. Instead of the lengthy speech she was anticipating, Laurie simply said, "Is that so?" Those three words seemed to be loaded with meaning. Unfortunately, Beth had no idea what it was.

"Shall we go and rescue Steffi and Lia from the boy talk?" Laurie's mood changed from serious to smiling in an instant.

When they reached the kitchen, it was immediately obvious that no rescue was necessary. Lia, perched contentedly in the circle of Vincente's arms, was entertaining her captivated uncles while Steffi fixed drinks.

"She's going through her entire repertoire." The pride in Vincente's voice brought a sudden, unexpected lump to Beth's throat.

Lia obliged by giving a repeat performance. Clapping, pointing, waving and covering her eyes with her hands before peeking through her fingers…they were all her favorite actions. Then she turned her head to smile at Vincente. "Dada."

He looked at Beth, his expression stunned. "Did she just…?"

She laughed. "I think she did."

"Say it again, Lia. Say 'dada.'"

Lia's cheeks dimpled as her smile widened. "Woof."

There was general laughter, and Lia clapped her hands delightedly.

"I think your daughter just made her first joke," Cameron said.

"Yeah, she got me." Vincente ruffled Lia's curls.

She nestled her head against his shoulder. "Dada."

Laurie placed a hand over her heart. "Vincente, you used to be the big bad brother. Now you're overloading my kitchen with cuteness."

Beth couldn't figure out the look in Vincente's eyes as he accepted a beer from Steffi and handed Lia over to her. The big bad brother. That was his reputation, and Vincente didn't try to play it down. If anything, he encouraged it. *You may be big, Vincente, but I know you too well. You're not bad.* She watched his face as he smiled at something Bryce was saying. *The problem is, I don't know if you've figured it out yet.*

Sixteen months ago, when she ran out on the life she'd known, Beth would have said she knew everything there was to know about Vincente Delaney. Yet, over the last few weeks, he had surprised her. She thought there was a good chance he had surprised himself, even if he might never admit it. Not all heroes wore capes. Sometimes, they even had to overcome their own fears.

To an outsider, Vincente was the ultimate alpha male. He had worked hard to create that illusion, including the impression that he lived only for himself. Other people were allowed into his world by invitation only. He was dominant. Vincente gave orders, he didn't take them. Even though Cameron was the founder and CEO of Delaney Transportation, Beth had never seen Vincente act like his brother's employee. And Vincente exuded the sort of confidence that bordered on arrogance. His whole attitude said it all. He didn't need anything or anybody.

Oh, he was a proud man. He was strong, reliable and capable. Perhaps it was because she was the only person who had ever looked deep enough into his eyes that she knew what was hidden beneath the commanding surface. She knew the frightened little boy whose mom had run out on him still lived inside Vincente. He was still wondering what he'd done that meant he was no longer worthy of his mother's love. And he was trying desperately to make sure no one could ever break through his barriers and hurt him that way again.

But, ever since she had placed her cares—and her life—in his hands, Beth had seen a difference in Vincente. She had seen his underlying quiet confidence shine through. There was no longer any need for pretense. She had needed him, and he had come through. Coolly, calmly and with the self-esteem that had been so deeply buried it might have been hidden forever. That scared child hadn't gone away, but he was growing up.

As the chatter and the laughter ebbed and flowed around her, Beth finally acknowledged what she had always known. She loved Vincente. She loved the strong, bold, brave man who made her heart sing and her body thrum. But she also loved the insecure person he kept hidden deep inside, the one who had persuaded himself he was unworthy of love. And, having convinced himself of that, he had, with classic Delaney hardheadedness, decided he would never try to find it.

*Not even with me.* She almost laughed at the thought. It had taken her long enough to acknowledge that they were meant to be together. Would Vincente ever see it? They had a lot of problems to solve before they could focus on themselves. And then?

Who knew what the future held for them? Because Beth had changed, too. A return to their former relationship wasn't going to be enough for her now. She knew exactly what she wanted. She wanted Vincente. And she wanted everything with him. She wanted his heart. She wanted to hear him say "I love you." Wanted the hugs and kisses and touches that went with those words. Wanted to ease his sorrow and share his joy. Wanted to see that same look of pride and wonder on his face when their next child came along…

If they hadn't been thrust into this dangerous situation together, would she ever have understood the depth of her feelings for him? Beth wasn't sure. But she knew it now, and there was no going back.

*Yes, I want everything. And if I can't have that?* A tiny splinter of despair pierced her heart. *Then I'll have to settle for nothing at all.*

## Chapter 13

Although the next few days were calm, the atmosphere was one of anticipation. To Vincente, it felt as though they were waiting for something momentous to happen, like war to break out or the government to fall.

Beth started working part-time for Edgar Powell, undertaking some research to help him with court depositions. Although she said the jobs he gave her barely stretched her brain, Vincente could tell she was glad to be exercising her legal mind again.

Laurie had nothing new to report on the case. They had shared Beth's unsettling memories about Peter Sharp's part in Cory Taylor's death with her. Laurie had persuaded her chief that the new murders provided sufficient cause for the Stillwater Detective Division to reinvestigate Cory's murder. Peter had been the first person she had interviewed.

Although he couldn't refuse to speak to a detective in the same manner he had snubbed Beth, Peter had been reluctant to talk about what had happened on the Devil's Peak ten years ago. Laurie had come away with no new information. In fact, when she compared what Peter had told her with his original statement, they were almost identical. It was as if he was repeating a well-rehearsed speech.

"But that doesn't make him guilty." She had sighed as she left the lake house. "We still haven't found Rick Sterling, and I have four other people to talk to, including Tania."

Lia had come down with a cold and wasn't sleeping well. On the third day, her cheeks were flushed and her temperature was elevated. When she kept covering her right ear with her hand and crying, Beth decided it was more than just a minor ailment.

"She needs to see a doctor." She rocked Lia in her arms, soothing her tears. "But we can't take her into town."

"I'll call Leon Sinclair. We can trust him." Vincente reached for his cell phone.

"This is not a good time for jokes, Vincente." Beth gave him a look of horror at the mention of Leon's name.

Vincente had forgotten that Beth had been away from Stillwater for some time. There wasn't much about the city that had changed in her absence, but one of the most striking things was probably the status of Dr. Leon Sinclair. Leon was one of Bryce's friends. A former army medic, he had been given a medical discharge for mental health reasons, although he had retained his license to practice. Upon leaving the army, Leon had come home to Stillwater and proceeded to raise every kind of hell his inventive mind could devise. He had become known as the only man who had been thrown out of every bar in Stillwater in one night. That would have been his reputation around the time Beth left town.

Since then, Leon had undergone a remarkable transformation. A spell in rehab had followed and, although the fight against his demons had been a long one, he had won the battle. He had redeemed himself so successfully that, when there was a recruitment crisis at the Main Street Clinic, the lead clinician had approached Leon with a job offer. It had started out as a short-term position, but there was no sign of it coming to an end anytime soon. To everyone's surprise, especially his own, Leon was proving to be extremely popular with the residents of Stillwater.

"Trust me on this, Beth. Leon is not the same man he was. He's a respectable doctor now, he'll come straight out when I call him, and he won't tell anyone where you and Lia are living." Vincente could say those things with confidence. There had been a lengthy period during which Bryce was the only person in town who had any faith in Leon. He had encouraged his brothers to share his trust in the troubled medic, with the result that the Delaney brothers had occasionally called upon Leon to help them in times of difficulty. He had never let them down. "Leon is a friend and he is completely sober these days."

Beth huffed out a breath. "Okay. But if there is so much as a suspicion of alcohol on that man's breath, he is not coming within a yard of our daughter."

Leon repaid Vincente's praise by arriving within half an hour. Vincente could tell by Beth's face that she barely recognized the former hell-raiser. Leon was still way too pale and thin, and the stammer that had disappeared while he was drinking was evident as he examined Lia. But it was clear he knew what he was doing and that, as Vincente had promised, he was sober. He was even rewarded with a watered-down version of Lia's chuckle, after which the baby rested her head against Beth's shoulder and closed her eyes, succumbing to the slumber that had eluded her for much of the previous night.

"She has an ear infection," Leon said, having shone a light into Lia's ears. "I'll give you antibiotics and she can take infant pain relief, as well. It should clear up in a day or two, but if it doesn't give me another call."

"Thank you." Vincente could see relief replacing the worry that had gripped Beth's features. Because she had confided in him about her postpartum depression, he could see when the signs appeared. He knew when she was fighting an inner battle. But with each struggle, she seemed to grow stronger. And this time, that inner strength appeared almost immediately.

Leon had placed his medical bag on the kitchen counter, and he retrieved it now. As he closed it, he paused, gazing at the item next to it. It was Beth's photograph of the West County Climbing Club.

"How old is this picture?" Leon's gaze became intent as he looked at it.

Beth frowned. "It's ten years old. Why?"

Leon beckoned her over. "If it's that old, I'm guessing this guy—" he pointed to Cory "—has already gotten treatment for his condition?"

A cold feeling tracked its way down Vincente's spine. He could see the same feelings of dread and fascination reflected on Beth's face. What new twist was this? "He's dead."

"What condition did he have?" Vincente asked. "And how can you possibly diagnose it from a photograph?"

"Retinoblastoma. It's a rare form of eye cancer, usually only affecting babies or young children. It occurs very occasionally in adults. As far as I know, there are only a handful of documented cases. See how his eyes are glowing white and it hasn't happened to anyone else in the picture? That was caused by the abnormal reflection of the camera flash, a sign of a tumor in the eye… or, in this guy's case, in both eyes. I'm no expert, but it appears quite advanced. It's fatal if left untreated." Leon glanced from Vincente to Beth and back again. "Hey, I didn't mean to upset you by telling you this. A camera flash is a commonly used method of detecting retinoblastoma in kids these days. It's so successful that some organizations run ad campaigns targeted at parents of young children. There wasn't the same awareness of it ten years ago."

Vincente gestured to the photograph. "This guy's name was Cory Taylor. He was the climber who died in the Devil's Peak incident."

Leon nodded. "I remember that. It happened just before I joined the army."

"Would Cory have been aware of his condition?"

"I can't tell that from this picture," Leon said. "I don't know enough about the illness, and I don't know enough about him. Like I said, this appears advanced, but I can't say that for sure. If it *was* advanced, I'd have expected him to be in considerable pain and for his vision to have been affected. If the cancer had been present for some time but had gone undetected, it's possible it had already spread to other parts of his body."

"So there's a good chance that, when this photograph was taken, Cory Taylor was very ill?" Vincente asked.

Leon nodded. "I'd say there was a strong possibility he was dying."

"She's sleeping soundly, catching up on the hours of rest she missed last night." Vincente returned from checking on Lia. "Maybe you should try to do the same?"

"I don't know if I could sleep. I can't stop thinking about what Leon said." He flopped down into the seat next to her, and she turned to face him, wanting to share the jumble of thoughts that had been worrying her. "If Cory knew he was dying, it changes everything."

"Do you think he would have gone on a climb like that if he was in pain and his eyesight was failing? From what you've told me about him, he doesn't sound like the sort of guy who would put himself and others in danger."

"Who knows how anyone would act if they knew they didn't have long to live?" While he had been checking on Lia, she had been going over and over it in her mind. Her thoughts kept returning to one memory. One tiny phrase that altered her view of what had happened on that stormy mountain peak. It was so simple, yet so awful, it took her breath away. "Hear me out on something?"

Vincente nodded, his eyes on her face. "Of course."

"When I was alone in the tent with Cory, most of the sounds he made were incoherent. Just moans and cries of pain. He only spoke clearly twice. Just fragments of sentences. He said 'Let me die' and 'Wanted to die so bad.'"

"They both sound like the sort of things a man with a broken neck and a broken back might say," Vincente said.

"No." Beth shook her head. "Listen carefully to that second phrase. Cory said '*wanted* to die so bad.' Not '*want* to die so bad.'"

Vincente frowned. "He was talking in the past tense, but does it change the meaning? He was still expressing his wish to die."

Beth drew a breath. "I think the tense really matters. He was telling me what he *had* wanted. Not at that moment, but as we climbed the Keyhole. I don't believe his fall was an accident. I think Cory tried to kill himself."

Vincente whistled softly. "That's a hell of a big conjecture from just a single word. Particularly as the speaker was a man who was out of his mind with pain, both from his injuries and probably, as we've just learned, from cancer."

"I know." Despite Vincente's skepticism, Beth couldn't let go of her growing certainty. "But what if I'm right?"

Vincente leaned his head back, gazing up at the ceiling. He was silent for a long time before he turned to look at her. "If you're right, he planned it. Cory knew when your team set out for the Devil's Peak that he was going to take his life. And that means Peter Sharp must have agreed to help him."

Beth nodded. "If Cory hadn't confided in Peter, his plan wouldn't have worked. You can't throw yourself off a rock face when you are attached to another person. Not unless you want to take your partner with you. But if Cory and Peter had arranged it between them, then it was simple. When Cory was ready, he would give Peter a signal. Cory would fall—or jump—from the rock, and because Peter was prepared for it to happen, he would have been able to make sure he wasn't dragged to his death, as well. They hadn't counted on the storm. We should have been more spread out along the rock face, with no chance of anyone coming to Cory's aid. Peter should have let go of the rope."

"But he hadn't counted on Tania coming to the rescue."

"It was a superhuman effort on her part," Beth said. "Even in the blizzard, she managed to pull Cory part of the way back up before Danielle, her partner, joined in and helped. Then Peter roused himself from what appeared to be shock and got involved. Rick and I moved across from our position to assist, as well."

"I can't picture the woman we saw at the climbing club having the strength to haul an injured man up a cliff face."

"She was very different back then. Tania was strong, both physically and mentally. And don't they say you find reserves of energy you didn't know you had in difficult situations?" Beth asked.

"You should know." Vincente's gaze moved over her face, touching her skin like a caress, warming and soothing. "You've had so much thrown at you, yet you still keep fighting."

Beth felt a blush heat her cheeks. "This murderer hasn't left me much choice."

"If you're right—and it still feels like a huge leap—then we finally know who killed Cory Taylor…"

They said the name together. "Peter Sharp."

Once the antibiotics kicked in, Lia made a remarkable recovery and was soon back to her lively, beard-and-tail-pulling self.

"I think it's time to pay Peter Sharp a visit," Vincente said as they finished breakfast.

"You don't think we should speak to Laurie first?"

He decided Beth was looking outrageously sexy. Since she had just crawled out of bed, there was no particular reason for his conclusion. Her hair was mussed up, her eyes were slightly bleary and she wore one of his shirts and a pair of his socks. And he would never get tired of seeing her that way in the mornings. He would never get tired of *her*…

He forced his mind back to her question. "No, I don't think we should tell Laurie about Cory's illness. Not yet."

She poured milk onto Lia's cereal in response to the increasingly noisy demands from the high chair. "Any particular reason for this decision?"

"Several. But one of the most important ones concerns Cory Taylor's family. What if they didn't know about his cancer?" He poured coffee into two cups and handed one to Beth. "Hell, what if Leon is wrong and it's just a faulty, ten-year-old photograph? I don't want to put Cory's family through any more pain for something that may just be a hunch."

Beth walked past him with Lia's breakfast, pausing to rise on the tips of her toes and plant a kiss on the corner of his mouth. "You, Vincente Delaney, are a very nice man."

He pretended to look startled. "Don't tell anyone. You'll ruin my reputation."

She pulled a chair up next to Lia's high chair and commenced the feeding routine. One spoon for Beth, one for Lia. While Beth scooped cereal into the baby's mouth, Lia splashed in the milk, hammered out a drumbeat with her spoon and rubbed soggy cereal into her hair. She batted milky eyelashes at Vincente and held her spoon out to him.

"Sweetheart, as tempting as that is, I'm going to pass," he said. "How would you like to spend some time with Aunt Steffi today?"

Having called Steffi to agree on a time, they set off a few hours later. Leaving an excited Lia at the animal sanctuary, Vincente took the road toward Whitebridge.

"At least we know from the information Tania let slip where Peter lives. And it's Saturday, so there's a chance of him being at home. But what if he refuses to talk to us like he did last time?" Beth asked.

"Then we use the threat of the police. He has had one visit from Laurie—he won't want another."

"If Peter did help Cory in his suicide attempt and subsequently assisted his death, he isn't going to confess to it. He's gotten away with it for all these years. All he has to do is keep quiet." Beth shifted restlessly in her seat. "We have no proof and he'll know that."

"Did he look like a man who was at peace with himself?" Vincente asked.

"No, but…"

"Maybe he doesn't want to get away with it anymore. Maybe it's time for the secrets of the Devil's Peak to be told."

Beth didn't appear convinced, but she lapsed into silence for the remainder of the journey. She continued to amaze him with her fortitude. There had always been an incredible connection between them, but how she had dealt with this crisis had shown him her true character. She was handling this whole thing with an emotional and mental strength that was beyond anything he would have believed possible. That she was doing it having fought her way back from the debilitating depths of depression only added to his admiration.

Vincente had been reconsidering a lot of things lately. One of them was just how well he had known Beth. He had believed he knew everything about her. Now he wondered how much of that knowledge had been superficial. She had always been the person he wanted to hang out with, the person to whom he could talk for hours; she shared his interests and his sense of humor more than anyone else he knew. And, of course, he wanted to drag her off to bed at every available opportunity.

*That last one will never change.*

They had been driven into an incredibly tough situation. They were living in close proximity 24/7, constantly looking over their shoulders to see if a serial killer was lurking in the shadows, sharing the care of Lia, and obliged to form new bonds with Vincente's family. Everything had changed, including the way Vincente viewed Beth. There were depths to her he had never considered until now. The things he had known about her before still mattered. She preferred mountains to beaches, romance novels to horror stories, beer to champagne, and pizza to caviar.

Now he also knew that she had a fighting spirit that would put a world championship boxer to shame. She possessed a grace and poise that meant she could present a calm face to the world even when her nerves were worn raw with stress. Even under duress, she had the sort of generosity that meant she could sympathize with the sufferings of Tania Blake and try to reach out by sharing her own experience to help reduce the other woman's pain. Her physical attractiveness was obvious. He had also discovered that her inner beauty was endless.

*Just what the hell are you going to do about all these new feelings?*

Even with everything else that was going on, it was the question that had been tormenting him for days. The only thing he knew for sure was that doing nothing wasn't an option. He sensed the final confrontation was looming, and, once this nightmare was over, it would signal the end to the intimacy they now shared. Was he prepared to let Beth walk away?

He flicked a sidelong glance in her direction, and his whole body blazed with the force of his feelings. That was what being with her did to him. When he was with Beth, her presence acted like a mute button on the rest of the world. Fear, anger, pain…they all faded away when he looked into her eyes.

*And yet you still have to think about this? You have to ask yourself what this is called, and whether it's forever.*

He bit back the laugh that almost rose to his lips. He could call himself every kind of fool there was, but he'd wasted enough time already. His biggest problem wasn't sorting out his own head and heart. They were finally aligned and telling him exactly what he needed to do. No. He had more important things to worry about.

Starting with how the hell, in the middle of all this mayhem, he was going to find the time for a conversation that started with persuading Beth he had loved her all along.

## Chapter 14

The Whitebridge Episcopal Church was a pretty, tradi-
tional building with white wooden walls and green trim.
Its spire could be seen from the approach to the town,
and Vincente parked the car in the street opposite. Beth
had become so used to wearing her disguise of baseball
cap and shades that it was second nature to her now. She
tilted the brim down low over her face as she followed
Vincente toward the church.

"Tania said Peter lived in the house next to the
church."

There was only one house matching that description.
Nestling within a protective apron of white-barked and
gold-topped aspens, the tiny dwelling looked like the
sort of home that belonged to a storybook character. It
was perfectly maintained, with not a single leaf daring
to mar the flawless, emerald lawn. As they drew closer,

Beth was certain they were being watched by someone inside the house. Her suspicions appeared to be confirmed when the door was opened almost as soon as Vincente knocked.

She had been prepared for anger. Even possibly the threat of violence. But the look on Peter's expression made her step back in shock. Not because she was afraid for herself, but because she was frightened for him. Vincente had asked if she thought Peter Sharp was at peace with himself. Looking at him now, there was no doubt about the answer to that question. He was in hell.

Although Beth's face was hidden, Peter must have remembered Vincente from the last time they had met and made the association with her, because he gave a tortured groan. "I told you, I don't want to talk."

As he began to close the door, Beth stepped up close. She would only get one chance at this and she didn't have time for tact or hesitation. "Did Cory try to kill himself?"

The door's forward motion halted. Peter's face crumpled. "How can you ask me that…?" The words lacked heat.

"Because someone is trying to kill us all, and what happened to Cory is the key."

His shoulders slumped in an attitude of defeat. "You'd better come in."

The interior of the house was as new and pin neat as the outside. Peter led them to a small sitting room that overlooked a flower garden and gestured to a sofa. "A police officer came to see me." There was a haunted look in his eyes as he took a seat opposite theirs. "Why is this happening now? After all this time?"

"Because Andy Smith and Danielle Penn are dead,

and it's possible they were murdered." Beth decided not to mention Rick Sterling. "Did you get sent a copy of the newspaper article, and then a letter and the photographs with people's faces crossed out?" Beth asked.

Peter nodded miserably. "That's what I mean. Why now? Whoever is doing this must have felt all this hatred ever since Cory died. Why wait until now to start attacking us?"

"You're right." She turned her head to look at Vincente. "It's an aspect that hadn't occurred to me. Cory died a decade ago, yet the murderer waited eight years before sending the newspaper article, letter and photographs. What was the trigger two years ago that made him want to start killing us?"

"I can't believe this is happening. When I agreed—" Peter broke off, burying his face in his hands.

"So it's true? You agreed to help Cory kill himself?" Beth jumped on the words as proof. Until now, she had only half believed her own theory.

When Peter raised his head, his face was streaked with tears. "Cory was my best friend." He made a sound that could have been a laugh. "Who am I kidding? Cory was my *only* friend. You know what he was like. He had this big personality that wrapped itself around you. For a long time after we became climbing partners, I couldn't understand how someone so popular and with so many gifts would want to be friends with me. He wore me down. We'd hang out sometimes. I'm sure other people looked at us and wondered what the hell the guy with the movie-star looks had in common with the geek."

"Cory had a mind of his own. If he chose you as his friend, it was because he liked you." It was strange how, ten years on, she was getting a glimpse into a friendship she hadn't understood back then. This intensely shy man was clearly uncomfortable talking to them, and yet she sensed a part of him wanted to open up and tell them about Cory.

"That was what he used to say." Peter's expression had taken on a faraway quality, as though he was looking back in time. "When he was diagnosed with eye cancer, he didn't tell anyone except me. Not even his family. He'd left it too late, you see, and it had already spread throughout his body. He'd been ignoring the symptoms, hoping they'd go away. When he told me about it, he was quite calm, but he was already in pain and was losing his sight. He knew the next thing would be complete blindness."

He turned his head and looked at one of the pictures on the wall. The scene was unmistakable. Tenderness Lake was a focal point on the Stillwater Trail. The artist had captured a perfect moment. The mirror-smooth surface of the lake, the majesty of the mountain range, the ribbon of low-hanging clouds, the rounded pebbles peeking through the water's edge in the foreground… the palette was exclusively blue, teasing out every shade and nuance. The visual impact was stunning.

Beth raised a hand to her lips. "Oh, poor Cory! His eyesight was everything to him."

"That was the hardest part. He said he could cope with the pain and the thought of dying, but he couldn't stand to go blind." Peter dragged his gaze away from the picture with an obvious effort. "When he made the decision to take his life, he was quite calm about it. He thought it through carefully. For the sake of his family, he wanted it to look like an accident. He had convinced himself it would be easier that way. He wanted them to remember him as an active person, a person who died doing what he loved, rather than—and these were his words—'the guy who swallowed a bottle of pills rather than facing the end with dignity.'"

"But why did he need to involve you?" Beth asked. "If he was going to make it appear that he had died in a fall, he could have gone out on a solo climb and not come back."

Her thoughts went to Rick Sterling, who, it appeared, had staged his own death in an accident. There were so many twists and turns to this story, it felt like they would never get to the truth.

"Because his eyesight was already failing. If he was alone, he couldn't be sure he wouldn't fall and injure himself badly at a lower height. He risked a horrible impairment that left him in agony, but didn't kill him. The irony was, of course, that it happened anyway." Peter scrubbed a hand over his face as though trying to rub away the memory. "He needed my help to get him to a high point. A place where, once he decided to stage a fall, he couldn't possibly survive."

"And you agreed to help him because he was your friend."

He nodded, the tears beginning to flow again. "At that time, he was my only friend." Beth recalled Tania's words that he had recently found someone with whom he was happy. She was glad. The thought of his loneliness was painful.

"Why don't I make coffee?" Vincente raised his brows at Beth and she nodded gratefully.

While Vincente found the kitchen and could be heard clanking cups, Beth moved across to kneel on the rug beside Peter's chair. Clasping his hand in both of hers, she looked up into his face. Bleak sadness clouded his features.

"I made Cory a promise I would make sure he didn't come back down from that mountain. I had to see it through. When it was my turn to take over and watch him, I decided that would be the time to do it. Killing him was the hardest thing I've ever done. When I held the pillow over his face, he didn't even fight. It was like he knew what was happening and he welcomed it." He gulped back a sob. "Although I don't regret it, there is one thing I'm sorry about… I wish it hadn't been necessary to hit you."

Beth lifted a hand to the back of her head. "I don't think there's even a scar."

"How did you figure out I was the person who killed him?"

"It was something Cory said when we were alone in his tent. He said he wanted to die so bad, and I guessed that he was talking about what happened when he fell," Beth said. "I was the only person who heard him say it, so whoever is sending these pictures still doesn't know that it was you who killed Cory."

"I wonder if he, or she, cares?" Peter drew a perfectly folded handkerchief from his pocket and dried his eyes.

"What do you mean?"

"The letter addressed us all as murderers and said he would come for us one by one. I may have held the pillow over Cory's face, but that rage was directed at all of us. This person blames everyone who took part in that climb." Peter returned the clasp of her hands. "Although I said I have no regrets, I do feel guilty about the effects of what happened. And I've kept silent for too long. I had already decided to tell my story to that supereffcient Stillwater detective. My partner persuaded me it would be the right thing to do, but don't count on it stopping this killer."

Beth sat back on her heels, considering his words. "I wonder how he decides on the order of the victims? Is it random, or is there a pattern?"

"What do you mean?" Vincente asked as he returned with the coffee cups.

"Andy, then Rick, then Danielle. That's the order the photographs were sent. If Peter is right, and the killer blames all of us equally for Cory's death, I wonder why he selected the victims in that order? Is it to do with location?" She shook her head. "No, it can't be that. Andy was in Elmville and Danielle in Toronto."

She left Rick out of the conversation. Even though his face had been crossed out of a photograph, she knew he wasn't dead.

"Maybe he is apportioning blame?" Vincente hazarded a guess. "Killing those he considers most guilty first."

"If you use that logic, Peter and I should have been the first people killed." She gave Peter an apologetic smile. "I was with Cory when he died, and Peter was the person who was with him when he fell."

"And I'm next."

Peter's words sent a chill down Beth's spine. "How do you know that?"

"Haven't you received the latest picture?" He got to his feet, moving to a desk that was piled high with books. Reaching into the top drawer, he withdrew a photograph and brought it to Beth.

She didn't want to look at it. Every instinct told her to throw it down on the floor and run. Just like she had wanted to do when they found the picture in Lia's crib back in Casper. Run and keep on running. Instead, she took the picture from Peter and forced herself to look at it. There were five red crosses on this copy. Cory, Andy, Rick, Danielle and now Peter. Bold red lines slashing through their faces. She could feel the killer's rage as he took his pen and marked them off, one by one.

"When did you get this?" Her hand shook as she gave the picture back to Peter.

"What day did you come to the climbing club meeting? It was in my mailbox the next day." He frowned. "I wonder why you didn't get a copy."

"He doesn't know where I live." The words provided a measure of relief from the shock of looking at the picture. Ten people. Five crosses. Half of them should be dead. Peter was the next target…and Rick was still on the run.

Before they could discuss it further, there was a knock on the door. Beth cast a scared look in Vincente's direction, but Peter reassured her. "I'm expecting a delivery. Wait in here."

As he left the room to answer the door, Beth moved closer to Vincente anyway. The house was so small they could hear every sound as Peter drew back the catch on the front door. "Can you carry it through to the kitchen?"

There was the sound of two sets of footsteps walking along the wooden floorboards in the hall. A moment or two of silence followed, then Peter uttered a startled exclamation. "You!"

The gunshot was horribly loud, freezing Vincente and Beth into a moment of immobility. Then, springing into action together, they darted out of the room and into the hall. They were in time to see a black-clad figure dash out of the open front door. They saw nothing of the killer's face, only catching a glimpse of the back of a hooded sweatshirt before the door slammed closed.

In the kitchen, Peter lay in a crumpled heap. The perfect circle of a bullet wound was in the center of his right temple and a puddle of blood was forming on the floor beneath his head. A gun lay close to his right hand, placed to look as if he had dropped it when he fell.

Vincente muttered a curse, and Beth could read his dilemma on his face. The killer was seconds away from them. But if Vincente chased after him and left Beth alone, he exposed her to a possible trap. If he took her with him and they confronted an armed murderer who had already sworn to kill her...

Keeping an arm around Beth and holding her tight against his side, he reached for his cell phone. "Laurie? I need you in Whitebridge right now. You're going to need backup."

Two uniformed police officers from the Whitebridge Police Department arrived five minutes after Vincente called Laurie. Vincente showed them through to the kitchen.

"The caller didn't say anything about a body." One of the officers frowned as they surveyed the scene.

"The caller? Aren't you here because Detective Delaney from the Stillwater Police Department called you?" The feeling that he and Beth were in a shared nightmare was growing stronger.

"Detective who?"

After several minutes of trying to explain the situation, Vincente called Laurie. Although she was already in her car, she was able to speak on her hands-free cell phone and assure the police officers that Vincente had indeed been the person to call in the murder. No one was able to explain the confusion surrounding the call, but Vincente and Beth waited in Peter's sitting room until Laurie finally arrived with a Whitebridge detective.

"Looks like a suicide." One of the Whitebridge police officers studied Peter's body from the kitchen doorway.

It took Laurie about two and a half minutes of relaying cold, hard facts about Andy Smith and Danielle Penn to change his mind.

"Forensics will show that there is no gunshot residue on his clothing and his fingerprints are not on the gun."

She never once used the words *jumping* or *conclusions*, but they were obvious from her attitude. The uniformed officer grew red in the face and shuffled his feet as she spoke.

Laurie then questioned Vincente and Beth about what happened. With her usual relentless focus on detail, she missed nothing. When the forensic team turned up, she told Vincente and Beth to go home and informed them that she would call at the lake house later.

They were silent for most of the drive, the horror of what had happened still sinking in.

"Just before he was shot, Peter said 'you.' That means he knew who it was," Beth said.

It was the first time Vincente had thought of it that way. She was right. When he uttered that single word, Peter signaled that he had recognized his killer. Peter, who had been Cory's friend, could have gotten to know the other man's acquaintances. Would he still be in touch with them after ten years? It wasn't impossible, but that single word made it seem less likely that the killer was a member of Cory's family or one of his friends. It felt more like Peter had recognized the person instantly and been shocked at who it was.

*So who are you?*

Vincente had been close enough to the killer to reach out a hand and touch him. The frustration that he had let him get away left a sour taste in his mouth.

"Although the murderer placed the gun next to Peter's body, it wasn't going to work as a staged suicide this time." He voiced his thoughts out loud. "Apart from the forensic evidence Laurie talked about, we were in the house. There were witnesses this time. It was only a half-hearted attempt to disguise the killing as something else."

"Why is that?" Beth asked. "Did the killer panic because we were with Peter? Did he think that, between us, we might come up with the truth? Or did he just want to scare me even more by showing how daring he is?"

"Maybe it was both of those things…or neither." Vincente briefly placed a reassuring hand on her knee. "Who knows what's going on inside this person's mind? And possibly it's that simple. The killer could be starting to unravel."

"A violent, unpredictable criminal who is becoming more volatile? That makes me feel a whole lot better."

"I'm here." He tightened his grip on her leg. "He won't get past me."

The easiest way to reach Bryce and Steffi's home on the way back from Whitebridge was to drive through the center of Stillwater, then take the lake road out toward the Stillwater Trail. Their house, with the animal sanctuary located in its rambling grounds, was nestled in the foothills of the mountain range. Vincente had deliberately avoided the route through town the last few times he had driven out to collect Lia. Even though the car he was using had tinted windows, meaning Beth was unlikely to be recognized as they drove through Main Street, he didn't want to take any risks with her safety. It would only take a flat tire in the center of town or another unforeseen holdup, and her cover would be blown.

Just as he was about to drive past the turn that would have taken them along Main Street, Beth cried out, startling him.

"Stop!" The exclamation appeared to have been caused when she saw a man jogging toward them along the edge of the highway.

Vincente braked hard. "What the hell…?"

The jogger ran past them, taking the right turn that led into Stillwater.

"Back up and follow him."

Even though he did as she asked, he issued a warning. "Beth, this is dangerous. We're right on the edge of town here."

"Keep going but slow down." Her voice was urgent as she slewed around in her seat to get another look at the jogger. "Now pull over. Look in the rearview mirror." Vincente did as she instructed. "See this guy running along as though he doesn't have a care in the world?" Her hand was on the door handle as she prepared to jump out of the car. "It's Rick Sterling."

"Wait—" Beth was gone before he finished speaking. There weren't enough curse words in the world to summarize what he was feeling, so Vincente settled for one or two as he slammed the car door and ran after her.

Beth couldn't have chosen a worse place for a confrontation. Up ahead, just a few hundred yards away, was the start of Main Street itself. Vincente could see the giant, skillet-shaped sign of the Pancake Parlor swinging in the breeze and glimpses of the whiteboards of the cab company office were just visible through the trees. In the opposite direction, he could still hear the sounds of the highway they had just exited. To their right was the brutal scar that slashed across the landscape, the knife-sharp fissure known as Savage Canyon. It was a wilderness packed with forest so dense it was almost impossible to plow through it.

To their left was the Ryerson River and the Eternal Springs. At least the local scenic attraction wasn't likely to be busy with tourists at this time of year.

"Rick?"

As soon as Beth said his name, the guy's head snapped up and he stopped running. Beth halted as well, giving Vincente time to catch up to her. Although Vincente had never met Rick Sterling, there was no doubt in his mind. They had the right man. The wary look on his face confirmed it. Side by side, Vincente and Beth faced him across a distance of several feet for a few seconds. Then Rick turned and ran in the direction of the waterfall.

Beth didn't hesitate. She took off after him with the speed of an eagle swooping on its prey. Although Rick was bigger, Beth had determination on her side and she was closing on him as he neared the top of the cliff from which the river took a sharp downward plunge. Vincente muttered another curse. Beth had no idea what kind of danger she would be in if she caught up to this guy. Rick had faked his own death, been in Toronto the day before Danielle Penn died and was likely to have been the person on their deck in the middle of the night. Taking those things into account, Vincente decided to concentrate on running after her instead of swearing or shouting a warning.

When Rick reached the top of the waterfall, he cast a glance over his shoulder at Beth, who was close behind him. Crouching low, he placed his hands on the cliff edge and lowered himself into the water. Vincente blinked as the other man disappeared into the spray. He had a horrible premonition about what was going to happen next.

"Beth, don't—"

It was too late. Beth had already launched herself into the waterfall.

## Chapter 15

This was a first. Beth had climbed *up* waterfalls in the past, always using ropes and protective gear. She had never climbed *down* a waterfall. At first, the biggest problem was lack of visibility. She took care of that by moving to one side of the cascade itself. The difference was immediately apparent. Although she was drenched, cold as ice and her hands felt numb, moving out of the fast-flowing water at least allowed her to see. Planning a route down the steep rock face had to be her first priority…after clinging on.

She could see Rick below her, moving swiftly and nimbly as a cat. If she didn't act fast, he would be gone. The thought spurred her on. Probing to find places for her fingers and feet, she began her descent. The conditions were just about as bad as they could get. Ten years ago, she had been experienced at climbing on ice and in winter weather, but this surface was even more unpredictable. As she moved downward, she didn't know whether her next handhold would be rock that was loose, mossy or wet. She quickly discovered that the only certainty was it wouldn't be solid.

Everything seemed to be conspiring against her. The pounding of the falls, the freezing spray, the slippery surface…her descending path was more a scramble and a slide than a climb. About a third of the way down, she risked another glance below her in time to see Rick duck across to an exposed section of rock. Determinedly, she followed his course. There was no way she was letting him get away.

Swinging out over a sharp ledge, she hung on by her fingertips the way she had just seen Rick do, scrabbling wildly for a foothold. *Damn!* By taking the same route as Rick, she had miscalculated. He was at least six inches taller than she was. When he had dangled from this overhang, his feet had found a place to grip the rock. Because she was shorter, she wasn't going to make it. Could she pull herself back up? She seriously doubted it.

A glance down told her how much trouble she was in. Her hands were tiring already. When she dropped, she was going to fall at least forty feet onto solid rock.

*Lia.* Her daughter's face flashed into her mind and she tried desperately to struggle back up. *I can't die like this. She needs me. And I need a chance to tell that stubborn Italian how much I love him.*

Another glance down kicked her heart rate up another level. Rick had seen her and was climbing back up.

Panic seized her. She was helpless. It was no good telling herself he wasn't ready to kill her because he hadn't sent a photograph with her picture crossed out.

He was a serial killer and he was in charge of how he did this. By following him, she had presented him with the perfect opportunity. He could kill her now simply by releasing the grip her fingers had on the ledge. She would drop onto the rocks below. Vincente would know what had happened. He would tell Laurie, but there would never be any proof. Why the hell had she run after Rick?

The answer was simple. She had pursued Rick because she was tired of being scared. Tired of hiding. Tired of living half a life. She wanted normality. A life in which she could walk along Main Street and say hi to her old friends, reserve a table at Dino's and go there on a date with Vincente, take Lia to the park and push her on the swings, and walk Melon along the riverbank so he could play with the other dogs and attempt to herd the wildfowl.

Rick was a few feet below her now and she bit back the sob that rose to her lips as she aimed a wild kick at his head.

He grunted, ducking out of her way. Seconds later, he was alongside her. No matter how hard she tried to retain her grip on the rock, he was too strong for her, prying her fingers away easily. Instead of allowing her to fall immediately, he placed an arm around her waist, pinning her against him with her arms trapped at her sides.

Beth had no idea what torture he had planned for her, but she didn't intend to submit without a fight. Racing heart. Tight chest. Breathing hard. Light-headed. She was a panic attack checklist. With good reason. She squirmed wildly, trying to get her hands free.

"Keep still." Rick's tone held the same authoritative note he'd used when he ran the climbing club all those years ago. He had been her climbing partner. The man she had trusted with her life. How had they gotten to this point? His voice was so evocative, Beth almost obeyed. Even though she was fighting for her life, the temptation to do as he asked was close to overwhelming.

His strength must be phenomenal. Carrying her with one hand, he used the other to swing down from the ledge. She recalled that Rick had always been superbly fit. Clearly, he had maintained that level of physical ability. A wave of despair washed over her. How the hell was she going to fight a man who could climb down a cliff face one-handed?

After he had descended for a few minutes, Beth felt her feet touch a flat surface. Rick released his hold on her, turning her to face the cliff wall and pressing her hands up against the rocky surface. She trembled in anticipation. Was this it? Was this the moment he was going to push her over the edge and into oblivion? If it was, he was stringing it out, tormenting her with his silence.

After long, anxious seconds had passed and nothing happened, she risked a glance over her shoulder. She was alone on a wide ledge, just about as safe as she could be. Glancing down, she saw Rick almost at the bottom of the falls.

Vincente had never known fear like it. When he saw Beth disappear into the mist of Eternal Springs, he faced a split-second choice: follow her or find another way to track down Rick Sterling. If he went after her and Rick, he would be at a disadvantage. Chasing two experienced climbers down any rock face was going to be tricky enough. Down a waterfall? Vincente could only foresee one outcome…and it wasn't a pretty one.

Leaving Beth as he raced back to the car felt like the ultimate betrayal. Like he was running toward an abyss. Because if he'd gotten this wrong that was what he might as well be doing. As he ran, he experienced everything with perfect clarity. The breeze was so cool it felt like icy needles stinging his exposed skin. The blue of the sky hurt his eyes. Stillwater had its own scent. Sagebrush and pine, with a hint of juniper. It reminded him of licorice and root beer. It was the smell of home, but right now it made Vincente want to retch. Although his limbs seemed heavy, his body felt light, as though it had been hollowed out. But his heart…oh, his heart. That hurt too much to bear. He wanted to rip it out and cast it aside so he could think straight. Because his damn heart wouldn't let him get past one single, awful thought. If anything happened to Beth…

Jumping into the car, he gunned the engine. The falls cascaded into a large plunge pool before the Ryerson River continued its meandering journey toward Elmville. The lake road passed close to the pool. Vincente planned to drive out that way, leave the car and cut through the forest. Depending on how fast Rick and Beth climbed down, he should be able to catch up with them at the bottom of the cliff face.

If he misjudged it and Beth confronted Rick before he got there to back her up… No, he wasn't going to let himself think about that. Wasn't going to picture her alone with the man who might have threatened to kill her. Who might have already killed three people.

Once Vincente was on the highway, he pushed the car to its limit, scorching up the road until he reached the point where he could pull over. The distance from the highway to the plunge pool was short, but it wasn't easy to make his way through the trees and undergrowth that covered the ground between them. By the time he heard the roar of the falls, he felt like he had battled a dozen sharp-clawed monsters. His arms ached from pulling aside heavy branches and the backs of his hands were scratched and bleeding.

When he finally broke through the cover of the trees, the first thing he saw was Rick descending the last few feet of the rock face. Covering the distance between them at a sprint, Vincente was waiting for the other man as he stepped onto level ground. Gripping the collar of his shirt, Vincente swung Rick around. The look of surprise on the other man's face lasted about as long as it took for Vincente's fist to smash into his face. Blood spurted from Rick's nose. The feeling of intense satisfaction didn't quite replace Vincente's fear, but it sure as hell helped.

"Where is she?" Vincente raised his fist in preparation for another blow.

As he swung the second punch, Rick shifted his weight, bringing his leg up and kicking Vincente in the shin. The two men toppled to the ground together, trading blows as they fell.

"Where. Is. She?" Vincente punctuated each word with a jab.

Rick grunted and hit back. The guy had a punch like the kick of a horse. They rolled onto the edge of the plunge pool, and Vincente's head rocked back as Rick's fist connected with his cheekbone. He scrabbled wildly for something to hold on to, felt himself falling backward, grabbed hold of Rick's shirtfront and pulled him over the edge with him as he toppled into the water.

The plunge pool was deep. Vincente already knew

that from summer days spent out here diving into it, trying to reach the bottom. When they were kids, Bryce claimed he'd done it one time, but Vincente hadn't believed him. There was a local legend that the pool was bottomless. It sure as hell felt like it now, as Rick's hands closed around his throat and he sank down and down. The blood pounded in his head and the edges of his vision darkened.

Just as everything began to fade, Rick released his grip. Vincente didn't know why, but he kicked out for the surface. When he broke through, he drew in what felt like several lungs full of air. He spent a few minutes just concentrating on breathing. Yes, he still wanted to kill that bastard Rick Sterling, but first he needed to make sure he wasn't going to die himself.

When he felt his strength had returned sufficiently, Vincente swam to the edge of the pool and hauled himself onto the side. A quick glance around confirmed his worst fears. There was no sign of Rick. How the hell had the guy managed to get away so fast? Slumping forward, Vincente let his head drop between his raised knees. Despair washed over him, sour and dark. What now? Rick was gone and he still had no idea where Beth was.

It took him a moment to register a movement at his side. Turning his head, he looked into Beth's eyes as she knelt and draped an arm around his shoulders.

"How…?" The word rasped over his damaged throat muscles.

She looked up at the cliff face. "I'm not sure you'll believe me when I tell you. I don't know if I believe it myself."

They staggered, shivering and wet, from the plunge pool through the trees to the car. Bryce had already been home when they arrived to collect Lia, and the look of shock on his face and Steffi's had been more effective than a mirror.

"You need a doctor." Bryce helped Vincente to a chair in the big, comfortable kitchen.

"I need a drink." His voice was working again by then. Just about.

They both took hot showers and borrowed clean clothing. Vincente's cheekbone was cut and the eye above had swelled half-shut. A mass of deep red bruises mottled his neck, making it look like a lump of raw hamburger. His whole body felt like it had been pounded with a plastic mallet. Although Bryce and Steffi had tried to persuade them to stay the night, they had wanted to get home. Bryce carried Lia out to the car and Vincente promised to give him a full account of what had happened in a day or two.

It was late when Laurie, having spent most of the day in Whitebridge, had stopped by to let them know what was happening. "I wish you'd told me what you suspected, but I don't believe you could have prevented Peter Sharp's death."

"It was just a hunch," Beth said. "And it felt like a crazy one. No one was more surprised than I was when Peter came right out and confirmed it."

"What makes you think we couldn't have prevented Peter's death by telling you?" It still hurt a little to talk, but Vincente's voice was getting back to normal.

"Because, just like the other killings, this was carefully planned. The murderer wants these deaths to look like accidents or suicides. He's not going to risk getting caught. Not until every single person who was on that mountain ten years ago is dead."

"That's what Peter said. He said it wasn't about the individual who killed Cory. The killer has a grudge against all of us." Beth had reached the point where her whole body was drooping with exhaustion.

"The problem was that, this time, you two got in the way of the plan. I don't believe the killer didn't know you were in the house. That's just too coincidental. I imagine Peter's killing would have been more carefully staged, but possibly the murderer panicked. He didn't know what you were talking about. Even the smallest piece of information could have revealed his identity. Peter had to die immediately." Laurie glanced from Vincente to Beth with a grimace. "You both look like hell."

"You have such a way with words, Detective."

Although Vincente responded with flippancy, he had to acknowledge the truth of what she was saying.

Although Beth hadn't sustained any physical injury from her ordeal, she was aching all over and clearly so tired she could barely move. Steffi had helped them out by preparing dinner for them to bring home. Luckily it had been one of those evenings when Lia, tired out by her day with the animals, had gone straight to sleep.

"None of this business with Rick Sterling makes sense." Just when they didn't have the energy or inclination to do any more thinking, Laurie was forcing them into it. "From what you're saying, Beth, he actually rescued you when you were in difficulties?"

"Yes, he could have got away at that point, or killed me, but he saw I was in danger and he helped me."

"He's a wanted man. So why the hell was he out jogging in plain view in the middle of the afternoon?"

Vincente shrugged, wincing as the action caused his

aching muscles to protest. "He was running along the edge of the highway, then he turned into the road."

Laurie drummed her fingers as she considered the matter. "Maybe he had car trouble and was jogging into town to get help?"

"That would be a hell of a coincidence. The guy's car happened break down just outside the town where Beth is staying? The same town he most likely visited a week ago so he could climb down onto our deck in the middle of the night?"

"Another alternative could be that he got a ride as far as Stillwater. The person he was with dropped him on the side of the highway, and Rick was jogging into town when you came by."

Vincente considered Laurie's suggestion. "It still bothers me that he was here in Stillwater. Where Beth is."

"That can't be a fluke. Beth is the only member of the Devil's Peak team who is in Stillwater, even though her location is supposed to be a secret." Laurie shook her head, confusion evident in her expression. "Yet Rick didn't kill you today when he had the chance, Beth. On the contrary. He saved your life."

"Rick is a good guy." They were the words Beth had said when they'd driven out to the West County Climbing Club. She repeated them now as though she was clinging to the lifeline she hadn't had as she went down Eternal Springs.

"We can't rule out his involvement in the other murders, even Peter Sharp's. He had plenty of time to get from Whitebridge to Stillwater today. Which reminds me… I'm sorry to have to do official stuff, but I need a description of the person you saw." Laurie took her

faithful notebook out of her bag. "Because of the connection to the Devil's Peak Murder, I'm working with
the Whitebridge Police Department on this case. I'll
take full statements from you tomorrow, but I find it's
better to get a description as soon as possible after the
incident."

"I didn't see much." Beth shook her head. "It happened so fast. I barely saw him."

"Me, too," Vincente said. "I saw his back view as he
ran out the door."

"Let's start with what he was wearing."

"Black clothing," Beth said. "Sweatpants and a top
with the hood pulled up."

Vincente nodded. "And black sneakers."

"Did you notice anything else about the sneakers?
The brand? Was there a logo?"

He shook his head. "They could have had a gold flash
along the side, but he was moving fast."

"Oh, and he wore gloves," Beth said. "I just remembered that."

"Okay." Laurie scribbled a brief note. "What about
his size? Did you get any impression about that?"

Beth hesitated. "I didn't think he was big…"

Vincente thought back to what he'd seen in that brief
instant. "Beth's right. He wasn't tall, and he didn't appear
muscular, but—" he shook his head "—this is based on
what I saw in a split second, you understand? He moved
like lightning. That had to take some power."

Laurie wrote some more before returning her notebook and pen to her bag. "From what you're saying,
this is not the same person who climbed down the cliff
here and onto your deck. Although you've only gained

a brief impression of each of them, Beth, you described that man as tall and muscular."

Beth nodded decisively. "They were two different people. The guy at Peter's house was smaller, both in height and width."

"I agree. Having been up close to Rick Sterling today, I can say for sure he was not the person I saw at Peter's house." Vincente lifted a hand to his damaged throat. "Rick may have tried to choke and drown me, but he was fighting for his life after I attacked him first. He wasn't the person who killed Peter...and he did save Beth."

"This is the strangest case I have ever known. Right from the start, no one has been who they seem. Cory Taylor wasn't the carefree charmer everyone thought he was. He was harboring a heartbreaking secret. We thought Rick Sterling was dead, but the person with his hands around your throat in the plunge pool today was very much alive, Vincente. Behind his mild-mannered exterior, Peter Sharp was hiding the fact that he killed his best friend." Laurie got to her feet. "Someone else is hiding something. When we find out what it is, we'll find the killer."

## Chapter 16

Vincente checked all the locks and closed all the drapes before coming to sit next to Beth on the sofa.

"It's Lia's birthday next week." She let her head flop onto his shoulder. "We can't let him take that away from her."

"No." He ran a hand down her hair, the touch soothing, both of them too tired for anything more heated. "Lia will have the best celebration we can give her."

His hand spread wider to cup the back of her head and Beth looked up into those midnight eyes. They drew her in exactly the same way as they had done on the first day she saw him. He moved closer and tenderly brushed his lips over hers. She parted her mouth beneath his, needing his taste and warmth. Vincente's tongue caressed hers in a firm sweep. Nothing could have worked as well as this to restore her damaged spirits. His touch was so right, so perfect. When they ended the kiss, Vincente rested his forehead against hers and they stayed like that, breathing each other in.

"I thought I'd lost you today." His voice was hoarse and she didn't know if it was because of his injury, or because of the force of his emotions.

"You won't lose me, Vincente."

There was so much that was unspoken between them, but now wasn't the time. They could say more with their bodies than they could with words. That had always been the way they communicated best.

Beth's hands tugged at his shirt, pulling it free from his jeans. Without bothering to undo the buttons, Vincente pulled it over his shoulders and tossed it onto the floor. Beth ran a hand over his chest and abdomen, tracing the bruises that were already darkening in color.

"Are you sure about this?"

He caught her hand and pressed a kiss into the center of her palm. "Just be gentle with me."

"I can't make you any promises, but I don't think you have too much to worry about. I'm not sure I have it in me to be energetic."

She lifted her sweater over her head as Vincente pulled down her borrowed sweatpants and her underwear at the same time. Getting to his feet, he removed his jeans and boxer briefs and kicked them aside.

Kneeling between her legs, he let his fingers wander over her body. Trails of fire followed in their wake. Beth reached up, cupping the back of his head and pulling him down to her for another kiss.

"I may have lied." Her breathing was coming a little harder. "I can feel my energy returning."

Their tongues joined in a heated dance as his hands

moved lightly down her sides, grazing her breasts and hips. He spread her legs wider as his tongue massaged hers with long, strong strokes. When his hand cupped her sex, Beth moaned softly against his mouth. How had she gone from utter exhaustion to full-on raging desire in the space of a few seconds? The answer was simple. It lay in the magic of Vincente's touch.

Lining his erection up with her entrance, he pressed into her waiting heat, driving his full length in all the way to the hilt. Beth gasped, breaking the kiss as she threw her head back against the cushions. Vincente paused, taking his time, letting her feel every delicious inch. Those wonderful hands continued to stroke and soothe. He traced sweet, tiny kisses along her jaw, her neck and her breasts as her nails dug into his shoulders. When her back arched, he began to move. And then it was as if he couldn't stop. The gentleness was gone as the fire took over, blazing out of control within seconds. As soon as Vincente began to pound into her it was too much, but not enough. Beth craved more, even though her whole body was bowing under the pressure of his demands.

She called out his name, and Vincente increased the pace. Harder. Faster. Slamming into her. Her body jerked up from the sofa in time with his relentless thrusts. Her eyes fluttered closed as the first spasms hit. Waves of pleasure crashed through her as she trembled until she was limp. Vincente lowered his head, pumping short and shallow as his own climax hit. Fatigue hit them both and their bodies grew limp and their breathing became heavy and rhythmic.

They kissed slowly, as if they had all the time in the world. Beth lifted her arms and twisted them around his neck. In that instant, everything felt so perfect. If only they could stay just like that, wrapped in each other's arms, maybe they did have all the time in the world. Maybe it would all be okay.

"I don't recommend hanging from a rock by your arms when you haven't done any serious climbing for years." Beth groaned with each movement. "Edgar is going to think there's something wrong with me when I can't concentrate on our meeting because I keep wincing."

"Call him and postpone." Although Vincente's body was a rainbow of bruises, he appeared to be suffering fewer ill effects from their encounter with Rick the previous day than Beth. His face looked like he'd gone the distance with a world-champion boxer, but he was aching less than he'd expected and the tightness in his throat had eased.

Beth shook her head. "Edgar has put his trust in me, even though I've been unable to let him in on the details of what's going on in my life. He hasn't once asked me why we have to meet in such a cloak-and-dagger way, even though he must wonder what's going on every time he comes to your apartment to hand over my next lot of research for his court depositions. The least I can do in return is remain professional."

Vincente let the subject drop. He knew how much she was enjoying the work she did for Edgar, and guessed that had more to do with her reluctance to cancel than anything else. He understood how important it was to her to keep everything normal. Or to at least create that illusion.

With that in mind, they set off after lunch for the

planned meeting with Edgar. "Why is he here?" Vincente regarded Melon with surprise as the dog bounded onto the passenger seat. "What use will he be in a legal meeting?"

"He hasn't been anywhere different for a long time. I thought, once the meeting was over, we could take him for a walk along the riverbank. I've brought Lia's carrier, as well."

Beth was right. After the drama of the previous day, they needed something ordinary like a walk with a dog and a baby to restore their vigor. It was a perfect day. Sunny and clear with stinging blue skies and hint of chill in the air.

"Why not?" He spoke to Melon as he started the engine. "Just behave yourself in my apartment. I don't want any complaints from the neighbors." Obviously feeling a response was required, Melon wagged his tail and lolled his tongue out of the side of his mouth.

When they arrived at Ryerson Heights and left the car, Melon tried to drag Vincente by the leash toward Savage Canyon.

"That is one place we will never be taking a walk, my friend."

Vincente hauled him away and into the building while Beth carried Lia inside. She also took the carrier Vincente would use to hold Lia on his back when they went for their walk later. They mounted the stairs to the second floor and entered the apartment. Vincente always enjoyed the views from the full-length windows across the river. The raw power of the Wyoming landscape was incredible.

Edgar was due in twenty minutes. Beth prepared by setting up her laptop and papers on the dining table while

Lia crawled around, pulling herself up by the furniture. Melon embarked on a thorough inspection of each room, dashing in and out with his nose pressed to the floor. When Beth called him, he glanced up briefly with the don't-bother-me-now expression of a dog who was far too busy to be distracted by human business before returning to his meandering exploration.

When Vincente's phone buzzed, he expected the caller to be Laurie. Things were happening so fast with the case it seemed impossible nothing dramatic had occurred yet that day. When he glanced at the display, it was Trey Reid. With a pang of guilt, he realized it had been two days since he'd last spoken to his temporary replacement. He signaled to Beth that he needed to take the call, and she nodded her understanding.

"Trey. I'm sorry I haven't been in touch."

"Bryce told me things had been busy at home." Trey sounded apologetic. "And it hasn't been a problem until now. I hate to bother you, but…" Vincente could hear the concern in the other man's voice.

"Go ahead."

"I'm doing the monthly audit and everything was going fine until I ran the final program yesterday. I've made several attempts now, but there seems to be a glitch and the totals are all wrong." Trey's frustrated sigh resonated in Vincente's ear. "I've been in the office all night trying to figure it out."

"I've had that problem myself. Let me check my notes and I'll call you back." Vincente groaned at the prospect of attempting to sort the problem out over the phone.

"What is it?" Detecting his annoyance, Beth glanced up from her paperwork.

"Trey has screwed up the audit program." Vincente

ran a hand through his hair. "Actually, that's unfair. It's a complex system and if you don't know what you're doing, one wrong step can mess the whole process up. If I was in the office with him, I could sort it out in five minutes, but talking him through it in a phone call is going to be a nightmare."

She tapped her pen on the edge of the table. He could tell by the look on her face that half her mind was on her work. "Why don't you go down there?"

He gave an emphatic shake of his head. "Because you come first and there is a maniac on your tail, remember?"

"I'm not likely to forget it. Seriously, your office is five minutes' drive from here. Go and sort out your problem. Lia and I will be fine until you get back."

He hesitated. It would be the perfect solution. But... He thought of what was at stake. Saw Peter Sharp's body lying on his kitchen floor, a thick, dark red puddle forming beneath his head. "No."

Beth got to her feet. Coming around the table, she took his hands. "We can't let him do this to us, Vincente. We can't become prisoners because of him. You chose this apartment for my meetings with Edgar because it's safe. The only people who know we're here are Edgar and Laurie. And I'm meeting *Edgar*. After your family, there is no one more trustworthy."

She was right, of course. He was being paranoid. And it would be so much easier to fix the computer glitch in person. "I would be gone fifteen minutes at the most."

Beth grinned. "Now you're talking sense. Don't forget we have Melon to take care of us."

He rolled his eyes. "Now you're *not* talking sense."

"Don't insult my dog." She pushed him toward the door. "Go."

He kissed her before going out. Closing the door carefully behind him, he ran down the stairs and made his way out to the parking lot. The sooner he sorted this damn program out, the sooner he could get back and they could have their family walk by the river.

*Family.* The word was warm in his thoughts as he started the car. Not frightening. Not like a steel trap coming down. Not something that he would someday run from, hurting Beth and Lia in the process. It was what they already were. His family. All he had to do was make it official.

He was still smiling as he stepped into the familiar foyer of Delaney Transportation. A flurry of greetings followed him as he made his way down the corridor to his office. Trey looked up from his desktop computer, his expression both relieved and embarrassed when he saw who it was.

"I didn't want to call you in here…"

Vincente dragged a chair over to the desk. "Let's see if we can't sort this out between us." He knew he could solve the problem in minutes, but it seemed insensitive to say that when Trey had spent all night worrying about it.

Five minutes later, he had explained to Trey exactly which combination of figures weren't working together and the other man was pretending to bang his head on the desk at the simplicity of the solution. "It's so straightforward now you've explained it. I feel like an idiot for not seeing it."

"Everything is easy once you know how it works…"

Vincente frowned as his cell phone buzzed. A nasty

little worm of dread began to writhe around in his stomach when he saw Laurie's name on the display.

*Not now. Not when I've left them alone.*

"Vincente." Laurie didn't give him time to speak. Just the way she said his name, the way she was shaken out of her usual composure, had him on his feet and heading for the door. "I've found out who the other person hiding a secret is. Cory Taylor was Edgar Powell's nephew."

Even though Beth had encouraged Vincente to go, as soon as the door closed behind him, the apartment started to feel like a scary place.

*This is crazy.* She tried out a laugh and it sounded false. *The reasons you gave Vincente for why it was okay to go still apply.*

She scooped Lia up and carried her over to the window to show her the view. Lia was unimpressed and wriggled to be put down again. Deciding to make coffee while she waited for Edgar, Beth took Lia through to the kitchen with her. Vincente's cupboards were as chaotic as ever, and she smiled at old memories of trying to make sense of where he kept things. Salt next to powdered detergent. Sugar with the beer.

She had just located the coffee when the buzzer sounded. Trust Edgar to be exactly on time. Not a minute too early or too late. Bouncing Lia up and down on her hip, Beth went to the intercom.

"Come on up, Edgar. You must have smelled the coffee."

She pressed the button that would release the door of the building and went through to the hall. Her smile faded as she opened the front door of the apartment.

"Hello, Beth."

Instead of Edgar's familiar, reassuring figure, Tania Blake stepped over the doorstep and closed the door behind her. Her eyes glittered triumphantly and a curious smile twisted her lips.

Beth took a moment to gather her thoughts, but in reality, the situation didn't take much working out. Her eyes were telling her everything she needed to know. Tania was dressed in black clothing. Sweatpants and a hooded top. Her eyes dropped to Tania's feet. Beth recalled what Vincente had said to Laurie last night.

*Black sneakers. They could have had a gold flash along the side, but he was moving fast.*

Tania was wearing black sneakers with a gold flash along the outside. And gloves. The same gloves Beth had noticed her wearing the day before.

*When she killed Peter.*

The thought didn't need any confirmation, but Tania provided it anyway. "I have something for you."

She held out a photograph. It was the one Beth had been dreading. Six red crosses. Cory, Andy, Rick, Danielle, Peter…and now Beth.

*My turn.*

There was no longer any sign of Tania's depressed demeanor. Beth wondered if she had been faking her illness, or if there were two sides to her personality.

Before Beth could move, Melon emerged from the sitting room. Vincente might mock the dog's intuition, but he immediately picked up on Beth's mood. Throwing back his head, he launched into a volley of menacing barks, directing his threats at Tania.

Tania withdrew a gun from the pocket of her sweatpants and leveled it at the dog. "Get rid of it, or I'll shoot it."

Grabbing Melon by his collar while still holding Lia tightly with her other arm, Beth wrestled the dog into the bedroom.

"Not the baby. I have plans for her."

The words sent Beth's nerves into panic mode as she shut the door. Melon's howls sounded like something from a low-budget horror movie, and he started scratching wildly at the bottom of the door.

Tania frowned. "The neighbors will wonder what the hell is going on. Maybe I should shoot it anyway."

"He'll calm down in a minute." Beth tried to keep the pleading note out of her voice. She should probably save that for herself and Lia.

"We won't be here long anyway."

Before Beth could ask what Tania meant by that comment, the buzzer startled her.

"It's my boss. If I don't answer it, he'll call the police." Would Tania swallow the lie? Beth was desperate. She was prepared to try anything.

"Let him in." Tania moved to stand at one side of the apartment door, concealing herself behind it. "But don't try anything."

Beth pressed the button on the intercom. "Beth, I'm sorry to be so late."

She wanted to sob when she heard Edgar's voice. Should she risk calling out to him? Tell him to contact Vincente? Maybe she could wrestle the weapon from Tania? Beth ventured a quick glance at the gun. Her blood ran cold when she saw where it was pointing. Tania wasn't aiming it at her. It was leveled at Lia.

"Come on up, Edgar."

Tears filled her eyes as she opened the door and Edgar stepped into the apartment. His smile was apologetic. "A last-minute crisis at the office—" a frown chased away the smile "—is everything okay?"

His eyes widened as Tania stepped into view. He barely had time to raise a defensive hand before the gun barrel came down on his temple. Edgar's body seemed to fold in on itself as he toppled to the floor.

Beth cried out and made a move toward him, but Tania grabbed her arm.

"Leave him. We're going for a walk." Tania used the gun to gesture toward the door.

"I need to put Lia in the carrier," Beth said. "I hurt my arms yesterday and I can't hold her for long."

It was true, although she didn't know how far they'd be walking. Another reason for wanting her hands free was that, if the possibility presented itself, she would do anything she could to get away from Tania. Having Lia in a carrier on her back would make escape easier than having a baby in her arms.

Tania made a huffing noise, but folded her arms across her chest as Beth got Lia into her coat and then into the carrier. Since being restrained in any way was what her daughter hated more than anything, this action provoked an immediate protest from Lia. The sound of her distress caused Melon to renew his barking. Between them, they were making so much noise that Beth was half hopeful, half fearful that someone might decide to investigate. She hoisted Lia onto her back and secured the carrier in place.

"The gun will be in my pocket. I don't advise you to do anything stupid." Tania gestured for Beth leave the apartment first.

Why hadn't she noticed that Tania was as physically fit as ever?

*Because she hid it beneath those baggy clothes. I saw what she wanted me to see. She drew me in and made me believe she was a pitiful figure who couldn't possibly hurt anyone.*

Beth had fallen for Tania's illusion and now she and Lia were about to pay the price.

# Chapter 17

Vincente and Laurie screeched into the parking lot of Ryerson Heights at the same time. They exited their vehicles in the same instant.

"Edgar?" Vincente was still stunned. "He's worked with Beth for years. He must have known she was part of the Devil's Peak team. If he wanted to harm her, he could have done it anytime he chose. Why would he suddenly start sending letters and photographs two years ago?"

"Edgar's sister was Cory's mother. They had been estranged for many years, but there was a reconciliation just before she died after a lengthy illness. That was two years ago. Who knows what happened? Cory's mother could have been harboring a grudge against the Devil's Peak team and passed that hatred on to Edgar before she died. She may even have asked him to take revenge on her behalf."

"I know the fact he never told Beth he was Cory's uncle makes it likely he's guilty, but I'm still struggling with it," Vincente said as they raced toward the entrance.

"That's Edgar's car." Laurie gestured to the battered old Fiat that was parked close to the front of the building. She was pulling her gun out of her shoulder holster as they dashed up the stairs.

Vincente reached the second floor just ahead of Laurie. His heart plummeted when he saw the door to his apartment was open. He was moving toward it, when Laurie's voice halted him.

"I need to call for backup before we go in there."

It took him about thirty seconds to consider what she was saying. "It's *Beth*. And my daughter."

"Vincente, I understand how you feel. But I can't let you go do this—"

He placed his hand on the door handle. "The only way you're going to stop me is if you shoot me."

"Why do you Delaney men always have to be so damn stubborn?" There was a note of defeat in the question, but he heard her footsteps right behind him as he stepped into the apartment.

The first thing they saw was Edgar crumpled in a heap on the floor. Laurie dropped on one knee beside him.

"He's alive. It looks like someone hit him over the head."

As she spoke, Edgar stirred. He moaned, opening his eyes and blinking at Laurie as though he didn't recognize her. After a few seconds, he attempted to sit up. The effort was too much for him and he collapsed back onto the floor. "Beth… The baby…"

His words were all the confirmation Vincente needed that Edgar was not the killer.

"What happened, Edgar? Can you remember?"

Vincente leaned over him. As he did, he saw a photograph. His whole body went cold as he picked it up and handed it to Laurie. It was proof of what they were dealing with. It was the familiar picture of the Devil's Peak team. In this one, there was a sixth red $X$. Beth's face had been eliminated.

Vincente hadn't believed the pain he was experiencing could get any worse. In that moment when Laurie called him and he realized he had left Beth and Lia in danger, he had experienced pure agony. Every part of his body had been battered by terror. And every second since had felt like he was being beaten with a bag of bricks. But this? Looking at that picture took the feeling one step higher, made it spin further out of control, gripped his spine and tried to draw it out through the top of his body until he was a useless, whimpering mass. For Beth's sake, he forced emotion aside and concentrated on what Edgar was saying.

"A woman…dressed all in black. She was hiding behind the door when I came in. Had a gun on Beth and the baby." His voice shook. "Hit me over the head."

"Do you know where they went?"

"No. I blacked out."

A desperate howl almost drowned out what Edgar was saying. "It's Melon. He must be in one of the bedrooms."

Vincente went to let the dog out. Melon went wild, jumping all over him, licking his hands and whining pitifully. When Vincente tried to go back and finish his conversation with Edgar, Melon circled his legs, trying to herd him out of the apartment.

"He's stressed," he told Laurie as Melon sniffed a path to the door and back again. "If he heard what was going on and couldn't do anything, the poor dog will feel like he wasn't doing his job."

"He definitely wants to take you somewhere," Laurie said.

She was right. Melon wasn't giving up. He kept returning to Vincente, nudging his legs and whining as he attempted to drive him to the door. At the start of their acquaintance, Vincente hadn't rated Melon's intelligence as particularly high. He had revised his opinion of the dog over time, but maintained the joke with Beth, who always got fired up and defended her beloved pet. Now, he realized Melon wasn't stressed. He was trying to tell him something. He wondered if it was possible Melon might be remembering his search-and-rescue training.

"Can you take me to her, Melon?" It was a long shot. If the person who had taken Beth and Lia had forced them into a car, Melon wouldn't be able to follow their scent. But the dog was so damn insistent. "Can you find your mistress?"

Melon gave an excited bark and dashed to the door. Vincente followed him.

"I'll call the paramedics and get them to come out here to you, Edgar." Laurie shouted the words over her shoulder.

"Just find them." Edgar's voice was still weak, but he managed to make himself heard as they ran for the stairs.

They emerged from the apartment building and Vincente wondered just how crazy he had to be to entrust a task of this magnitude to a dog. But he was desperate, and Melon was all he had right now. There was no question that he was following a scent. His nose was down and his plumy tail was waving.

As they followed him across the parking lot, Vincente paused. "That car—" he pointed to the scarred and battered Ford Mustang "—I saw it at the West County Climbing Club."

It was unmistakable. He remembered the sticker in the rear window. *Rock climbers do it up against the wall!* He'd made a lame joke to Beth about not going to the Christmas party if that was the standard of the humor he could expect.

"Edgar said it was a woman who hit him. Tania Blake was at the climbing club when Laurie and I went there. It could be her car."

Laurie was on her cell phone, calling in the license plate and registration as Melon led them to the rear of the building.

"That dog sure seems to know what he's doing." Laurie panted as they ran to keep up.

Vincente nodded. "I agree. But if he does, our problems are getting bigger by the minute."

"What do you mean?"

"He's taking us into Savage Canyon."

"How did you find me?" Beth asked.

Although Tania was urging her to go faster, the ground underfoot was a minefield of deep fissures and lethal tree roots. Savage Canyon was an alien landscape. Growing up in Stillwater, kids were warned never to come to this place. Beth remembered the way it had assumed almost mystical proportions in her mind. If she had a nightmare, it was always set here, home of the boogeyman, witches and hobgoblins; no one in their right mind stepped foot in Savage Canyon.

In reality, it was a place in which, over millions of years of relentless slashing and slicing, the Ryerson River had carved a brutal path through the Wyoming landscape. With its red-rocked, knife-sharp walls, the canyon was so narrow that little light pierced through to river level. As they penetrated deeper into the trees, it grew increasingly primitive. Beth felt as though they were leaving civilization behind them. Twenty-first-century Stillwater felt a million miles away. She wouldn't be surprised if they were the first people to ever walk this path. Boogeyman? She wasn't scared of meeting a creature from her childhood nightmares. But it felt like dinosaurs might still roam this forest.

Not that any of it mattered when a killer with a gun was at her side. Surreptitiously, she loosened Lia's light-weight sneaker. Slipping it off her daughter's little foot, she dropped it on the ground. A bright pink shoe in the middle of the dark vegetation should be a marker for anyone following them. She bit back the harsh sob that rose in her throat. Why would anyone follow them *here*?

"It wasn't easy." Tania seemed to feel she should be congratulated for her ingenuity. "Not once you left Casper. While you were there, it wasn't a problem." She laughed at Beth's look of surprise. "I'm a computer systems analyst. Hacking is child's play for me. I kept track of all of you through your medical records. I needed to give you the photograph of Danielle, so I was watching you the day the detective and the handsome hero turned up."

Beth allowed that information to sink in. She thought back to the time when she'd been scared and asked the doctor not to keep any notes about her. It turned out she'd been right to be fearful. She saw the open window in Lia's bedroom and the ladder up against the wall. All the time she'd believed she was hidden away, Tania had been able to get to her anytime she wanted.

"Once you left Casper, I lost track of you for a while. But you helped me out by coming to the climbing club, and your boyfriend—" she spat the word out with such venom that Beth felt a fresh wave of alarm "—isn't an ordinary-looking guy. Tall, handsome, with that dark, smoldering thing going on…you really hit the jackpot with him, didn't you?" The mocking edge in Tania's voice made Beth shiver more than ever. "I remembered you used to live in Stillwater. So I started here. It's amazing what people will tell you." Her voice took on a different note. Warm and singsong. "Oh, hey, I just love your town. So quaint and Old Western. I had a friend who used to live here. We're going back…let me see, must be ten years now. Beth Wade. You remember her? You don't say. Disappeared? Maybe murdered? Oh, my sweet Lord. Is Vincente an Italian name? Oh, half-Italian. And his brother is the mayor, you say?" Tania switched back to her mocking tone. "Yeah, people can be so dumb."

She appeared to be enjoying herself now. Talking about her achievements had brought a little smile to her lips. "Of course, even when I found out who he was and where he lived, it was obvious you had gone into hiding somewhere. But I'm a patient woman. I checked Vincente's apartment out every few days. Sat in the parking lot with my memories to keep me warm. I figured he'd come along there eventually to get his mail or pick up some clothes, and he'd lead me to you. Today was my lucky day. Your little family showed up, and then—just as I was on my way in to surprise you all—your body-guard left you alone."

*My memories to keep me warm.* What did that mean? Would Tania tell her all of it? If Beth was going to die, she'd like to know the real reason. "I'm not the person who killed Cory."

"You all killed him." Tania's voice had taken on a dreamy quality. "By not saving him, you ruined my life."

"You loved him." It was obvious from her face and the quality of her voice.

"Yes, I loved him." Tania's lips twisted into a bitter smile. "And he would have loved me, too, you know. If he'd been allowed to live, we'd have had what you have."

"Cory was dying. He had incurable cancer." Beth didn't know if telling her was going to make things better or worse, but she figured the truth was the only weapon she had right now. "His fall wasn't an accident. He wanted to die on Devil's Peak that day."

"No!" It was the wail of a wounded animal. "You're lying."

"He had tumors in both eyes. By the time he found out, it was too late to save his sight and the cancer had already spread throughout his body. Peter knew and had promised to help him commit suicide. When you saved Cory, you did it with the best of intentions, but it wasn't what he wanted." The gun was pointed at the ground and Beth kept her gaze on it, willing it to stay there as she kept her voice calm and gentle. "Peter was the one who killed Cory. He did it because that was the agreement they had made."

Tania started shivering wildly, shaking her head as though she could make the words go away.

Even as she talked, Beth was remembering what Peter

had said. That this whole nightmare was about more than who killed Cory. He had wondered about the order in which the victims were selected. Andy, Rick—even though he wasn't dead—Danielle, Peter and now Beth. *We'd have had what you have.* Those words that Tania had just spoken were the key. That was what she had been searching for with Cory, what she felt had been snatched away from her with his death.

*Happiness. Love. Romance.* Each of the victims had found a partner with whom they were happy. Tania was killing the people who had what she thought she'd lost.

"Keep moving." Tania seemed to have recovered her composure as she gestured with the gun. "Cory dying of cancer? I've got to hand it to you. That's quite a story."

They stumbled onward, taking a slight upward path. It hadn't worked. Tania was going to believe what she wanted to believe.

"Why did you start with Andy?" Maybe if she got Tania back on the subject of her achievements, she could distract her. Lia had fallen asleep, and Beth was glad. At least her daughter wasn't picking up on any distressing vibes. Carefully, she began to undo Lia's other shoe.

"Because he was always so damn smug." Tania's voice became high-pitched and jeering. "'Oh, I'm so happy. I have such a great relationship. No one could ever be as much in love as me and my wife.'"

"You killed him because he was happy?" As the incline became steeper, Beth dropped Lia's other shoe.

"I killed him because I could. But, yeah, the happiness thing didn't help him. And yet, when I got to him, he wasn't happy at all. He was a drunken mess. And killing him was easy. All I had to do was get him to swallow some pills with his next few drinks. He didn't even notice what was happening." Tania seemed disappointed. "I had to make it look like suicide, or an accident, of course. If there was any chance of it appearing to be murder, I might be caught before I could move on and get the rest of you. One by one, remember. Just like I promised in my letter."

Beth swallowed to try to get rid of the hard lump in her throat. How could she be here, having this conversation? Trying to sound normal as she walked alongside a serial killer? *With my baby asleep in the carrier on my back?*

"If I couldn't have Cory, the people who walked down off that mountain sure as hell weren't going to be happy."

"Why did you wait eight years to decide that?" Beth asked.

"I already told you." Tania sounded impatient. "I had a few problems. They hospitalized me."

When they met at the climbing club, Tania had told Beth she had been diagnosed with severe depression. If Tania's problems had lasted eight years, they had been more complex than she'd revealed and must have included something more serious than depression. Tania had said she was tracking them by hacking their medical records. *She knew I suffered from depression.* Beth felt a flare of anger at the way Tania had callously used that information to provoke sympathy from her.

"And Rick?" Did Tania know he was still alive? Surely, she must be aware if one of her murder victims had gotten away from her. Much as Beth would love to know the story of what had happened to Rick on that ledge in the Grand Teton National Park, she wasn't sure she was going to hear it from Tania. "He always kept his private life quiet. How could you know whether he was happy or not?"

Tania's top lip curled back, showing her teeth in a near snarl. Beth was willing to bet that meant she did know Rick was still alive. Did she know he was in Stillwater? That was an interesting question. Were they working together? She had never considered the possibility until now. "I don't want to talk about him."

"So, you killed Danielle next." She moved on, since it seemed they were skipping over what happened with Rick.

"She wasn't quite as easy as Andy. She tried to fight me, but I was too strong for her." That faraway note was back in Tania's voice, as though she was recalling a pleasant memory. "She begged and pleaded with me as I got her head into the noose. I enjoyed that part." She turned to look at Beth. "I hope you'll beg. I like begging."

Beth choked back a sob. Of course she would beg. She would do anything to protect Lia.

"Peter was right on your doorstep. You saw him all the time at climbing club meetings. Why did you wait until after you'd killed Andy and Danielle to go after him?"

Tania gave a derisive snort. "Because he didn't count. Not at first. He wasn't *happy*. Not until he met her."

Beth remembered her meeting with Tania at Betty's Bakery. How she'd dismissed Tania's rambling speech about Peter's new partner and wondered if Tania might have some sort of prejudice against people who used internet dating sites. But that wasn't what Tania's problem had been. Her scorn had been about Peter's happiness, not how he found it.

"That's how you decided what order you were going to kill us. It was according to how happy we were."

Tania nodded. "You moved right up my list when I saw you gazing into the eyes of your Italian lover when you came to the climbing club. It was like you were waving a flag with the words *me next* at me."

If it hadn't been so awful, it might almost have been funny. Beth had taken such care to protect herself and Lia. Vincente had done everything he could to look after them. But the one thing they had tried so hard to deny had been the thing that had given them away. Tania had seen it in a simple exchange of glances.

*We love each other. We hid from everything else, but there was no hiding from that.*

They were alongside the top of the trees now. The narrow path they were following was leading out onto the top of the canyon. Beth wasn't sure what the plan was, but she didn't like the way this was going. High up above the cruel fault in the earth's crust, there were too many ways a disturbed mind could make it look like she had tripped or slipped.

"Did Cory know how you felt?" Beth tried a new approach. "Did you ever tell him you loved him?"

Tania swung around so sharply Beth almost lost her footing there and then. "He would have loved me. We just never got the chance to be together."

Beth wasn't so sure, although she had no intention of saying so. She thought back to ten years ago, contrasting Tania's personality with Cory's. They had been steel and silk. Tania had been arrogant and inflexible. Cory had been easygoing and modest. It would have been difficult to find two people more different. She guessed Tania had fallen in love with Cory's looks. Had she known, on some level, that her feelings would not be returned?

*I had a few problems.* Did Tania's problems start with Cory's murder, or had they been present before he died? Had she developed an obsession with him, one that had been allowed to spiral out of control in an already unstable mind after his death? Looking at Tania's face as they paused on top of the canyon, it was hard to picture a time when reason had been a feature of her personality.

"Ever since I knew about your postpartum depression, I've been planning how I would do this." Tania smiled, turning her face into the breeze as though they were out for a pleasant hike. "I even came and checked this place out. It all got too much for you—that's what they'll believe when they find out you killed yourself and your baby."

"Not her." Beth couldn't keep the sob out of her voice. "Please…"

"But it won't work as well without her." Tania pouted as she drew a slip of paper out of her pocket. "I typed this note for Vincente from you, explaining everything. How sorry you are. How much you loved him. How you just couldn't take the stress anymore." She looked down into the canyon. "There won't be much of you left when they find your bodies, but I hope they'll be able to read the note. I spent so long getting it just right."

# *Chapter 18*

Panic would be his worst enemy. That was what Vincente kept telling himself. He needed a clear head if he was going to get Beth and Lia out of this. He had to keep regulating his breathing, stopping his mind from racing, taking time to place his feet carefully instead of storming ahead and breaking an ankle on a tree root.

Melon dashed on ahead of them, occasionally darting back to either check they were still with him, or to hurry them along.

Laurie had been speaking on her cell phone to her chief, keeping him updated about what was going on, but she muttered an exclamation. "The signal keeps fading."

"I'm not surprised. This is like going back in time to the Jurassic Period."

Waist-high ferns clung damply to his legs and thick ropes of tangled vine hung down to meet them. The scent of loam, pine and wild garlic was thick and cloying. Vincente saw this view every day from his bedroom window. *Never felt tempted to come down here.* Savage Canyon was the sort of place people admired from a distance. It was nature at its most raw and untouchable. Would the killer really bring Beth and Lia into this alien scene? Melon clearly thought so, and the dog's instinct was the only thing keeping Vincente going.

As Melon followed the route of the river, an object lying among the gnarled tree trunks caught Vincente's eye. "Over there."

Melon got to the bright pink item before them. Snatching it up between his teeth, he brought it to Vincente. Wagging his tail with delight, he dropped what he was carrying at Vincente's feet, nudging it closer with his nose.

"It's Lia's shoe." Vincente managed to get the words out, even though his throat felt like it was closing. He squatted, ruffling the fur on Melon's neck. "I take it all back. You are the best damn dog ever. Now, let's go find them."

Melon needed no further encouragement. Uttering a joyful bark, he ran ahead of them again, snuffling in the undergrowth as he picked up the trail he had been following. Although Melon had been right to bring them this way, Vincente didn't feel able to allow any glimmer of hope to shine through his despair. The killer had chosen this hostile environment for a reason, and it wasn't going to be a good one. Somewhere up ahead, Beth and Lia were facing a dangerous ordeal. He had to get to them in time.

Melon was taking them on an upward path, leading them gradually out of the canyon itself and toward the ridge that overlooked it. Vincente judged that when they emerged, they would be in an isolated part of the countryside, outside of town and miles from any dwellings. The murderer had selected a place that was lonely and inhospitable, away from prying eyes and any chance of interruption. There was a reason for that choice.

They found Lia's other shoe as they ascended. "Beth did this deliberately," Vincente said as he tucked the little sneaker into his pocket. "She's letting us know they came this way."

Laurie placed a hand on his arm, her expression softening as she scanned his face. "We'll find them."

"But will we be in time?"

Before Laurie could reply, her cell phone buzzed, the signal kicking back in as they moved out of the canyon. Her face was serious as she answered and listened carefully to what the caller was telling her. It was several minutes later when she returned her cell phone to her pocket.

"That was Chief Wilkinson. The car in the parking lot outside your apartment, the one you saw at the West County Climbing Club? It does belong to Tania Blake."

"So she is the killer?" Vincente shook his head in amazement. "She seemed so harmless."

"Tania is very dangerous. Long before Cory's death, she had a history of obsessive behavior, including stalking. Although she was never convicted, she was ordered by a judge to seek psychiatric help."

"She told Beth she suffered from depression after Cory's death and had been hospitalized," Vincente said.

"That's only partly true. She spent several years in and out of the hospital, but it was due to a psychotic disorder. Her family used the term 'depression' as a cover story," Laurie explained. "When Tania was discharged from the hospital, she was supposed to remain in her parents' home, under their supervision. When her mother died, Tania left home."

"When was that?" Although Vincente asked the question, he suspected he could guess the answer.

"Two years ago," Laurie said. "The chief is coordinating with the West County Sheriff's Department. They're mobilizing a helicopter to search this area."

Melon interrupted them by giving a low growl and pinning his ears back. "What is it, boy?"

Vincente followed the direction of the dog's gaze. On the ridge, high above them, he could see two figures. They were too far away to hear if he called out to them, but he knew who they were. His heart made a wild attempt to escape through his throat. Beth was standing with her back to the canyon. He could tell from her body shape she was wearing the baby carrier. Tania was facing her with her right arm outstretched. He guessed from her stance that she was aiming a gun at Beth.

What neither of the women on the ravine edge could see was something that was clear from Vincente's viewpoint. There was a third figure. A man was stealthily making his way toward them, closing the distance inch by inch. Rick Sterling was doing a good job of creeping up on them unseen.

"If you shoot me, it won't look like suicide or an accident." Beth remained where she was, refusing to do what Tania wanted. Declining to step off the edge of the ravine and into certain death.

"I'm not planning on shooting *you*." Tania's smile was

smug. "The bullet is for the baby. I have it all planned. You shot her and then jumped. It's all in the note."

Tania had stuffed the fake suicide note into the back pocket of Beth's jeans and now she was forcing her closer to the canyon. Beth knew she was running out of time. If she tried to fight Tania, she risked both her and Lia being shot. If she jumped before Tania fired…her eyes skittered to the chasm behind her. How could anyone possibly survive that fall?

Tania took a step closer, raising the gun. "Time to say goodbye."

A movement behind her caught Beth's eye and she blinked, attempting to clear her vision. She must be imagining things. No one knew they were here. There wasn't going to be any last-minute rescue… She froze as Rick moved into view.

Beth desperately needed something on which to pin her hopes. Every fiber of her being wanted this to be a positive development. Wanted Rick to be the hero who had come to her rescue. But how could that be? Just yesterday, he had his hands around Vincente's throat as he tried to kill him. And Rick had been in Toronto when Danielle died.

Wasn't it more likely that these two were somehow in this together? Beth knew from her experience yesterday that Rick was capable of picking her up and throwing her over the edge of the ravine. Her defiance was in tatters, her thoughts scattering in every direction.

*Rick saved my life yesterday. Why would he do that only to kill me today?*

"No more, Tania."

The cool, calm words acted like bucket of cold water thrown over Tania. She shuddered violently before swinging around to face Rick, her face an almost comical picture of outrage.

Maybe hope wasn't out of Beth's reach. She wished she could run, but there was nowhere to go. And there was still that damn gun to consider.

"You shouldn't be here." Tania's lip trembled. "You were supposed to die."

"I know you planned to kill me right after you murdered Andy," Rick said. His face was a mess. It looked like his nose was broken, but Beth doubted he had sought medical help. "I figured out right from the start it was you. Cory told me you had a thing for him. He didn't know what to do about it, and he wanted my advice. I told him to act normal, continue to treat you like a friend and maybe you'd move on from it. The problem with Cory was he could be too kindhearted sometimes. I wondered if acting normal for him might make you think he returned your feelings."

"He did." Tania's lips were thin and white. "He loved me, too. He just never got a chance to say it because he died." She waved the gun. "Because you killed him. All of you."

Rick shook his head. "You're wrong, and people are dying because of it. When the letter and the photographs came, I knew they must be from you. Then Andy died, and my picture was next. I couldn't prove anything, but I decided it would be safer if I ducked out of sight for a while. You can't kill a man who is already dead."

"You cheated." Tania sounded like a child playing a game.

"You call it cheating, I call it taking care of myself and looking out for my friends…continuing the job I was supposed to do up on that mountain all those years ago. I wanted to try to keep the rest of the team safe." Rick's voice was regretful. "I haven't done a great job so far. Even though I was at Danielle's wedding, I couldn't stop you getting to her."

"No, you couldn't." Tania's expression brightened. "I was too smart for you in Toronto. I was too smart for you when I killed Peter. I'm too smart for you now."

"Give me the gun, Tania." Rick held out his hand. There it was again. That powerful note of authority. On every climb, he had been the person in charge. It didn't matter what the situation was—whether they were deciding when to stop for lunch or to push on to a summit in poor weather conditions—everyone deferred to Rick. His experience, skills and assurance made him a natural leader. Would the conditioning that had been so much a feature of their team kick in now? Would Tania obey him? "It's over."

"You say he didn't love me, but you can't know that. You can't be sure."

"Tania, I can be more sure of that than anyone." Rick's voice was calm, quiet and filled with memories. "We didn't last long, but for one wonderful summer twelve years ago, Cory and I were an item."

It happened so fast Beth didn't have time to react. Tania covered her mouth with her left hand. She was half-turned toward Beth and, as she staggered under the shock of what she had just heard, the gun in her right hand went off. The bullet hit Beth in the left hip and she reeled backward from the impact of the shot. Her feet teetered on the edge of the ravine. Time slowed to a crawl as she stared down at the Ryerson River. From this height, it looked like a silver ribbon, trickling though the canyon. She swung out, high above the trees as her arms flailed wildly and uselessly. This was it. There was nothing to grab on to. She was going to fall.

She thought she must be hallucinating as Vincente appeared. He crested the top of the ravine at a run with Laurie just behind him. With reflexes like lightning, he dashed to her and caught hold of one of the straps of the baby carrier. For an instant, Beth was suspended over the crevice, only Vincente's fingers preventing her and Lia from going into free fall and plummeting to the canyon floor. Then Rick was beside him, grabbing Vincente around the waist and the two men were working together to haul her back to safety. Sobbing, she clung to Vincente, clawing at his chest as though checking he was real.

Lia's screams were the only thing she could hear. The bullet felt like red-hot wire tearing into her hip. Blood, thick and sticky, soaked through her jeans.

"Lia?" She clutched Vincente's hand.

"She's okay." He eased her down onto her right side on the ground, kneeling beside her. "She's not hit, just scared."

"Don't let her watch…you know…" It was getting hard to talk. Everything seemed to be fading. "If anything bad happens to me, I don't want her to see it."

He was undoing the clips of the carrier and lifting Lia free. His face was ashen and his voice shook. "Nothing bad is going to happen." She could tell he was trying to convince himself as much as her.

As darkness swept over her, she felt Melon licking her hand.

"I'll take her." Rick held out his hands for Lia, and Vincente took a moment to consider the offer. Whatever was going on here, Rick had just helped him save Beth's and Lia's lives. He wasn't the bad guy. Dropping a kiss onto Lia's head, he handed her over to Rick, who patted her shoulder awkwardly.

Vincente turned his attention back to Beth, only vaguely aware of what was going on around him. His hearing seemed to be supercharged. Laurie's voice was clear and decisive, cutting across Lia's cries, as she removed the gun from Tania and began to inform her of her rights. Tania was gazing into space, her eyes unblinking.

In the distance, he thought he could also hear the whumping sound of helicopter blades. Maybe that was wishful thinking.

*Don't let it get here too late to save Beth.*

She had told him not to let Lia see if anything bad happened to her. The thought caused a choking feeling to rip up from Vincente's chest and tighten his throat. That was typical of Beth. *His* Beth. Putting Lia first even when she was...

No. He tried to push the fear away, but it persisted. Beth couldn't be dying. He wouldn't let her. Fate couldn't be cruel enough to show him what his life could be like with Beth at his side, only to take her away from him again.

Her face looked too pale. Like a beautiful waxwork imitation of the real thing. She was still breathing. Short and shallow, her chest rose and fell with a trace of precious movement. When he took her hand, it felt alarmingly cold. He tried to focus on comforting her, not on how much blood there was. Because there was so much blood... Stripping off his shirt, he pressed it against her hip, trying to stanch the flow.

"Hey." He bent to kiss her cheek. "This has to be the worst plan you could have come up with for getting out of a meeting with Edgar."

To his amazement her eyelids fluttered. "Lia." It was barely a whisper.

"Rick has her." He still wasn't quite sure what to do with that piece of information. The guy almost killed him yesterday, although, to be fair, it was in self-defense after Vincente had attacked him first. Today, Vincente was trusting Rick with his daughter. But this was far from a normal situation. Beth came first right now, and whatever Rick was doing, Lia's snuffles were subsiding.

"He saved us." Beth groped for his hand. "When Tania was going to shoot Lia and make me jump, he kept her talking."

Gratitude flooded Vincente's being, replacing every other emotion he had felt toward Rick. Without his intervention, Vincente and Laurie would have gotten here too late and found Beth and Lia had plunged to their deaths. How could he ever thank Rick for something of such magnitude? He had given them a priceless gift. Because of him, they had a future…if only Beth would make it.

The chopping sound of the helicopter blades was unmistakable now. Looking up, Vincente could see the pilot seeking somewhere to land. The terrain here at the top of the ravine was flat and uninterrupted by trees. Before long, the helicopter was touching down nearby, throwing up great clouds of dust.

Vincente spared a quick glance around. Lia's face was tearstained, but she had stopped crying and had rested her head on Rick's shoulder. That meant she felt safe with him. Vincente could leave her for a few more minutes while he stayed with Beth.

Laurie had worked fast. Tania was now sitting on the ground with her hands cuffed behind her. She was still staring into space as though unaware of what was going on. Vincente didn't know what had happened, but she looked like her whole world had been tilted off course. Her gun lay on the ground some distance away from her. The cartridge had been removed.

Laurie hurried over the helicopter, ducking beneath the blades as a passenger jumped down to meet her. Vincente recognized Glen Harvey. Glen had been through a tough time. He was the deputy sheriff of West County when it was discovered that Grant Becker, his boss, was the Red Rose Killer. Glen had been the one to pick up the pieces, pull the Sheriff's Department back together, and restore some pride to the team. He had recently replaced Grant as sheriff and was doing a good job in tough circumstances.

Laurie was gesturing to where Beth lay, and Glen spoke briefly to the pilot before coming over to them.

"Vincente." He tipped his hat, his handsome face concerned. "We're going to get Beth and the baby into the chopper and take them to Elmville District Hospital. They specialize in gunshot wounds there."

"Can I go with her?" The thought of not knowing what was happening to her, even just for the duration of the journey, was unbearable.

"Yes. It's a four-person helicopter." Glen turned to Laurie. "Chief Wilkinson said he has a vehicle on its way here, right?"

She nodded. "I'll wait here and take the suspect and Mr. Sterling back to Stillwater—"

Her words were cut short as Tania struggled to her

feet and staggered to the brink of the ravine. Moving quickly, Rick handed Lia to Laurie.

Edging closer to Tania, he held out a hand toward her. "This isn't the way."

"Cory didn't love me." Her voice was forlorn.

Tania's feet were inches from the rim. Tiny stones slithered under her sneakers and spilled out into the ravine. She bit her lip as she cast a glance over her shoulder.

"We can get you the help you need." Rick risked taking another step.

"Rick, be careful," Vincente warned as he carefully lifted Beth into his arms. "She's dangerous."

Rick got close enough to hook an arm around Tania's waist. A look of pure cunning crossed her features as she smiled up at him. "I'm still smarter."

Leaning backward, she toppled into the ravine, taking Rick with her.

## Chapter 19

Vincente hated hospitals. The thought of all those rooms containing people who were suffering in varying degrees made him uncomfortable. Or maybe it was a metaphor for his fear of loneliness? Although why the hell he was indulging in this level of self-analysis when Beth was in surgery was a complete mystery.

Laurie had contacted Bryce and Steffi, who had turned up a few hours ago. Steffi had taken Lia home with her, but Bryce stayed.

"You don't need to do this."

"You stayed with me when I got shot in the leg, remember? Being a brother works both ways."

The words had provoked an emotional reaction so intense Vincente had been unable to speak. Bryce, who seemed to understand, had gripped his shoulder before going off to get coffee and sandwiches. The surgeon had warned them it could be a long night.

Cameron and Laurie arrived in the early hours of the morning.

"We couldn't stand waiting around at home," Laurie said, hugging Vincente then Bryce.

"This is going to sound like a crazy first question given everything else that's happened, but where's Melon? And is he okay?" Throughout this whole nightmare, the occasional fear that the dog may have been left all alone out at Savage Canyon had bothered him.

"He's at our place, and he's fine." She smiled. "There was a slight problem when he insisted on sitting up front in the patrol car."

"Yeah, he does that." He managed a shaky laugh.

"Is there any news on Beth?" Cameron asked.

"They're still operating. They know she has hip and pelvic fractures, but they aren't sure what other damage the bullet may have done." Vincente leaned his head against the back of the plastic seat and gazed up at the fluorescent strip lighting, something he seemed to have done many times over the last few hours. "And she had lost so much blood…"

The image of Beth lying on the ground at the top of Savage Canyon came into his mind. Despite the drama of Tania throwing herself over the edge of the precipice and taking Rick with her, there hadn't been a moment to lose. Their priority had been to get Beth to the hospital fast. He had left Laurie to deal with the repercussions of the latest sensational twist in a story that had begun ten years ago.

Between them, Vincente and Glen Harvey had carried her to the helicopter. Despite the care they had taken not to hurt her, she had lost consciousness as they placed her inside. Lia had sat on Vincente's knee during the journey, and he was pleased that, although she was quiet, she didn't seem unduly distressed. When they arrived at the hospital, a nurse had taken Lia and given her some food while the trauma team got to work on Beth.

"Did you find the bodies?" He turned to Laurie, seeking a distraction from his thoughts.

"Yes. A combined team of police officers and rangers went into the ravine. They took search-and-rescue dogs with them. Both bodies were on the canyon floor a few hundred yards apart." Laurie didn't need to tell him what sort of terrible state Tania and Rick must have been in. The look on her face said it all. "No one could have survived that fall."

That was what Tania had planned for Beth and Lia. Vincente felt physically ill at the thought. When they had lifted her into the helicopter, he had noticed a blood-stained note sticking out of the right-hand back pocket of Beth's jeans. It had his name on it. With a feeling of dread, he had skimmed through it. As he did, something fiercer than rage tore into him. If Tania had been there, she would have felt his fury pierce her soul.

There was no way Beth would have written such helpless pulp. He had thought of her strength, her pride, her dignity and wanted to crush the hateful note in his hand, obliterating the words forever. Instead, he had handed it to Glen. Tania might be dead, but the investigation wasn't. The people she had murdered deserved some answers.

*Just don't let Beth be another of her victims. Let her live.*

The same thought had been playing over and over in his mind since he had pulled her back from the edge of that precipice. He closed his eyes as the image drained his energy one more time. When he opened them, the surgeon was coming toward them.

As he tried to stand, Vincente wasn't sure if his legs were going to work. Luckily, he found the strength from somewhere to get to his feet. "Is she...?"

He stopped short of saying the word *okay*, because it was such an ineffective way of asking all the things he wanted to know. Would she be able to walk? Would she be able to swing Lia up into her arms? Would she be able to have other children? Would she be the strong, independent woman she had always been?

"Beth is heavily sedated. We've pinned the fractures to her hip and pelvis and, although it's going to take some time, she should make a complete recovery." The doctor smiled when he saw Vincente's look of relief. "I've conducted a surgical examination of her pelvic organs and found no evidence of any lasting damage. She had lost a great deal of blood and needed a transfusion."

"That's it?" Vincente took a moment to process what he was hearing. He'd worked so hard at convincing himself not to hope—because not hoping was what he did, it was what he was good at—that he wasn't prepared for this outcome. "She's going to be okay?"

"She's been through a major trauma and it's going to be a long, painful recovery...but, yes, she's going to be okay."

"Can I see her?" Although he phrased it as a question, there was no way he was taking no for an answer.

"Beth won't come around from the anesthetic for several hours," the doctor said. "She won't know you're there."

Vincente smiled. "She'll know."

\* \* \*

Beth wanted to wake up, but it was too hard. Every time she tried, sleep grabbed her and dragged her back under. *Not sleep*, her mind insisted. There was a reason for this groggy feeling. If she could focus on one thing, maybe this drifting sensation would stop.

There was a warm hand wrapped around hers. She would concentrate on that. She knew that hand. It was strong and capable, slightly callused. There were scratches on the back. She loved that hand...

"Vincente." The word was somewhere between a whisper and a croak. Her throat felt raw, her mouth dry and her lips scratchy.

The grip on her fingers tightened. "I'm here."

"Water."

He held a specially adapted cup with a straw to her lips, and Beth sucked greedily at it. "The nurse said not to give you too much at first."

She murmured a protest when he took the water away. Then another thought drove everything else from her mind. "Where's Lia?"

"She's with Steffi. I spoke to her earlier. She'd tried to force-feed Steffi's cat her own breakfast cereal, so it sounds like she's fine." He took her hand again. "And Melon is at Cameron and Laurie's place."

Snippets of what had happened were starting to come back to her like flashes of a bad dream, half remembered because she'd tried to bury them. *I was shot!* The memory was like another bullet ricocheting through her and she turned her head to gaze at Vincente. He looked exhausted. Even though he smiled, the lines of worry around his eyes were etched deep. *It must be bad.* She couldn't feel any pain. Couldn't feel anything from the waist down.

No matter how scared she was, she had to ask. "My legs?"

"You're going to be fine." The look in his eyes was like a blanket wrapping around her. She felt it warming every part of her. "The bullet shattered bones in your hip and pelvis, but the surgeon was able to pin them back together. You'll be walking on crutches at first, then with a cane, but you'll make a full recovery."

"My pelvis?" That meant the bullet had passed close to her uterus and other vital parts of her body.

"Apart from the damage the bullet caused to your skin and muscles, there were no other injuries." Vincente seemed to read her mind. "Your internal organs weren't harmed."

She lay quietly for a few moments, allowing the words to sink in. The time after she had been shot was a blur of pain, noise and confusion. A horrible blackness had been trying to pull her under and, no matter how hard she tried to fight back, it had been too strong for her. She knew now, of course, that it had been caused by shock and blood loss.

"What happened to Tania?"

"She's dead." There was something in Vincente's face as he said those words. It meant he had something bad he needed to tell her. "She threw herself into the ravine... but she took Rick with her."

Helpless tears rolled down her cheeks, and Vincente shifted closer so he could cradle her head against his shoulder. The doctors must have used some powerful painkillers on her body, but they couldn't touch the hurt in her heart. Rick Sterling had been her idol when she was learning to climb. Other girls her age had crushes on pop stars. Beth didn't have a crush, but she had hero-worshiped Rick. In return, he had been patient, wise, and good-humored, teaching her everything he knew. Then he had come back into her life two days ago in the strangest of circumstances and saved her life. Twice. He had saved Lia's life, too. Now she would never get a chance to thank him.

"He was a hero."

"He was." Vincente found a Kleenex and dried her tears before giving her some more water. "Laurie is investigating how and why he did what he did, but we owe him everything."

"Is Edgar okay? Tania hit him with the butt of her gun and knocked him out."

There was a slight hesitation before Vincente answered, a fleeting sense of him wanting to say more and deciding against it. Beth was too tired to pursue it. "He's fine. I'm sure he'll come to see you and will want to talk to you."

His face was next to hers on the pillow and she examined every beloved feature. Lifting her hand was hard work, but she managed to trace her thumb along his cheekbone. "When that bullet hit me, the first thing I thought was that I'd fall into that ravine and never see you again."

His dark eyes shimmered with unshed tears as he raised her hand to his lips. For a second or two, he struggled to speak. "Three times now, I've faced the prospect of losing you. The first time was when you left Stillwater. Then there was the other day at Eternal Springs. But this—" the words became choked, and he broke off.

"I've already said you won't lose me, Vincente."

"No, I won't." He got his voice back under control. "I won't, because I'm never letting you go again. I love you, Beth. I just wish I'd had the courage to recognize it and say it years ago."

She smiled through her own tears. "Don't be too hard on yourself. I don't think either of us were ready for forever back then. You might have been the one fighting commitment, but I wasn't doing a lot to tie you down. We both enjoyed the craziness we created."

He laughed. "It was fun, wasn't it?"

"It was. But then it got real…and we found out real was even better than fun."

"If we can be together through what life has thrown at us these last few weeks, then bring on the future." His kiss was featherlight on her lips. "I can't wait to share it with you."

"I love you, Vincente. I've been waiting such a long time to say that." She gestured to the cage that covered the lower half of her body. "I promised myself that once this nightmare was over, I'd walk down Main Street holding your hand and carrying Lia. Looks like we may have to postpone."

"We can take our time. We have forever."

It was a few days before Beth was allowed to see anyone other than Vincente and Lia. Just as she was growing increasingly impatient at lying flat on her back, the doctor judged it was time for her to progress to a wheelchair. On the day Bryce, Steffi and Laurie came to visit, she was clearly delighted to be upright and to have a measure of independence.

They brought balloons, cake and presents. It was Lia's first birthday.

"You said she'd have the best day we could give her." Beth clutched Vincente's hand as tears filled her eyes.

"She still has her mom. That's the best gift ever."

Lia clapped her hands delightedly as she opened her presents, scattering paper and ribbon everywhere. Even when Bryce joined her on the floor and tried to engage her interest in her new toys, it was clear she found the wrapping more interesting than the contents.

"You look so well," Steffi said as she studied Beth's face.

"I feel it. Apart from after the physiotherapist comes to see me and tries to get my legs moving. Then I feel like hell." Beth's smile lit up the room. *Or maybe it's just me she affects that way*, Vincente thought. Every time he looked at her, he felt as though he was the one who had been given a gift.

"We have a surprise for you." Laurie indicated the full-length glass doors that opened onto the hospital garden. "Don't worry. Cameron cleared it with the nurses."

She opened the door, and Vincente wheeled Beth's chair to the opening. When she saw Melon coming across the grass on his leash, with Cameron holding on to him, she clapped her hands with delight. Melon noticed Beth and threw back his head, giving a single, high-pitched yowl.

"My hero." Beth buried her face in Melon's coat as he placed his front paws on her shoulder.

"This hero of yours has been teaching our dogs some very dubious tricks." Cameron's face was expressionless.

Beth turned her head to look up at him, a look of resignation on her face. "What has he been doing?"

"Let's just say things may never be the same in our house again. Our dogs have been taught the benefits of sleeping on the furniture, drinking out of the bathrooms and stealing food from the kitchen counters." Cameron's lips twitched. "Oh, and shredding newspapers. They particularly enjoyed that lesson."

"Melon—" Beth caught hold of his collar, giving him a little shake "—have you been disgracing yourself?"

Melon placed his head on her lap, his expression one of complete innocence.

"Take no notice," Laurie said. "If Melon hadn't led us to you, I wouldn't have been able to disarm and handcuff Tania. She would have killed you and Lia as well as Rick. Melon deserves an award for bravery. In fact, I think the mayor of Stillwater should organize a special ceremony."

"I can think of a few things that dog deserves, but awards are not top of my list." Although the words were caustic, Cameron was biting back a smile as Melon noticed Lia and wagged his tail delightedly before holding out a paw in her direction.

"If it's a problem, Melon can come and stay with us instead," Steffi offered.

Beth and Vincente exchanged horrified looks. "There's just one problem with that…the herding. He's a collie, so he has all the instincts, but he doesn't know how to do it properly…your animals would be traumatized."

"Don't worry." Cameron rubbed Melon's head and the dog rolled his eyes with delight. "It's not as bad as it sounds. I can live with my well-trained hounds being turned into delinquents while Beth recovers."

Although the others visited for only half an hour, Laurie stayed after they had gone. "I wanted to let you know what we had found out about Rick."

Beth was tired after being in her chair for the first time, so Vincente helped her back into bed. Lia curled up contentedly at her side and began to doze. Laurie took her notebook out and began to read from her jottings.

"Rick had been staying in a hostel right here in Still-water. It's a place that's popular with climbers and hikers, so possibly it's somewhere he stayed in the past when he did climbs on the Stillwater Trail. We found a journal with his possessions. In it, he had kept a detailed account of his own actions after he faked his death, but he was also following what Tania was doing, and, where possible, tracking the movements of the other members of the Devil's Peak team."

"He said he was trying to protect us," Beth said.

"That seems to have been his sole intention. His notes are dated, and right from the start—the first photograph and letter—he was onto Tania. He kept newspaper cuttings about Andy Smith's death, and there was a sense of frustration in his notes that it wasn't seen as suspicious. He appeared to know something about Tania's obsessive behavior in the past. When he got the picture with his own face crossed out, he decided to fake his own death."

"But Tania was killing people who were happy. If she chose Rick for that reason, didn't he leave a partner behind who was devastated by his pretense?" Vincente asked.

"Rick was intensely private. He never spoke about his personal life or his relationships. But he was also very comfortable with who he was. People, including Tania, often mistook that to mean he had found happiness in his private life. In reality, at the time he faked his death, Rick was single.

"When we were on the top of the ravine, he told Tania he and Cory had once been in a relationship," Beth said.

"Rick was gay," Laurie confirmed. "That may be the reason why he was so keen to protect his privacy. We'll never know for sure."

"So, having faked his death, he set about trying to stop Tania from killing the rest of us? Why didn't he go to the police?" Beth asked.

"Rick did make several anonymous calls to the Whitebridge Police Department when Tania sent the first letters and photographs. He told them they might want to talk to her about it. Even told them she had a previous history of stalking. Unfortunately, it looks like he was written off as a crank. There will be some red faces among my Whitebridge colleagues, but hindsight is a wonderful thing."

"If Rick was in hiding, he couldn't know whose face was crossed out in the next picture," Vincente pointed out.

"That's right. But he was keeping track of what was happening with each of the team and when he found out that Danielle was getting married, he thought there was a good chance she would be next. He traveled to Toronto, and, sure enough, Danielle confirmed his worst fears. She had received a photograph with her face crossed out. Rick urged her to go to the police and name Tania as the suspect."

"She would have refused because of the threat to her loved ones." Beth sounded certain.

"That's almost word for word what Rick wrote in his journal. He offered to stay for the wedding to watch over Danielle—" Laurie's expression twisted momentarily out of her businesslike composure "—but the one time he couldn't be with her was when she was dressing in her bridal clothes."

"And that's when Tania got to her." Beth shook her head in sorrow. "She knew how to find a weakness and exploit it."

"You were the person who worried Rick most," Laurie said. "He felt particularly protective toward you, Beth. He even attempted to analyze why he felt that way in his journal. He stated it stemmed back to your partnership on the Devil's Peak and the fact that he had an added responsibility toward you as the youngest member of the team. He also felt you got an unfair amount of attention over Cory's death. But he was frustrated because he couldn't find out where you were living. Until you walked into the West County Climbing Club a few weeks ago."

"How could Rick know that if he was in hiding himself?" Vincente asked.

"He was watching Tania's every move. He couldn't get up close to her, obviously, but he was watching who went in and out of the club that evening. When he saw you and Vincente were…what was the exact phrase he used—" Laurie flipped through her notes "—here it is. *Head over heels in love…*" She looked up with a smile, lightening the mood momentarily. "Funny how a guy looking through a pair of binoculars got that, but you two never noticed."

"We've figured it out now." Vincente flapped a hand, indicating that Laurie could continue. "You can stop matchmaking and keep policing, Detective."

"Rick knew immediately that, by walking into the club and showing Tania you were happy with Vincente, you had moved your name right up her list. He followed you back to Stillwater after the meeting. When he came out to the lake house that night and climbed down the cliff onto the deck, he wasn't intending to harm or threaten you. He was checking out your security. Rick was making sure you were safe. He couldn't approach you and warn you because he was supposed to be dead."

"Even though Rick was doing all he could to keep us safe, it wasn't enough to save Peter," Beth said.

"Like you, Rick didn't know Peter was Tania's next target. He didn't know Peter was in a new relationship and never saw the photograph with Peter's face crossed out. Rick was in Whitebridge the day Peter was killed because he was following you and Vincente. When he saw Tania arrive at Peter's house, he called the police. That was how the Whitebridge officers got there before I did. When he saw you leaving the house, Rick drove back to Stillwater. He even passed you on the highway."

"If that was the case, why did he end up jogging toward us along the edge of the highway?"

"My theory about car trouble was right. He ran out of gas. He was so focused on everything else that was going on, he didn't look at the fuel needle until it was on empty. And he didn't have a gas container in his vehicle. His plan was to jog into Stillwater, buy a container at the gas station, fill it there and jog back to his car. He wrote in his journal that it was just bad timing he encountered you before he reached the turning into Stillwater. A minute later and he'd have missed you."

Vincente lifted a hand to his throat. The bruises had faded, but the memory of those strong hands closing around it lingered. He knew now that Rick had been fighting for his life because Vincente had given him no choice by attacking him, but at the time Vincente had believed he was up against the murderer.

"Why did he run when we confronted him? At that point, he could have told us the whole story," Beth asked.

"He knew his cover was blown, but he was worried you would go to the police and we wouldn't believe him about Tania. If he'd been arrested, she'd have been free to continue killing people and there'd have been no one to protect his friends. With only a split second to make a decision, he wasn't willing to take that chance," Laurie explained. "What Rick hadn't expected was that you would go after him, Beth. When he saw you were in trouble partway down the waterfall, he couldn't leave you, so he turned back to help. Having saved you, he reached the bottom and was tackled by Vincente. Even though he didn't plan on killing you, he had no choice but to fight back."

"You're sure about that?" Vincente touched his throat. "It sure felt like he planned on killing me."

"In his notes, he said he let you go once he knew you were incapacitated. While you were struggling out of the pool, Rick hightailed out of there as fast as he could. He knew if you caught up with him, he wouldn't stand a chance."

"He was right." Vincente remembered his feelings of anger toward Rick on that day. He thought he was dealing with the murderer. If only he'd known the truth.

"After that, Rick was on Tania's tail the whole time. He'd seen her checking out Vincente's apartment block and Savage Canyon. When she led you out of the building, Beth, I guess he was right behind you all the way."

Vincente shook his head. "You and Lia were rescued by a man who should have been dead, and a dog."

Beth gripped his hand tighter. "You rescued us, Vincente, from the moment you found us in Casper to the moment you pulled us back from the edge of that canyon."

"Home." As Vincente carried Beth through the door of the lake house, the word meant so much more to her than ever before. "It's so good to be back here at last."

"Steffi's bringing Lia over later, and Cameron said he'll drop Melon off this evening. Although he'll never admit it, I think he's going to miss him." Vincente set her down on the sofa in the family room and knelt beside her, rearranging cushions and lifting her feet onto a footstool. "We have the place to ourselves for a few hours."

"I don't know what you were planning." She smiled into his eyes. "But I'm not quite ready for any bedroom gymnastics just yet."

"That wasn't what I was planning. Not yet, anyway." Although he returned the smile, she could tell he was nervous. He reached into his pocket. When he withdrew his hand, he was holding a black velvet box. He flipped open the lid, revealing a vintage ring. The single, square-cut diamond was displayed to perfect advantage by a pretty, engraved band. It was the most beautiful ring Beth had ever seen.

"This was my grandmother's engagement ring. My mother doesn't get many things right when it comes to love, but she told me that she shouldn't be trusted with something as precious as this. She gave it to me on one condition. I would only ever give it away if I was sure the hand that wore it would hold mine for the rest of my life." Vincente lifted Beth's left hand and took the ring from the box. "You can choose another ring, or wear this on a different finger, but…"

She shook her head, blinking back tears. "I love it. I can't believe after everything that's happened to us I'm going to cry because I'm so happy."

"Don't cry. Not yet." As he said the words, Vincente's own eyes glistened. "Bethany Wade, you already make me the happiest man in the world. Will you make it official and marry me?"

The tears spilled over then as she started to laugh and cry. "Vincente Delaney, I would love to."

Vincente slid the ring onto her finger. "It's a bit big. We'll take it into town and have it adjusted."

"Can we go tomorrow? And can we stop at The Daily Grind and get coffee and cake?" Vincente came to sit next to her, and Beth held her hand up, twisting and turning it so she could admire the ring from different angles. "Do normal things? Show Lia off?"

"We can do anything you want, as long as you remember the doctors said slow and steady was the way to approach your recovery."

"I feel so much better already just being home."

Vincente placed an arm around her shoulders. "I wanted to talk to you about that." Beth tilted her head up to look at him. "About this house being our home. Cameron will sell it to us if we want it."

"If?" Beth was surprised by the hesitant note in his voice. "I love this house. I thought you did, too. Why wouldn't we want it?"

"It's not very big."

"There's only three of us. We fit perfectly into this space…" His smile told its own story. "Oh!"

He laughed. "Beth, are you blushing?"

"Well, I didn't know you wanted more children."

"Nor did I. But now I think I would." He twined a length of her hair around his finger. "What about you?"

She nodded. "I would love for Lia to have a little brother or sister in a year or two."

"Maybe more than one?" His voice had dropped to a persuasive murmur. "Melon needs a few if he's going to really hone those herding skills."

"My goodness, you've been giving this some thought, haven't you?" Beth regarded him in wonder. "Now I see why you think the house is too small."

"It is, but while you were in the hospital, I consulted an architect. We can't expand outward because of the cliffs and the lake, but there's nothing to stop us going upward."

Beth laughed. "This is turning out to be quite a day. I get an engagement ring and the house of my dreams. Do you have anything else in store for me?"

His face became serious. "I don't, but there is someone else who would like to talk to you. Do you feel strong enough for a visit from Edgar?"

*Four months later*

"Whose idea was it to put ribbons on the guard dog?" Bryce muttered the words to Cameron as the three Delaney brothers stood at the front of the church.

"Laurie thought it would be sweet if Melon had a bow on his collar to match Lia's bridesmaid's dress," Cameron said.

"Sweet? He's just ripped it off and shredded it all over the lawn outside. Someone will need to clear the mess up before Beth arrives."

"I can't do it." Vincente smiled at his younger brother. "I'm exempt from Melon duty today. I can't see the bride until she arrives at the altar. It's probably one of the best men's responsibilities." He held up a finger before Bryce could speak. "And remember not to swear in church."

Bryce stomped outside, and Cameron choked back a laugh. "This is probably the first wedding I've been to where a dog is likely to be the most troublesome guest."

"I think you're forgetting something." Vincente rolled his eyes. "My mother is here with her latest billionaire. Although I have warned her against any attempts to divert attention away from the bride."

"That hat is a diversion in its own right."

Giovanna was as out of place here in Wyoming as a designer ball gown at a rodeo. She had arrived in Stillwater a few days ago, and had surprised Vincente by taking an instant liking to Beth. The feeling was mutual. Beth regarded Giovanna with the amused tolerance Vincente wished he could cultivate toward his mother. Lia had also helped establish a new family bond, although Giovanna was outraged at the idea that anyone would know she was old enough to be a grandmother.

"You must bring the *bambina* to visit me in Firenze." Giovanna had extended the invitation in her usual vague way, and Vincente had decided they wouldn't be in any hurry to take her up on it. One day they would take Lia to Italy and introduce her to the other part of her heritage. For now, their priority was to enjoy being a family right here in Stillwater.

"They're here." Bryce resumed his place. "I got all the ribbon cleaned up in time."

The music started up. Vincente looked around to watch Lia walk down the aisle holding Steffi's hand.

Even though she had been doing it for a few months, he was still getting used to the idea that his daughter could walk. It seemed so grown-up. Yet watching her now, she looked so tiny. Oblivious to tradition, Lia spotted Vincente and tottered the last few feet toward him.

"Kiss, Dada." She raised her arms. Vincente obediently lifted her up, kissed her cheek and handed her back to Steffi. The maneuver was swift and didn't hold up the process of Beth proceeding down the aisle on Edgar's arm.

Every time Vincente looked at Beth, he thought she was the most beautiful woman in the world. Today, her white lace dress and shy smile only added to his conviction. As she drew level with him they gazed at each other for what felt like an eternity. The sense of peace and perfection that swept over him in that instant was overwhelming.

Edgar placed Beth's hand in Vincente's and moved to one side. Vincente knew how much it meant to him to be here. It had been hard for both him and Beth when he explained why he had kept his relationship to Cory a secret from her.

"I knew you'd been part of the Devil's Peak team, but I didn't speak to my family and you never mentioned what happened back then. It wasn't something I could talk to a junior employee about," Edgar had said. "Then, when I knew you better, the silence had gone on too long. There was never a right time for me to say 'By the way, I'm Cory Taylor's uncle.'"

Beth had understood. Edgar was a reserved man. There had been enough losses because of what happened on that mountain. She wasn't prepared to lose Edgar as well as Rick. Instead, she had asked him if he would escort her down the aisle when she got married. Edgar had remembered her injuries just in time to refrain from embracing her.

Vincente had been determined to remember every second of the ceremony, but suddenly it was over and he was being told he could kiss his bride. Not that he could find any fault with that instruction.

"I think the idea is we have to stop kissing at some point," Beth whispered.

"It's my wedding. I'll do this my way." Vincente kissed her again. "Are you okay with all this standing?"

"I'm fine." She hooked her arm through his as they turned to walk up the aisle. Although there was a slight hesitation in her walk, the limp was barely noticeable now, and it was getting better every day. "More than fine. I'm happy."

"Me, too. And happy is the way we're going to stay."

\* \* \* \* \*

*If you loved this thrilling romance,
don't miss the previous titles in Jane Godman's*
SONS OF STILLWATER *miniseries:*

*THE SOLDIER'S SEDUCTION
COVERT KISSES*

*Available now from Harlequin Romantic Suspense!*

### #1979 COLTON'S DEADLY ENGAGEMENT
*The Coltons of Red Ridge* • by Addison Fox

When Finn Colton, the Red Ridge police chief, goes undercover as Darby Gage's fiancé to catch The Groom Killer, his only goal is to close the case. Until he realizes he's falling in love with his fake bride-to-be!

### #1980 GUARDIAN COWBOY
*Cowboys of Holiday Ranch* • by Carla Cassidy

Sawyer Quincy is *trying* to get to know the woman he's certain he had a one-night stand with, but someone is going to great lengths to keep him away from Janis Little—and it looks like they'll even kill to make sure he does!

### #1981 HER MISSION WITH A SEAL
*Code: Warrior SEALs* • by Cindy Dees

Navy SEAL commander Cole Perriman and CIA analyst Nissa Beck are in a race against time to catch a notorious Russian spy only Nissa can recognize. But with a hurricane bearing down on New Orleans and feelings neither of them expected taking them by surprise, they'll need to pool all of their skills to succeed—on the mission and in love!

### #1982 UNDERCOVER PROTECTOR
*Undercover Justice* • by Melinda Di Lorenzo

A decade ago, Nadine Stuart lost her father and her memory in a fire. Now the man who caused the fire is determined to ensure Nadine never remembers. Her only hope is Detective Anderson Somers, but they must race to find the link between the conspiracy that killed her father and the cold case Anderson is undercover to investigate.

HRSCNM0118

# Get 2 Free Books,
## Plus 2 Free Gifts—
### just for trying the Reader Service!

HARLEQUIN®
ROMANTIC suspense

HRS17R3

"Demi Colton is not the sort of woman who murders a guy who can't appreciate her. Especially if that guy was dumb enough to dump her for Hayley."

"So you think it's someone else?"

"Yes, I do. And that someone isn't me," she added in a rush.

That tempting idea snaked through his mind once more, sly in its promise of a solution to his current dilemma.

*Catch a killer and keep an eye on Darby Gage. It's not exactly a hardship to spend time with her.*

"Maybe you can help me, then."

"Help you how? I thought you were convinced I'm the town murderess."

"I'm neither judge nor jury. It's my job to find evidence to put away a killer, and that's what I'm looking to do."

"Then what do you want with me?" The skepticism that had painted her features was further telegraphed in her words. Finn heard the clear notes of disbelief, but underneath them he heard something else.

Curiosity.

"Fingers pointing at my cousin isn't all that's going around town. What began as whispers has gotten louder with Michael Hayden's murder."

"What are people saying?"

Finn weighed his stupid idea, quickly racing through a mental list of pros and cons. Since the list was pretty evenly matched, it was only his desperation to find a killer that tipped the scales toward the pro.

With that goal in mind—closing this case and catching a killer as quickly as possible—he opted to go for broke.

"Bo Gage was killed the night of his bachelor party. Michael Hayden was killed the night of his rehearsal dinner. One thing the victims had in common—they were grooms-to-be. And in a matter of weeks half the town has called off any and all plans to get married or host an engagement party."

"I still can't see what this has to do with me."

"If you're as innocent as you say you are, surely you'd be willing to help me."

"Help you do what?"

"Pretend to be my fiancée, Darby. Help me catch a killer."

*Will Finn find the Groom Killer before the Groom Killer finds him?*

*Find out in* COLTON'S DEADLY ENGAGEMENT *by Addison Fox, available February 2018 wherever Harlequin® Romantic Suspense books and ebooks are sold.*

www.Harlequin.com

Need an adrenaline rush from nail-biting tales
(and irresistible males)?

Check out **Harlequin® Intrigue®**
and **Harlequin® Romantic Suspense** books!

**New books available every month!**

---

**CONNECT WITH US AT:**

Harlequin.com/Community

 Facebook.com/HarlequinBooks

 Twitter.com/HarlequinBooks

 Instagram.com/HarlequinBooks

 Pinterest.com/HarlequinBooks

ReaderService.com

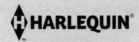

**ROMANCE WHEN
YOU NEED IT**

SGENRE2017

# *LOVE*
# Harlequin
# romance?

Join our Harlequin community to share your thoughts and connect with other romance readers!

Be the first to find out about promotions, news, and exclusive content!

Sign up for the Harlequin e-newsletter and download a free book from any series at

## **www.TryHarlequin.com**

---

**CONNECT WITH US AT:**

Harlequin.com/Community

 Facebook.com/HarlequinBooks

 Twitter.com/HarlequinBooks

 Instagram.com/HarlequinBooks

 Pinterest.com/HarlequinBooks

ReaderService.com

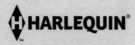

**ROMANCE WHEN
YOU NEED IT**

HSOCIAL2017

# Reward the book lover in you!

Earn points from all your Harlequin book purchases from wherever you shop.

Turn your points into *FREE BOOKS* of your choice
OR
*EXCLUSIVE GIFTS* from your favorite authors or series.

Join for FREE today at
**www.HarlequinMyRewards.com.**

Harlequin My Rewards is a free program (no fees) without any commitments or obligations.

MYR17